Whispers of the Silver Heart

Book One of the Highbloods Saga

Renee Remeta

ISBN: 8993563503
ISBN-13: 9798993563503

This book is dedicated to every single one of you still struggling to find your way.

Don't hide your scars from me, love. Show me how you battled this world...and won.

-Renee Remeta

Acknowledgements

First and foremost, I need to say thank you to my very own real life, fantasy book boyfriend, my husband, Nick. You give me more strength and more butterflies than you will ever know, and I love you now, forever and always.

To my sons, Alex and Stephen, thank you for your silly jokes when I was stressed, your constant belief that I could do this, and your intermittent forehead kisses when I was busy working, they helped more than you realize. I'm so proud of you both and I love you eternally.

To my very own Natalie, Willow and Eliana, thank you for the endless brainstorming sessions, conference calls, and feedback on every single version of this you ever read. This book would not be here without you.

To my parents who encouraged me to write ever since I could hold a pencil, and who were always my biggest and loudest fans. I love you.

To Ivy, thank you for the tireless edits, and equally tireless lunches where you listened to me ramble about this book incessantly. You're the best!

To my favorite crew over at Barnes & Noble on Haywood Road, so much of this book was fueled by your mocha lattes and the smell of books!

* * *

To SKZ and Stay, thank you for pushing me when I would have given up, for supporting me through all the twists and turns, and for being the most positive, most uplifting fandom I've ever been blessed enough to be a part of.

And lastly, this book is for my grandmother, Phoebe Ballengee Stacy. For making me promise so many years ago, that one day I would sit down and write a book, and give the rest of the world the chance to fall in love with the stories in my head. I fulfilled my promise, so ***I hope you're smiling up there****.*

1

"Missing? What do you *MEAN* missing?"

"I don't know. I thought maybe she was ghosting me, but when I drove by the shop today it was closed up tight. When I saw that I figured I should maybe give you a call."

"You figured you should maybe...," Mayla palmed her forehead, squeezing her temples in frustration while trying *really* hard not to climb through the phone and beat her best friend's useless boyfriend to a bloody pulp.

"Oh SHIT!!"

"What? Tyler, what is it? Did she text you?"

"Huh? Oh, uh, no, I was watching the game. My fantasy tight end just got hurt. That's gonna murder my score for this week."

Mayla Charles blew out an irritated breath as she replayed the conversation in her head for what seemed like the thousandth time. Her best friend Willow was *missing*.

And Willow's waste of space, fantasy football addicted boyfriend was way overdue for a solid kick in the jewels. Her best friend had been missing for an entire month and the clown only thought to call Mayla yesterday.

After a sleepless night of texting everyone she could think of and driving around town looking, Mayla was now well beyond furious Tyler hadn't contacted her sooner. And yes, admittedly, she was feeling a truckload of guilt as well. She'd texted Willow the last couple weekends, but when she hadn't received a response, it hadn't seemed like a big deal.

These days Willow was always at Green Tease, her tea and plant shop. Thanks to her friend's Lowblood druid magic, the plants were healthy and lush, the teas more fragrant and flavorful than anywhere else in town. The shop had been so successful lately, it often kept Willow busy from morning until night. When Willow and Tyler started dating a few months ago, her schedule had tightened up even more. The last time Mayla had even seen her best friend in person was when they'd accidentally run into each other at Starbucks. They'd hugged, grabbed their orders, and promised to get together for a lunch date soon.

That had been almost five weeks ago.

Mayla bit her lip, hard. Ugh, five weeks! The thought had her anxiety horse-kicking her in the gut as she eased her white Chevy Volt onto the interstate. In ten minutes she was supposed to meet an officer downtown to file a missing persons report, and her anxiety was riding her hard. She tried to ignore the trembling in her hands and the doomsday feeling building in her chest, focusing instead on merging onto the exit to downtown Miradea. Two lefts later, she pulled into a massive gray and green concrete parking garage and waited for the machine to spit out a ticket.

Mayla'd spent her entire life fighting her crippling anxiety, but no medication or therapy she'd ever tried had helped her in the slightest. She'd even attempted to use her own minor healing magic on herself a few times, but there had been no noticeable improvement, and as a Lowblood, she wasn't all that surprised. Lowblood magics weren't very impressive to begin with, and Lowblood healing magic even less so. If she'd been lucky enough to be born Highblood, with all their strong fae blood, things might have been different, but unfortunately she'd had no such luck. Most of the city sought out Highblood healers whenever the need arose, all that strong magic making their quick treatments virtually painless.

Mayla pulled the Volt into a parking spot and turned off the car. Pulling in a slow, stabilizing breath, she climbed out, locking the car with a quick beep before stashing the keys in the pocket of her white hoodie. Her sister would be mortified that she was meeting anyone dressed so casually, but Mayla had never been a fancy outfit and matching purse kind of girl, much to Natalie's chagrin. She much preferred faded jeans, worn-in band t-shirts and her endless collection of random hoodies. Looking down she realized the Stray Kids hoodie she currently wore had been her birthday gift from Willow last year. The sudden memory of the grin on Willow's face when Mayla had unwrapped it, squealing in delight, took her breath away. And left a massive ache in the center of her chest.

Where could she be?

Was she ever going to see her best friend again?

The thought sent another deep kick of fear through her gut, and she hurried her steps as she left the parking garage. It was time to stop screwing around and start searching for her friend.

Anton Tevaris needed coffee, and he needed it *yesterday*. As he moved quickly across the downtown plaza, his long strides eating up the pavement beneath him, his jaw was set and his expression frigid. The citizens of Miradea scuttled out of his way like crabs, crossing to the edges of the sidewalk and ducking their heads to avoid the freezing air that was rolling off him in waves. His broad shoulders strained the seams of his white dress shirt, his black slacks fitting snug to his trim waist. On any normal day, his long silver-white hair, crystalline blue eyes, and unmistakable Highblood lineage would be drawing people toward him like bees to honey.

But today was not a normal day.

Today he had a headache the size of the Grand Canyon and his stomach was iffy at best. He'd only managed three hours of sleep before his alarm set off World War III in his temples this morning, and his mood had gone steadily downhill from there.

After letting his second-in-command talk him into 'one drink after shift' yesterday - a decision he known he would come to regret as soon as he made it - he'd found himself at CuePhoria, playing pool and drinking tequila and absinthe cocktails until three in the morning. The Lowblood bartender had called them Corpse Revivers.

Based on the way his head was currently pounding, and the quirky way his ice magic was misbehaving, he'd say he was feeling much more 'corpse' like than he was 'revived'. His ice magic was definitely hungover, his shower this morning ice cold no matter how far he'd turned the knob, and he'd incited a small snow flurry on the way to his car. All of that had only reinforced the old adage they'd been taught since grade school, 'booze and magic don't mix.'

Which was why he desperately needed a fresh, hot, entirely too strong cup of coffee as soon as physically possible.

As if his thoughts had somehow conjured it, the smell of fresh espresso wafted to him from across the plaza, a siren song calling straight to his pounding head. The huge glass windows of Well Grounded Coffee Shop glowed with warm light, a perfect beacon of invitation. The center of downtown was bustling this morning; the collection of coffee shops, bakeries and sandwich windows were overflowing with people looking to grab a quick breakfast before heading into work elsewhere downtown. Huge skyscrapers towered over the exterior of the plaza, clearly marking the area as the primary financial district of the city.

Two centuries ago, Miradea had been a well protected fae city hidden deep in the woodlands of upstate South Carolina. That was before the Great Unveiling of course, which had then led to the Blood War between the humans and the fae. When those fifteen years of bloodshed finally ended in a tentative peace, many humans chose to stay and settle in Miradea.

Less than two years later the first fae/human offspring had been born.

It had been something of a scandal back then, the idea of fae and human relationships and the mixing of bloodlines. Originally, those hybrid children had been completely shunned, mocked for their muddled genetics and haphazard magics. But as the years progressed and even more generations followed, the number of pure blooded fae had steadily gotten smaller and smaller.

Now, centuries later, there were no pure bloods anymore, the last one having died almost fifty years ago. Instead, Miradea found itself with two primary classes, Highbloods, those with more fae blood and significantly stronger magics, and Lowbloods, those with more human blood and weaker magics, if they'd been lucky enough to develop any at all.

Most of the time the two groups co-existed peacefully, but in a population where magical bloodlines were constantly being mixed and muted, sometimes things got a little…unpredictable.

That's where the Miradea Police Department stepped in. They policed Highblood and Lowblood alike, and worked to keep the city as peaceful as possible. Anton had been on the force for seven years now, and a detective for five of those seven. Three years ago he'd been appointed head of the newly created Miradea Task Force when the higher ups had noticed a disturbing increase in Lowblood targeted crimes.

So when dispatch needed someone to take a report on a missing Lowblood woman early this morning, Anton had immediately arranged to meet the caller. He'd chosen downtown as the meeting location for one vitally important reason.

The plaza had coffee, and this morning, coffee was *everything*. Two birds, one stone and all that.

"Hey! A…wait up!"

Anton smothered a groan at the familiar voice. The very same voice that had sworn they would play one game of pool and have one round of beers last night.

Elijah approached him at a jog, his features relaxed and free of any sign that he'd put away enough alcohol last night to drop a rhino. Instead, his ridiculously handsome face was warm and welcoming, his sparkling amber eyes bright and his smile easy. With that face and his unruly mop of wavy brown hair, it was no surprise his best friend was getting nothing but long glances and inviting smiles from the same citizens who'd been desperately dodging Anton moments ago.

Not a single one knew the true deception behind that million dollar smile. As approachable and friendly looking as he was, Elijah was a stone cold *killer*.

Despite his Highblood genes and movie star good looks, the deepest parts of Elijah were locked away from the world in a tragedy of bloodshed. When he was only ten years old, his entire family had been murdered right in front of him. In one night he lost his parents, his little sister, and every ounce of empathy he'd ever had. Ever since that tragic night, Elijah had focused on two things and two things only, living life to the fullest and waiting for his shot at vengeance. He'd spent the last fifteen years studying how to make killing an art form, and he reveled in being top of his class. He was fully capable of cutting your throat on a whisper, or breaking your neck on a sigh. The guy could also drink like a damn fish and never suffer a single hangover.

Asshole.

Elijah's tactical boots came to a stuttering stop before Anton. "Hey man, dispatch told me you were headed down here to take an MP report. I was nearby, figured I'd join you."

"I'm not talking to you, Elijah. You said one beer. Not seventeen of those," Anton waved his hand haphazardly in the air, "those gut poisoning concoctions you had me drinking last night. So yeah, I'm not talking to you. In fact, I'm seriously thinking about knocking your ass out."

Elijah grinned, a lopsided, mischievous hitch of his lips.

"Come on A, don't be like that. You had a blast last night! Hell, you took $200 bucks off me in pool, and I'm pretty sure that blonde bartender put her number in your phone before we left. I was ready to go home after three, but you kept making excuses to go over and chat with her so," Elijah shoved his hands into the pockets of his brown bomber jacket, shrugging and rocking backward on his heels, looking only the slightest bit sheepish. "If it helps, I covered the tab. All of it, I swear."

Anton shook his head. He had only the vaguest recollection of the blonde bartender, and he certainly didn't remember getting her number, but that was something at least. He sighed. The most infuriating thing about Elijah? No matter how much he pissed you off, you could never stay mad at the guy. Sure he drank, he caroused, and he womanized. He was too loud, too obnoxious, too *everything*. And he'd step in front of a bullet for you without thinking twice.

Anton sighed, his irritation slowly dissolving, and Elijah's grin widened as they began walking once more.

"It's good you're here then," Anton told him. "I'll go grab a coffee, you can stay and take this report so I can head back to the office."

Elijah shook his head. "No can do, boss. I'm far too attractive to take reports from women solo. It's actually in my personnel file, remember?" Elijah pitched his voice into a high falsetto, mimicking the tone of a kindergarten teacher. "*Mr. Barrett is, unfortunately, not to be trusted in one-on-one situations with single female citizens. While he maintains overtly protective and affectionate tendencies, he also fails to respect his position of power in regards to instigating consensual sexual contact.*"

Anton blew out a breath, rolling his eyes in annoyance. Gods, even that slight movement made his head pound.

"You're the only man I know who could talk your way into a woman's bed right after a death notification for her husband, Elijah."

Elijah put a hand over his heart in mock offense.

"Hey, it only happened once and it wasn't my fault! Her husband was much older and she'd been taking care of him for a really long time. She left the hospital that night to try to catch up on sleep, and he had the nerve to get smothered by his mistress's husband the one night she's not there? The poor thing was so upset. She just really needed a pair of strong shoulders to climb on."

Anton sputtered, glancing around quickly to make sure no one had actually heard that. The last thing he needed today was a citizen complaint on top of everything else.

"Damnit E, I swear your mouth works faster than your brain sometimes. Don't you have actual work to do? Isn't there a knife sharpening seminar for dummies you could attend? I already know you have plenty of overdue case reports to finish. Or is harassing me the only thing on your schedule today? If so, I'm sure I can manage to come up with a list of welfare checks or something."

Elijah gave a derisive snort and threw a companionable arm over Anton's shoulders.

"Don't even try it. My knives are sharp enough to shave the peach fuzz off of your nuts, my friend. And I will NOT, I repeat, *WILL NOT* get conned into doing a welfare check on Maude Tilley again. That old crone smells like dead fish and wood rot got together and had a kid. Last time I let you talk me into a welfare check on her I couldn't get that smell out of my clothes for a week." He crinkled his nose in disgust.

It was Anton's turn to grin. "That 'old crone' is the oldest and most pure blooded fae still around, my friend. You might want to watch your words. There may come a time when you'll be praying to the gods for her to come save your sorry ass."

Despite his words to the contrary, they both knew Elijah

had developed a soft spot for Maude. Anton knew his friend checked in with the elderly wood nymph regularly, usually staying at least long enough to smoke a cheroot and play a hand of poker or two.

As they continued across the plaza, the sudden sound of squealing tires had both their heads snapping up.

A dark sedan careened around the far corner. Through the half-lowered window, they could just make out the figure behind the wheel. Wearing a red skull mask and a black hoodie. Gods damn it. A black hoodie and red skull mask meant only one thing.

The Anord.

Starting out as a historical preservation club for Highblood teens, the Anord's original focus had been studying the histories of Miradea's oldest fae families. They gave talks, passed out free pamphlets in schools, even hosted community events and fundraisers to grow their membership. But in the last twenty years, the focus of their work had shifted dramatically. These days they spouted Highblood entitlement propaganda and held secret rallies protesting the existence of Lowbloods in their city. They were a high powered street gang now, with vandalism and assault their business of choice. They set Lowblood owned businesses on fire, sold street level enhancers to children, even dabbled in Lowblood abduction and trafficking. As prolific as they were, there should have been plenty of them in prison by now. The only problem was, the Anord were somehow top level experts at keeping their identities anonymous. They never claimed credit for any of their crimes. They wore black hoodies to conceal their hair, covering their faces with those red masks. They left no fingerprints, no DNA, and no evidence at all at their crime scenes. They were well trained, insanely disciplined, and somehow ridiculously funded. They were also easily responsible for three-quarters of the unsolved cases in Anton's department.

All in all, they were really starting to piss him off.

At his side, Elijah sank his weight into his knees, his brown and gold wings appearing at his back before he leapt into the air to follow in the sedan's wake. Anton was momentarily stunned. Elijah hated flying.

"Being in the air takes my legs away, messes with my balance," he'd once explained. Though Anton was fairly certain it had less to do with his balance and more to do with the way it reminded his friend of the baby sister he'd lost. Elijah had taught his sister, Isabelle, how to fly when she was three, their father being far too busy to undertake such a task. Once she'd mastered it, the two had spent every waking moment in the air together. Three years after that her life had ended and Elijah had avoided flying as much as possible ever since.

Many citizens in the plaza stared and whispered as Elijah took to the air. Few Highbloods even had wings anymore; the ones that did were descendants of some of the oldest and purest fae bloodlines. He and Elijah were two of only a handful Anton knew of, but to be fair, most winged Highbloods avoided boasting about the ability if they had it. There were very real dangers to having wings. They were vulnerable to attack, made for huge targets, and were easily injured. Pure golden ichor ran through wing veins, and the loss of more than a cup or two of that ichor meant a swift and painful death for the Highblood attached.

Still, Elijah never took a risk that wasn't calculated, and he'd never pass up a clear chance to gain intel on the Anord. They'd been responsible for the death of his family, and he still had a long, bloody score to settle on that front.

Anton turned and kept walking. Whatever trouble the Anord were causing this time, hopefully it would wait at least long enough for him to get his cup of coffee.

As he neared the door to Well Grounded, Anton's headache wasn't prepared for the scream that pierced the air somewhere behind him. He spun, regretting the move instantly, but ignoring the hungover lurch in his gut. Scanning the area, he searched for the source of the scream. There were people everywhere, some strolling, others shopping, but none seemed to be in any major distress. He shook his head. It must have simply been an upset child.

His temples throbbed at him, reminding him he was only a few steps away from high-test salvation. Turning back, the glass window before him suddenly wavered. His eyes followed the ripple and time slowed to a crawl.

Only one thing caused an air pressure distortion like that.

A bomb.

His own massive wings shot out of his back on pure

instinct, but he already knew it was too late.

"LOOK OUT!"

The scream this time wasn't just startling, it was a pure feminine command, an order from a much higher, stronger power. He spun, had a single heartbeat to realize someone was running towards him, fast. He reached out, felt soft fingertips brush his for just a breath. Then he was yanked clean off his feet…

And the world *exploded* behind him.

2

Anton needed to do *something*, he just wasn't sure what that something was. He should probably start with opening his eyes but his eyelids didn't seem to be following his instructions anymore. They felt like lead curtains, heavy and completely immovable. He pulled in a breath, thinking he'd turn over and worry about it after a few more hours of sleep, when the pain in the rest of his body finally registered.

Blistering, pulsating, overwhelming *pain*.

Something was wrong. Something was very wrong. As his senses slowly returned, he could feel the asphalt beneath him, could feel every inch of his body screaming in pain. Then he felt the hollowing out of his mind. The chill settling into his bones. And the gradual slowing of his heart.

He was going to die.

For the briefest second he wondered why dying smelled like vanilla sunscreen and the ocean breeze.

"This is *not* me freaking out, this is me holding it together and doing what needs to be done. You and me, we're going to breathe together big guy. You're going to keep breathing and your heart is going to keep pumping, because it is *NOT* allowed to stop."

The feminine voice slid into his ears like smoke and wove through his mind, softening the sharpest edges of the radiating pain. The words were breathy and panicked, but they still felt like velvet stroking across his skin.

"Damnit, I *said* keep breathing! Come on you Highblood asshole, *DON'T YOU DARE* die on me!" The soft words from before were gone, replaced now with cold, demanding ones that made him feel as if he'd suddenly been slapped.

Though it took every ounce of energy he possessed, Anton managed to crack one eyelid open. When he didn't see anything but a blurry blue smudge above him, he slowly peeled open the other, 200 pounder that it was, and tried to blink slowly. His head was ringing like a gong and his wings were a silent scream of agony raging beneath him. He let out a low groan, feeling like he'd gone ten rounds with a drunk lion shifter.

On strength enhancers.

Forcing out another breath, and then another, still blinking. When both eyes finally came into focus at the same time, he quickly became aware of a small, distinctly female body leaning over him. When he looked down, he saw her hands gliding over his now filthy shirt, a muted golden glow seeping into his body everywhere they touched. When those gentle hands came up to his neck and slid around to the back of his head, he felt the sharpest edge of the pain there instantly ease, his skin warming. Amazed, he looked up to find long, midnight black hair framing a softly rounded face, a pair of big, dark blue eyes watching him intently.

Gods, that blue was...it was…stormy seas and clouds about to burst with rain. Those long dark lashes framed two tiny galaxies, ready to reel a man in and drown him with eternity. When they blinked back at him, he saw they were the tiniest bit big for the face they sat upon, giving the woman a slightly frightened, startled look.

How absolutely mesmerizing. His stomach churned with a sudden, overpowering need to throw her over his shoulder and take her somewhere isolated so he could protect her from everything and everyone.

He closed his eyes again, slowly resting his head back against the ground. What kind of territorial bullshit was going on in his brain? How hard had he hit his head? He shook it slightly, trying to clear the cobwebs, and immediately wished he hadn't. He felt like Humpty Dumpty after his header off the wall. Everything throbbed and his wings felt absolutely shredded. He knew he needed to move, he should get his body weight up and off them as soon as possible. He shifted, bracing to sit up.

"Don't move. I need a little more time. I've got healing magic, but it's not very strong I'm afraid. I need you to lie still and let me keep working."

There it was again, the softer version of that amazing voice. The words were filled with anxious panic, but still stern enough that he opened his eyes and lifted his head to watch her. Her eyes fixed on his intently.

"Don't even *think* of arguing with me, you hardheaded beast. Keep still." When she tugged her lip between her teeth in concentration, his gaze dropped, centering on that delicate mouth. He wondered idly if she'd been kissed anytime lately.

AAAnnndd that was enough of that. He was clearly concussed. Wait a minute, had she just called him a hardheaded beast? He opened his mouth to argue, but then sighed. He didn't have enough energy to dispute her assessment at the moment. Slowly turning his pounding head to the left, Anton saw shattered glass and busted tables, the scattered remains of the coffee shop littering the plaza in a wide arc. Citizens were running in every direction. Some away as fast as they could go, others towards the numerous citizens who were down and bleeding. Many were moaning or crying out for help, some sitting up with dazed expressions on their faces.

Still more lay eerily still.

He could have sworn he'd been standing right in front of the coffee shop, but he was now almost fifty yards away. Had the blast blown him this far? When pain started a protest in the muscles of his neck, he let his head fall back once more, closing his eyes against the glare from the sun. He could hear the healer's breath above him. Had she managed to pull him out of the way? Or maybe magicked them both? He brushed the thought aside. If she was a Lowblood healer like she claimed, there was no way she'd have the power to do anything like that.

"I'm almost done."

He opened his eyes and watched her, this small woman who smelled like the clean breeze over the ocean. When she made a move to sit back a moment later, his hands instinctively grabbed hers. Dark blue eyes darted up to his in shock, her muscles tense and a slow blush climbing up her cheeks.

He was clearly out of his mind.

"Sorry," he croaked, "I just need…a minute." He winced when another spear of pain shot through his head.

She watched his face, then slowly relaxed her hands against his chest. "What still hurts?"

He opened his mouth to answer when a sudden wave of nausea overtook him. He moistened his lips, swallowing down the bile rising in his throat. Gods damned Corpse Revivers.

"Just give me a minute to catch my breath. Everything seems to be spinning."

She tilted her dark head to one side and closed those beautiful eyes. A few moments later a soft thrumming feeling began moving slowly through his chest. It felt like a butterfly had just been set loose beneath his skin. When it fluttered up and around to the back of his head, his nausea eased, the spinning sensation slowing, then stopping altogether.

What kind of magic was *this*?

Anton was Highblood, his ancestors some of the most powerful fae ever to reside in Miradea. His natural healing ability was better than ninety percent of the population, but on the rare occasion when he did need additional help, he saw the top healers in the city. And he'd never once had any healer do - well, whatever the hell it was that she was currently doing.

The odd fluttering continued to move slowly through his body. It slid around to his back, lightly brushing his wings and he jerked, hissing out a curse. The pain centered there battered at him like a drum. The butterfly hovered, a cool breeze of relief dissolving more of the pain with each flutter. He sighed, relaxing into the easing, and took a long, slow breath.

Moments later the butterfly was gone, the beautiful woman above him now panting heavily. Her brow was furrowed, a pained expression on her face, and her hands were tense and stiff under his.

She cleared her throat, taking another moment to catch her breath before she spoke.

"Your head will be a little tender for a while, but nothing an ice pack and some good rest can't fix. Your wings will need a little more help from a stronger healer though. I did what I could, but there's still at least two small fractures you should have treated."

Anton stared at her, dumbfounded. Healers could mend obvious injury, but they couldn't diagnose. It was literally the only reason they still had med units and hospitals here in the city. How could she possibly know he had fractures?

A shadow blocked out the sun above and they both glanced up, Elijah dropping from the skies to land in a crouch beside them.

"Good gods, what the hell happened here? It looks like a bomb went off...," he stopped talking, realization dawning.

"Did you catch them?" Anton demanded.

Elijah shook his head. "No. I followed the sedan out to the badlands, but then I lost them in the damned fog." He took another long look around, spearing a hand roughly through his hair, leaving it as messy and confused as the look on his face. "Is this what those creeps were up to?"

Anton nodded, the ache in his temples continuing to ease. His hands finally released the beautiful young woman he'd been holding on to so fiercely, and she scrambled to her feet. Did he imagine the small moment of wistful regret passing over her face?

Elijah gripped her elbow to steady her for a moment, then stepped forward offering Anton a hand. A low groan escaped as he pulled himself to his feet, but the relief in Anton's wings once they were free of his weight was instantaneous. He tucked them away, rubbing plaster and concrete dust out of his hair as he answered.

"Seems like too much of a coincidence for it not to be, but we don't know anything for sure yet. Call headquarters. Have Asher bring a team down here and let's get started on processing this mess."

Elijah nodded. Asher was the best tracker either of them had ever known, and one hell of a good detective. He was a wolf shifter, Highblood ancestry without a doubt, but he had no memory of his biological parents. His adoptive parents were Lowbloods, and when Anton had been given the go ahead to form the task force three years ago, Asher had been one of the first to sign on.

"Have Callan start a deep dive on the owners of the coffee shop. Tell him to send down every healer we've got right away. We're going to need four or five unis as well for traffic control and heavy lifting. And for the gods sake, someone *please* find me a fucking coffee.

We've got a lot of injured citizens down here, and a huge crime scene to work. It's going to be a long day."

"I'm on it, Anton."

The young healer's mouth dropped open, the color swiftly draining from her face. "You're with the police department? He called you Anton, are you Anton Tevaris?"

Anton paused, watching her intently for a moment. "Yes, that's me, have we met before?" He asked out of sheer courtesy. If they'd ever met in the past he would have damn well remembered that face.

Those storm cloud eyes were now brimming with worry. His stomach twisted at that look, at the horror and shame now warring in her expression. Why would she—

"I'm the reason you're here," she said quietly, a slight tremor in her tone. "I'm the person you're supposed to meet. My name is Mayla."

"Mayla," he repeated, the sound sliding across his tongue like a caress. It took a moment for his battered brain to catch up, but when it all clicked into place his eyebrows raised in astonishment.

"Wait. You called in the missing person report?"

She was nodding, her face red. "For my friend, Willow. I'm so very sorry. Gods, you could have been killed!" Her hands flew up to cover her mouth, her big eyes huge and terrified. "If we hadn't agreed to meet *here*," she looked around them, as if him being in this exact spot at this exact time had been her fault. In reality, it was all *his*.

He was the hungover idiot who'd wanted coffee.

"Nonsense. This was in no way your fault. If anything it was mine, I chose the location." He smiled at her, pleased when her horror dissipated just a bit. Her hands lowered, the redness in her cheeks fading to a soft pink. "Look, I'm going to be busy with all this for a while, but, would you mind hanging around? We could really use your healing skills, and afterward I can get that information from you so we can start looking for your friend."

She offered him a tremulous smile and nodded. "I'm not as good as most healers, but I'm happy to do what I can." Looking around at the chaos she took a deep breath. "I'll find you later?"

He nodded, watching as she walked away, drywall dust making the back of her onyx hair look silver in spots. A small shiver slid through him. Now that he was upright, for some strange reason he felt cold.

"Anton," Elijah's voice was dark and ominous from a few steps behind him. "You really need to see this."

Turning, he followed his friends wide eyed gaze downward. The concrete where he'd been laying was drenched in a huge swath of shimmering golden ichor.

3

Mayla Charles walked away as steadily as she could physically manage. Her stomach had tied itself in a knot, flipped itself upside down, and was now trembling like a chihuahua in a thunderstorm.

What had just happened?

This was not how this morning was supposed to go. According to the dispatcher she'd spoken with earlier, she was to come downtown, meet Officer Anton Tevaris to fill out some information, and then sign a form so the police could start helping her look for Willow. After driving around to all their usual hang out spots last night with no luck, Mayla had been so worried, she hadn't even *thought* to go by Green Tease until the sun was already staring to peek over the horizon this morning.

When she pulled up in front of the shop to find the plants in the front windows starting to brown and wither, her stomach had bottomed out. Willow would never leave the shop that way, it was her pride and joy. Her friend had spent her entire life savings to buy the little building outright when it had gone into foreclosure, and had put in months of work to fix it up before opening. She would never abandon it…at least, not willingly.

Mayla had headed back to her apartment then, spent twenty minutes battling a full on panic attack, and finally decided to call the police. Ten minutes after that call, she'd been back in the car and on her way downtown to meet Officer Tevaris.

In no realm of possibility had she ever thought that within the hour she'd be involved in a bombing? Her life felt like it was somehow imploding, and she was just along for the ride. *A bombing.* How was that even possible?

She was still trying to wrap her head around what had happened. As she walked through the debris scattered across the plaza, her breath felt like it was burning in her chest, a fire battering against the wall of her ribs. She'd pushed herself too hard with the tall handsome Highblood, given so much of her magic to heal him that she was feeling waves of pain and fatigue. And her back was suddenly killing her. If she didn't know any better she would swear her skin was split open there, huge jagged cuts that screamed at her every time the fabric of her shirt brushed against them. But she didn't have to check to know there was nothing actually there.

This wasn't the first time she'd had phantom pain after a healing. Her magic wasn't just temperamental, it was an unpredictable pain in the ass. As she had so often growing up, Mayla secretly yearned for the same strength Highbloods had. With their level of magic she wouldn't have to deal with these crazy side effects. She wouldn't have to worry about the strange colors she saw in her mind or the sudden strong feelings that sometimes overwhelmed her. Instead she'd be able to help people and then just go on about her day.

Take Anton for instance. He definitely had strong magic, those wings were proof he was about as powerful as you could get. The man could probably snap and cause a hurricane, or maybe sneeze and set the world on fire. Meanwhile, here she was, struggling to heal bumps and bruises without feeling like she'd been hit by a car.

Speaking of cars, that stupid sedan had been her first hint that something horrible was going to happen. An image had flashed in her mind as soon as she saw the car. She'd seen someone wearing a red mask walking through a door. Then another image, this one of a strange looking briefcase sitting next to a wooden chair. She could see green striped wallpaper, could smell espresso, even heard the low din of people chatting. The mental images had been so clear she'd almost stumbled on the sidewalk. She'd been turning the corner onto the plaza when it had shifted from an image to a blaring warning inside her head. She'd seen multicolored wires and numbers on a clock face, a red and orange pulse counting down to something horrible.

She'd seen *him* then, broad and handsome and completely engrossed in whatever he was looking at through that damned window. Her mind disengaged and her mouth took over. She was screaming before she had the time to realize she was running towards the danger, not away from it like she should have been.

He'd looked around at the sound, why hadn't he moved? Still running, she'd had no idea how she was going to get a man of his size to move, but she had to try. The next heartbeat his wings snapped outward and gods they were so breathtakingly beautiful, a deep purple interlaced with silver. She'd wanted to reach out and touch them, run a finger down their edges, but it was already too late. They'd both taken too long. He'd spun to face her. Had she screamed again? She'd gotten just close enough to brush his fingertips, before they'd both been launched off their feet.

Mayla had been dazed, her head and her ears ringing. She'd lain there a moment, hearing only her hard breath pulling in and out, waiting for her body to register the pain. After a few moments she realized her backside had been seriously bruised, but not much else.

It was when she sat up that she saw him.

His larger body was lying right next to her, shielding her from the worst of the explosion. He was so very still. He'd landed on his side, those beautiful, stunning wings facing the decimated building and leaking some kind of golden liquid. She knew Highbloods healed quicker thanks to their stronger fae blood, but that wasn't going to be enough. Not for *this*. She needed to help him. She scrambled over, turning him as gently as she could onto his back and calling up her healing magic. She felt a tightness around her heart ease when she saw his chest slowly rise and then fall. He was still breathing, but barely. Thank the gods. She couldn't fix him completely, but hopefully, with any luck, she could at least keep him alive.

She pushed absolutely every bit of her magic she could into his chest, feeling the strain of it in her mind. She knew she'd pay for it later, that she would be exhausted, overwhelmed and in all sorts of pain before it was over with, but she'd worry about that later. When he finally stirred, opening the most amazing pair of light blue eyes she'd ever seen, her mouth had gone instantly dry. Her heart started fluttering around in her chest, but she kept working, thankful when he chose to listen to her and kept still.

Then he'd reached up and grabbed her hands. That contact sent a tingle of awareness down her spine and a warm wave of total calm through her body. She'd never felt so many different ways at once, excited yet at ease, scared but suddenly completely calm. How completely bizarre.

Shaking her head, Mayla tried to get her brain back on track. She was supposed to be helping people. Instead, her mind was all over the place, sky high and rock bottom at the same time. She knew her mind was trying to protect her, trying to buffer her from the pain and chaos of the explosion. Whatever people were feeling around her, she always seemed to be able to feel it too, she couldn't help it. Her parents told her it was all in her head, that she felt things too deeply. That she needed to stop worrying so much about everyone else and focus on living her own life.

And she'd tried, she really had. It just never seemed to work.

So now here she was, still determined to help, her nerves jangling and her head buzzing as she approached a frazzled looking woman climbing through the debris in front of the blasted out cafe windows. The woman's fear radiated from her. It was complete abject terror, a blood red, jagged entity in Mayla's mind.

The thin, caramel skinned woman in horn rimmed glasses looked up at her in a daze, her eyes unfocused as she picked up random, small pieces of debris and tossed them behind her. Blood trickled from a deep gash on her right temple. When she spoke her voice constantly changed pitch, high and panicked one moment, calm and collected the next. Shock, Mayla thought.

"My baby!! Please!! Where's Dustin?" Her tone softened, calming. "He's wearing his new outfit today, the one he just got from his granny. Did you see his little tennis shoes? He loves those shoes. Always kicking his feet and smiling at them. We just came out for a walk to enjoy the sunshine today. His father and I don't know his magics yet, the doctor said they usually manifest at around a year or two, but he's still too young."

When she raised a hand to cradle her injured temple, Mayla's own head throbbed in response and she blinked, trying to push away the discomfort.

"Dustin is such a good boy you know. He's so well behaved in his stroller the other moms get jealous. They're always asking me, 'Cassandra, how did you get so lucky? He's so happy all the time!' He was playing with his shoes while I drank my latte. Have you seen his shoes?"

She started to pace then, wringing her hands and looking around. "We must have come outside, but I just can't remember. It's so bright out today. Don't you think it's bright out?" The woman stopped mid stride, shielding her eyes and looking upwards towards the blazing sun.

Mayla's heart dropped like a heavy stone into a still pond. She turned a slow 360, but there wasn't a single stroller in sight.

No.

Oh gods, *no*.

They must have been inside when the explosion happened. If this woman was concussed or in shock, maybe even both, it would easily explain her confusion. But if she was out *here* that meant her child might still be…

Mayla's eyes shot to what remained of the coffee shop. One wall was crumpled inward, a deflated accordion of concrete and rebar. Huge shards of jagged glass outlined the edges of the window, a security alarm blaring somewhere deep within. A small fire burned in one corner, just under a sparking electrical wire that was hanging from the ceiling. A huge slab of concrete she was pretty sure used to be the sidewalk had been blown upward and leaned against one pillar, blocking any access. Smoke billowed out from behind the slab.

Crap. It was either through the concrete or around it, there was a no other way. Maybe, if she could just shove it off balance a little, it would fall forward and she could climb over. But when she tried yanking at the hunk of concrete, it didn't budge. She braced her palms against it and pushed, groaning with the effort. Even if she could somehow manage to move this thing and get in, sweet gods, what if the child was—

A stab of fear pierced Mayla's chest and she halted that thought before it could go any further. She was already overloaded and she knew it. Her mind was in full fledged trauma mode and wanted her to escape, *right now*, but she ignored it. She couldn't just stand here like a quivering idiot. She had to do something. And right now something meant moving this slab.

She switched tactics, pulling instead of pushing at the concrete. Her arms began burning under the strain, hands scraping and fingernails splitting as they scrambled for a better grip.

4

A pair of large masculine hands came over hers, strong fingers gently lifting hers loose. When she turned, Anton stood behind her, those ice blue eyes and ridiculously long lashes looking at her with concern. He'd found something to tie his white hair back with, and it drew attention to the strong line of his jaw. His mouth was set in a firm line, his brow deeply furrowed as he watched her. Mayla felt her heart rate slow, the frantic edge of Cassandra's terror slowly dissipating.

There it was again.

That feeling of crazy attraction yes, but even stronger, a sudden feeling of utter calm. It was exactly what she'd felt earlier when he'd held her hands. It soothed her, muting the raging red in her mind and easing the terror back into a steady, slow heartbeat. She took a deep breath in, letting it out on a long, slow exhale.

When he spoke his voice was low and even, as if they were simply chatting over coffee, not standing in the shattered remains of a bomb site.

"Tell me what you need."

"We have to get inside. There's—," her breath caught before she could steady herself. "There's a child missing."

His eyes went wide, and she watched his jaw tense. He didn't move immediately, just stared at her, noting every little movement, including the way the tension in her shoulders eased the longer he stood before her. When he raised his eyebrows in a silent question she nodded, stepping to the side and out of his way. Wrapping his muscled arms around the huge hunk of concrete, he braced his legs wide, then heaved it up and over his right shoulder, tossing it onto the street without so much as a grunt of effort. More debris blocked the storefront behind where the slab had been, but there was at least enough space for Mayla to squeeze through.

When Anton turned, small specks of gold oozed through the fabric of his shirt, and Mayla felt an answering throb in her own shoulders. Those beautiful purple wings were nowhere to be seen, but clearly they were not completely healed, Highblood genetics or no.

"You're still injured," she blurted.

"I'll be fine. There's only a little ache left thanks to you, and I can already feel it healing," he lied. His wings were still throbbing like someone had taken a sledgehammer to them, but he'd never admit it, especially not with that embarrassment coloring her cheeks. Could she truly have no idea what she'd managed to do? Did she not realize how much damage there had really been? How was it possible she didn't even know how strong her own magic was?

He worked to reel in his wayward thoughts. That was a question for another time. Right now, people needed their help. Over their heads, smoke was escaping the building in black billowing clouds. He looked over at Mayla, the blue of his eyes slowly dissipating to a pure glacial white.

"Hold still, things are going to get a bit…chilly."

The temperature around them suddenly plummeted, Mayla's breath coming out in little white puffs. Above the black smoke a gray cloud formed, moving quickly over their heads to press through the shattered window frame and into the building. Once inside the cloud paused, hovering, sleet beginning to fall in steady sheets. Ice formed over the edges of the sparking wires. The freezing rain spit and hissed as it extinguished the fire, the black smoke gradually clearing.

Mayla gaped. Mother of gods, he was an *ice wielder*.

Such a thing was so rare she'd never even met anyone with the ability before, she only knew they existed from the viral videos she'd seen online. As the last of the black smoke cleared, the white in Anton's eyes melted away, those irises slowly returning to their usual blue. He wasn't even out of breath.

Cassandra approached them, patting Anton's shoulder. "Have you seen Dustin's new shoes? He loves those shoes."

Mayla pointed to the woman. "Help her. I'll be back in a minute."

Anton started. "Wait, where do you think—"

Mayla turned, disappearing over the jagged edge of the window and into the darkness within. Once inside, she ducked a giant twisted metal beam, weaving around huge hunks of busted drywall. Before long, she had to crawl on all fours to get any farther. She'd considered, for the briefest moment, letting Anton try and retrieve the child, but with his height and those massive shoulders, he'd have never made it through. Plus, she wasn't at all sure what condition she would find the baby in, if she even managed to find him. If she did, there was a very real chance he would need healing.

"Please, please, *please* be okay. Please don't be dead. Sweet gods, *PLEASE,*" she whispered, trying - and failing miserably - to brace herself for the heartbreak she might find.

She inched deeper into the decimated coffee shop on her hands and knees. How was this happening? She was not the type of woman who crawled through mutilated buildings minutes after an explosion. She was the type of woman who processed insurance claims remotely from her living room because she couldn't stand the noise of a regular office. The type who ate an entire bag of cheese puffs while watching other people do this kind of thing on TV.

As she crawled around yet another pile of crumbled drywall, she spotted a black stroller. It lay on its side, one wheel spinning slowly…ominously. Bile rose in her throat and she pushed it back down, swallowing hard.

She couldn't do this. She didn't want to see this. Even as her mind screamed at her and her heart threatened to crack open in her chest, Mayla kept moving, inching closer. Squatting down, she pulled the stroller towards her slowly, then heaved out a huge breath.

There was nothing inside.

Sliding it out of the way, she kept moving forward, the knees of her jeans soaking up a dark liquid from the carpet. She tugged in a tremulous breath. Please be coffee. She'd give just about anything to have that liquid be a half caff, double pump, caramel skinny what-the-hell-ever right about now. She pushed two broken chairs out of her path, zigzagged between a collection of overturned tables, and the breath caught in her lungs.

There he was.

The tiny infant lay on the floor, a halo of white light covering him from head to toe. He looked back at her in quiet fascination, his small feet kicking at the air as he sucked industriously on a green, frog faced pacifier that matched his green overalls and tiny green and white tennis shoes. She reached out tentatively, touching a fingertip to the lightly pulsing white light. When her skin brushed the light, a zing of electricity shot painfully up her arm, and she pulled back, flexing her fingers to dispel the sting.

Shield magic!

Mayla couldn't suppress a sudden, hysterical giggle of relief. "What a good boy you are, Dustin! Look what you did!"

She kept her voice light and happy, her smile broad. Covering her eyes with her hand for a moment, she then popped her head up and over, grinning at him.

A peal of laughter sounded from the child and the white light surrounding him faded. Mayla laughed when he spit out his pacifier to give her a wide, toothless grin. Reaching over, she picked him up gently, talking happily while she did so. Holding him against her chest, she marveled at the small, heavy weight of him, cradling his head to her shoulder and laughing again when he grabbed a fistful of her hair.

"You can hold on to that for now," she cooed, backing up slowly and turning around.

She kept one arm braced tightly around his small body, the other sliding along the floor beneath them, determined to clear any impediment. The progress was agonizingly slow, but she was determined to protect him from every jagged edge, and every single splinter.

"Just don't try to take that hair with you when we part little man, there's no makeup to cover a bald spot." She kept up the soft chatter, hoping to keep him calm.

"I can't wait to see your mommy's face when she sees you're okay," she whispered. "She loves you and is very worried about you. Let's get you out of this mess and back to her, okay?"

Dustin gurgled in response and she felt a tiny wave of yellow happiness caress her cheek.

When Mayla finally stepped back over the jagged window ledge a few minutes later with Dustin in her arms, the warm sunshine on her face had never felt so amazing.

She'd done it. She'd gotten him out.

Dustin's mother let out a keening cry of joy. "My baby! Oh, thank the blessed gods! Dustin!!"

Mayla couldn't stop the tears of relief that began sliding down her own cheeks as she passed the child over. "Protection magic. He's a shield," she told the Cassandra and Anton with a watery smile. "A strong one too, I don't think there's a mark on him."

Her eyes found Anton's. At his look of concern she quickly swiped at the tears spilling down her cheeks, offering him a watery grin and a soft nod. The resulting change in his expression robbed her of breath. Those crystal blue eyes warmed, dancing with unexpected delight. Then his aquiline features spread into a glorious grin, revealing a small dimple in his left cheek.

Mayla forgot how to breathe.

Cassandra was inspecting her son from his head to tiny little tennis shoes.

"I couldn't find any injuries but..." Mayla's voice trailed off. Even the thought sent bone rattling chills down her spine and caused dark, anxious pools of terror to gather in her gut.

Cassandra was shaking her head, her expression pure wonder. "He's okay. He's fine. He's just, perfect."

Stepping forward, she balanced her son in the crook of one arm and wrapped her other arm fast and hard around Mayla's neck. "Thank you," she whispered fiercely.

Mayla gave her a tight squeeze in return and nodded.

Cassandra looked over to where Anton stood, arms crossed, but posture relaxed.

"Thank you both so much. Really, I," she started to tremble, "I can't thank you enough. I just, I don't know why I was so worried about his shoes." Her eyes glazed just a bit, but her grip on her son never wavered.

Anton moved quickly, placing an arm around the woman's shoulders and the other just under Dustin's behind as he smiled.

"There's an on site medical unit setting up just down the block. Let's go get you checked out and have them look over your boy just to be safe, okay? We'll call your husband once we get there, I'm sure he's worried sick. How about I walk you over? "

Mayla watched her release a shaky exhale and nod, leaning into Anton's comforting support. Throwing a grateful smile back in Mayla's direction, she and Anton walked down the chaos filled street, her son wrapped tightly in her arms.

An hour later, hands braced on her knees, Mayla struggled to catch her breath and ease the dull, pounding pain in her head.

She was exhausted. There was so much pain, so much fear, and so much disbelief everywhere. All three sensations battered at her like waves in an agitated surf. Fatigue rode her hard, and her legs felt like they were tied with heavy weights, the pressure dragging her down with every step.

Four more healers had arrived to help, and a group of officers had moved those that could not be helped into one location, a dark haired wolf-shifter Anton called Asher directing them. Word had spread quickly about the explosion, and a crowd of onlookers now gathered around the edges of the plaza. That rakish friend of Anton's that dropped from the sky earlier had introduced himself as Elijah, and he was now directing things, phone pressed to one ear, arms waving as he directed the injured into one group and spectators into another.

"If you were involved in the incident, please take a seat in *this* area. If you need a med unit and can walk, please go right down the block to your left and get in line, but make sure you give me your name and contact info before you go. If you cannot walk or need help, please let the big guy over there know," he pointed at Anton and paused. "Now I know what you're thinking. He's obviously not as good looking as I am, and you're right. We can't all be perfect. Overall he's still pretty friendly though, and he happens to be phenomenal at heavy lifting, so he's just about perfect for the job."

Anton rolled his eyes, his attention on helping a limping elderly gentleman and the man's terrified granddaughter. The little girl couldn't have been more than eight years old, and she was now transfixed, her stare jumping back and forth between Elijah and Anton. Narrowing his eyes at his best friend, Anton gave a quick jerk of his chin, a visual *get back to what the hell you're supposed to be doing* reprimand.

Elijah grinned, then spun on a heavily booted heel, moving back toward the crowd of spectators and speaking urgently into his phone.

"Callan, I need any and all video you can find of the explosion. Focus on the street cams and any socials that have stills or footage from just beforehand. I also need current video of EVERY SINGLE SPECTATOR THAT'S RECORDING ANYTHING RIGHT NOW."

He let his voice get loud at the last, turning to glare at the crowd, many of them quickly stashing phones into bags or pockets. Those that didn't he eyeballed directly, before speaking to the group as a whole.

"Any of you step foot onto this crime scene and I will take immense joy in removing you myself. It's been a rough morning folks, to be honest, I could really use the stress relief." After one more long, meaningful look at the crowd, Elijah directed his attention back to his phone.

"Callan, did you get it? Awesome, shoot it over to me will you?" There was a quick pause, then Elijah blew out a frustrated breath. "Seriously Cal, do we have to do this EVERY time? I just need —," he stopped again, his jaw clenched. When he spoke again, his voice had gone completely monotone, his expression utterly irritated.

"Fine. 'Cal is the absolute best vampire I've ever met. I promise to bring him boba next time I see him because he deserves it.' There, I said it. Yes, I will bring it. No, I won't forget. Just send me the damn footage, would you? Gods Cal, you really are a demon sometimes you know that?"

There was a loud squawking on the other end of the phone, and Elijah pulled the device away from his ear, cringing.

"Okay, I'm sorry! Vampire, not demon. Vam-pire, I got it." Elijah mashed a finger into the phone before stashing the device in his back pocket, rolling his eyes.

Anton was scraped and sore, his clothes saturated with sweat, blood, and gods knew what else. He'd traded his dress shirt for an MTF t-shirt, but the blue material looked black at this point. He'd moved debris, carried injured, directed traffic and then rinsed and repeated for what was starting to feel like an eternity. Asher had shown up a short time ago, the quiet man getting to work immediately in that quick, efficient way of his.

Anton rolled his shoulders back and pushed his chest out, grunting a little at the aching stretch. The pain in his wings was almost gone, easing more by the hour. Glancing sideways to check on Mayla's progress, his brow furrowed in concern. The woman looked ready to fall over. She was pale, clammy and not at all stable on her feet. Twenty minutes ago he'd tried to get her to sit, had given an officer an order to find her a water and a snack of some sort, but she'd refused.

"Thanks, but no. I'll rest when everyone that needs it has been helped. When I can't feel their pain anymore."

Interesting. He wasn't sure she even realized what she'd said, but the comment only worked to verify what he'd already started to suspect about her magic. He let the matter drop, but he'd started checking on her, scanning the crowd for her face every few minutes. Her color was steadily getting worse, and as hard as it was to believe, he was now certain she had no idea why. He studied her, wondering if it was really his place to share with her what he suspected.

How could he be so pompous as to try to tell her what her own magic was doing? Picking up a mangled chair, he carried it over and tossed it on an ever growing pile of debris, then turned to watch her once more. Whether he told her his suspicions or not, he was determined to keep a close eye on her. If she was what he thought she might be, her magic could only take so much.

Mayla crossed to the opposite corner of the plaza, working her way towards an older woman propped up against the side of one of the unaffected buildings. She had waved them off earlier, insisting she wasn't as injured as the others, and directing each healer to help the others first.

"Ma'am? My name is Mayla and I'm here to help. Everyone else has been taken care of now. You're the very last one. You are so very sweet to be patient. Can I at least help you over to the med unit?"

The woman's hair was a rich espresso color streaked with gray. It lay neatly braided over one shoulder, her dark brown skin stunningly beautiful. Her countenance was serene, her eyes closed like she may be meditating, but she let a small smile slip out at Mayla's words. When she finally spoke, the words came out in a rush, puffing out on a huff of pain.

"I may have waited too long, I'm sorry. I'm afraid I can't stand up. My leg is broken." She pulled her wine colored, bohemian style skirt up, revealing her legs beneath.

Mayla's eyes followed the skirt as it rose. One leg turned at an impossible angle down close to the ankle, a jagged, blood smeared bone sticking upright out of the skin. Mayla started to shake, her head swimming and her equilibrium tilting dangerously. She swallowed hard, turning, her eyes searching frantically for help, only to find Anton already striding quickly toward her, a look of sudden worry on his face. When she tried to take a step towards him, a brutal, searing pain shot up her leg and through her chest, slamming into her already throbbing head.

And the world went dark.

5

"No arguments, Mayla. I told you, my wings are fine. You however, just passed out right in the middle of the damn street. You let me fly you somewhere to get some rest - somewhere with friends or family to keep an eye on you just in case - or you march over to that med unit and get checked out right now."

Anton towered over the curb where she sat, still recovering. He had those powerful arms crossed over his chest, his feet braced apart, and Mayla knew there was no way she was going to get around this.

"I don't need to go to the med unit. I told you I'll be fine. I just overdid it a bit. My magic isn't very strong and I pushed it too hard."

Her hands were still trembling around the water bottle he'd shoved into her hands moments ago, a rough blanket that may have once been a tablecloth now draped over shoulders.

Anton simply raised an eyebrow.

"Still not a debate. Flying or med unit. Make your choice."

When Anton launched them into the air ten minutes later, Mayla felt her stomach flip-flop and her heartbeat skitter in her chest. Cool air rushed past them, the chill biting at her cheeks with sharp little teeth. She peeked her eyes open and looked down, then slammed them shut again. Bile rose, a swift tide of WTF-do-you-think-you-are-doing running through her mind. She turned her face into Anton's shoulder, sucking in deep lungfuls of air. His smell was clean and crisp, a blend of sandalwood and clove that instantly soothed her. He smelled like a campfire on a midwinter night, a spicy, woodsy scent that warmed her from the inside out.

The strong column of his throat started vibrating against her forehead and she realized he was laughing at her timidness, though trying gallantly to hide it. She pulled her head back and slitted her eyes at him, ignoring the skies around them to study his profile instead. First, those eyes. So blue they were almost shocking, framed with dark, ridiculously long lashes. Then the smooth brow and aquiline nose, those lips that managed to look both stern and velvet soft. When those lips opened, she dropped her gaze quickly to his neck, hoping he hadn't caught her staring.

"Let me get this straight. You can climb through an exploded building at a massive trauma scene, not bat an eyelash at bloody injuries and even death, but a little flying is what terrifies you?"

His chuckle, low and soft as it was, tickled against her forehead like a kiss.

She managed a small smile. In her defense, everything he'd complimented her on she'd managed to do on the ground.

"It's not the flying."

She turned her face into the wind, shoring up her courage and shoving her fear deep within. If she looked straight ahead at the horizon it wasn't quite so bad, though the swift moving air still stole her breath when she spoke.

"It's more the falling thousands of feet to my bloody, miserable death I'm uncomfortable with."

"No falling, got it," he agreed, his speed constant and unchanging as he glided smoothly through the air. "In an effort to increase your confidence in me, it may help you to know that I've been flying since I was four. I'm happy to say I haven't lost a passenger yet."

She eyed him suspiciously. "You promise?"

"I swear on the lives of the old gods and my mother's entire bridge club," he said with the utmost solemnity.

She giggled.

"I'm dead serious. Just a few years ago Mrs. Winston got her locations for bridge club mixed up. She showed up at my mother's front door with an entire platter of crudités, when in fact, she was supposed to be across town at the Smithstons townhouse. I offered to fly her over, as it would be so much faster than driving. Do you know that ungrateful woman screeched at me the entire time not to spill anything off her platter and to stop trying to look at her stockings? For reference, Mrs. Winston was at least seventy at the time. The very last thing I was doing was trying to look at her damn stockings."

Mayla snickered once, pressed a hand over her mouth, then gave up and laughed out loud. The mental image of this strong, stern man carting a complaining, sour old woman through the sky while she yelled at him was just too much.

His lips curled in a private little smile and she found her eyes drawn there, her laugh slowly fading. He was mesmerizing up close, and she was having a very hard time not looking at him. She watched as he blinked, those ridiculously long eyelashes brushing gently across his high cheekbones. She was close enough, if she wanted to she could lean up and press a kiss to the skin there. Her eyes dropped to his mouth once more.

His curious sideways glance had her yanking her thoughts back over the double yellow where they belonged, a flush of heat climbing up her cheeks.

His wings beat once and she clutched at the front of his shirt with both hands, but they simply rose a little higher before resuming their previous smooth glide. When she dared a quick peek downward, the city of Miradea sprawled beneath them, the buildings just starting to light up as dusk settled in around them. Far off in the distance, she could make out the black fog of the badlands.

Anton cleared his throat. "My point being, if I didn't drop Mrs. Winston - and trust me, I was sorely tempted - then you have absolutely nothing to worry about. Now how about you tell me exactly what happened to you today? You dropped like a stone. Hell, I thought your heart had stopped. I'm not going to lie, you scared the absolute shit out of me." The words were raspy and raw, as if they had scraped his throat on the way out.

Mayla's heart twisted and she sucked in a breath at his

confession. She supposed he did deserve some type of explanation.

"Sometimes I...well...," her words stalled out.

She *really* hated how weak this was going to make her sound. No doubt he'd never once worried about his magic not being strong enough, or his mind not working the same way as everyone else's. She took a deep breath, counting in her head until her racing heartbeat finally slowed, then started over.

"My magic can be pretty temperamental. I can get overwhelmed when I use it too much or I push too hard."

He waited patiently, eyes still on the horizon, strong arms cradling her close to his warm chest. He didn't push for more details or ask any questions. He just waited.

"Intense situations often get pretty rough. When I get really tired like that it's hard not to physically feel what I'm seeing." She stopped for a moment, thinking before she continued.

"Look, I'm just a Lowblood healer, I know that. No Highblood genetics or amazing abilities here. My magic, what little I have, it just tends to wear me out. I feel things before others do, or I sometimes feel them more. So, when I'm around a lot of intense situations, like what happened today, I get...overloaded."

Anton clenched his jaw, but she didn't seem to notice. He'd suspected that she had no idea what she was, but he still couldn't believe it. *How* could she not know? She'd been struggling her entire life to handle an ability that no one had even recognized? That she'd never been taught how to manage? Did she not even realize how much power she truly had?

"I think maybe it's a sensory issue, or an anxiety response. I've talked to other healers, tried all sorts of therapies and such, but nothing really works. When I go too far and pass out, like I did today, I'll be worn out for a day or two, but then I'm okay again. I've just sort of learned to live with it."

When Anton remained silent, she shifted, suddenly nervous. He probably thought she was a total nutcase. Rushing to fill the silence, she pushed on.

"Most of the time I can tell when it's too much. I know when I need to go somewhere quiet and just focus on calming myself down. It's just that sometimes that's kind of impossible, like it was today. I couldn't really say *sorry, I know you're bleeding and in pain, but I need a little mental health break, I'll be right back.* So yeah. I'm just a little bit crazy I guess." She forced a shrug. "But hey, who isn't these days, right?"

"You're not crazy, Mayla," he said sternly. His blue eyes looked down at her, his expression a mixture of awe and was that... disbelief?

"Sure, yeah, I just meant—"

"Don't ever say you're crazy, Mayla. You're not crazy at all, and you're not just a low level healer, either. Your mind isn't confused, and you're not weak by any stretch of the imagination. You saved my life today. Not just with your healing magic, but with something much, much stronger." The finality in his voice echoed in the skies around them.

He gave her a few moments to process what he'd said. A few moments of nothing but cool air brushing across her face before he turned her world upside down. A few moments before he told her what he'd realized the moment he saw that golden ichor spread across the pavement.

"Mayla, your power was what pulled us away from that blast today. Your magic did that because you wanted it to. Your magic went into my body and my mind, and healed injuries that should have been fatal. That only happened because you willed it to happen.

Mayla, you're not just a healer. You're an *empath.*

The strongest damn empath I've ever seen."

6

If Mayla reminded him of a tormented, stormy sea, the woman standing before Anton now seemed more like a wildfire blazing out of control. She had long, fiery red hair, a pert little nose spattered with a handful of freckles, and a pair of hazel eyes that were currently so intensely focused on him he could almost feel them scorch his skin.

Anton and Mayla had arrived at the split level modern farmhouse on the outskirts of the city just over half an hour ago. He'd landed on the front walk, wasting no time in striding right up to the door to knock heavily. When the bright red door opened, the three people standing inside took one look at Mayla, still pale and shaky in his arms, and ushered him inside immediately.

The strongest damn empath I've ever seen.

Mayla hadn't spoken a single word to him after that. She'd gone completely silent and her trembling had increased, though he couldn't be sure if that was from the cool air or from the information he'd just dumped all over her. He gave himself another mental kick in the ass.

Sure, why not give huge, life changing, massively overwhelming information to an empath after a completely traumatic day? He was such an asshole.

Mayla's mother and sister both fired more than a few questions at him, and he was getting a lot of '*if I find out this was your fault*' looks from the tall blonde man he assumed was Mayla's father. Throughout this chaos, a small white dog jumped around Anton's feet, barking in a ridiculously high pitched yip and threatening - in not so many words - to rip Anton's head off if he tried anything shady.

Still, when her parents directed them into the living room and motioned for him to put Mayla on the sofa, his arms had tightened around her just a fraction. He was in no hurry to get rid of her warm, slight weight. He'd much rather find a quiet room where they could talk. He wanted to apologize for his delivery, to swear he'd help her get all of this sorted out, and then tuck her into a nice warm bed where she could sleep, undisturbed for as long as she needed. One look at the rest of her family however, and he realized that was not going to happen.

He begrudgingly settled Mayla onto the couch, tucking a soft white blanket around her legs before turning to offer explanations. He'd told them everything he legally could, about the bombing, about how Mayla had helped so many and worn herself out. Partway through his explanation, Mayla's mother bent down and picked up the little white dog and the yipping finally ceased.

Thank the blessed gods.

Shortly thereafter, Mayla's sister pulled him aside, but he was finding it very hard to stay focused on what the woman was saying to him. His gaze continuously wandered back over to Mayla, searching her face for any signs of distress.

Even completely drained and clearly exhausted as she was, she made the effort to smile, grasping her mother's hand while letting her father pull her in for a bear hug. Her mother was small and active, flitting first to tuck a white sherpa pillow behind Mayla, then rushing to the kitchen before returning with a steaming mug that she pressed into her daughter's hands. After watching Mayla take a few tentative sips, the dark haired woman finally settled next to her on the couch, pulling her daughter into her arms.

Where her mother was small and thin, Mayla's father was quite the opposite, tall and broad with an easy smile and a quiet, calming nature. He was fair of complexion, his hair reddish blonde, his smile quick and comfortable. His eyes were Mayla's. That deep, dark, ever watchful blue. He sat on the opposite side of the couch, his arm wrapped around both women, his eyes regularly shifting between the two of them and his other daughter. Keeping an eye on all of his ladies just in case. Anton could respect the hell out of that.

Seeing Mayla finally settled, relaxed and tucked securely between both of her parents, he finally managed to tear his gaze away. For the first time in what felt like days, he took a deep breath.

Turning his gaze back to the redhead standing before him, he tried to focus. She was tall and curvaceous, those piercing hazel eyes framed with dark lashes, that thick red hair reaching down past her shoulders. She wore a green wraparound dress, a golden sunflower necklace, and knee high brown leather boots. She looked like she could manage a Fortune 500 company one minute and jump on a plane to Mykonos the next. At the moment however, she was standing with her hands on her hips, one eyebrow raised in clear irritation.

"Are you done now?" she asked in a snide tone.

Anton blinked at her. "I'm sorry, done?"

"Are you done eye banging my sister?" The question was quick, harsh, and completely serious.

Anton coughed to cover his snort of shock. That was certainly one way to make a first impression, he thought. Mayla's sister didn't pull any punches, and he smothered a smile at her overprotectiveness. He had a sudden vision of one of her boots kicking him in the backside, so he took a moment to choose his words carefully.

"I apologize if I gave you the wrong impression," he let the words hang in the air between them, blatantly waiting for her to offer her name.

"Natalie," she finally bit out, perturbed.

He nodded. "Nice to meet you, Natalie. I apologize if you got the wrong impression. I am absolutely not eye-ba-...err, what I mean to say is, I'm merely concerned for your sister's welfare. She quite literally saved my life today, and I owe her a little gratitude for that."

His eyes traveled back across the room, noting the dark circles and the way Mayla now leaned her head wearily against the back of the couch. Her color was starting to improve slowly, but she was still too pale. When she had dropped like that in the plaza...

A tremor went through him as he saw it again in his mind, her face going stone white, her body suddenly folding like paper toward the rough pavement. Thank the gods he'd been keeping an eye on her. He'd sprinted forward, catching her just before her head and shoulders could crash into the filthy, glass covered asphalt.

"When she passed out after helping so many people, it worried me. She seems very fragile just now and I need," he cleared his throat, correcting himself quickly, "I want to make sure she's okay. I tried to take her to the closest med unit, but she refused, insisted I bring her here instead."

He slid a hand through his hair and heaved a heavy sigh, some of the tension releasing in his shoulders. "It's been a very long day, Natalie," he finally muttered with a shrug.

Over on the couch, the tiny guard dog turned three circles in Mayla's lap before settling in with a sigh. Despite the relaxed position, its intense little black eyes never left Anton, the warning still clear.

Damn, tough room.

"Coffee shop explosion, yeah, we heard about it on the news. But it was your fault she was even there, wasn't it? Your dispatch sent her there. And now you're telling me my sister saved your ass, and in return you let her run herself ragged playing hero for everyone else?"

Anton took a quick step back, feeling like he'd just been sucker punched. Gods the fire in this woman! And the nerve! The idea that he would deliberately put Mayla in any kind of danger did strange things to both his mind and his equilibrium. Yes, he was the one who'd wanted coffee this morning, and yes, he'd picked the location. But how the hell was he supposed to know that the Anord were planning to bomb the place? The fact that he hadn't had any knowledge or inclination, especially considering his job as head of the MTF, was a separate wound altogether.

Still, he'd done absolutely everything he could have, hadn't he? Should he have just snatched Mayla up and flown her out of there right away? Packed her into a car and sent her straight home? Well, maybe. But with her healing abilities and so many injured, he couldn't pass up an extra pair of hands. He'd tried to stay as close as he could given the circumstances though.

His eyes narrowed. He had absolutely no obligation to Mayla or this family, so why was his gut on fire at her sister's accusation? Why did a small part of him feel like she was absolutely right? His hands curled into fists at his sides.

"I think your sister is fully capable of making her own adult decisions, don't you?" The temperature around them grew chilly with his words. His tone was cold, hard, and held a clear warning. Whatever her problem with him, Mayla's sister was tiptoeing onto dangerous ground.

The tall redhead must have realized she'd gone a bit too far, because the irritation in her face melted and she released a long sigh, running a graceful hand down her face.

"Look, I'm sorry. I don't mean to snap at you. There are - things - about my sister that you just don't understand. She's different than most people, better really, but she pushes herself too hard and I worry. And as you may have already figured out, I tend to get angry when I'm worried." She shrugged at the admission.

Anton relaxed, the air around them quickly losing its chill. Of course she was worried, they all were, even more so because they obviously didn't understand her magic. They thought she was struggling with anxiety or a similar issue. They would naturally step in and want to protect her.

His mind flashed back to when he'd been flat on his back in the plaza, to that amazing butterfly sensation dancing through his body. Mayla hadn't even known what she was doing at the time, had thought she was using simple healing magic, but it had been so much more than that. He wondered what her family would think when they found out their daughter's magic was not only incredibly rare, but also far more powerful than any of them realized.

7

Natalie was still speaking, but her tone was friendlier, more gentle. She'd even dashed into the kitchen for a moment and grabbed him a soda from the fridge.

"Mayla feels things more than most people do. Hell, sometimes I think she literally feels everything."

Anton nodded. It wasn't his place to tell to Mayla's family about her abilities, it was hers. He'd learned his lesson when he'd blurted out the truth and shocked her into stunned silence. He'd follow her lead on if and when she told her family. He would also be putting her in touch with someone to help her learn more about her abilities. He knew just the guy, was already planning to shoot him a text when he left here.

Sipping his soda, it took him a moment to realize realized Natalie was waiting for a response. Crap, what had they been talking about? Feelings, right?

"She does seem very perceptive to other people's feelings; I noticed that earlier today. She could tell when people were hurt and often figured out what they needed before they even had a chance to tell her. That seems like quite the skill."

Natalie's bright, answering smile was breathtaking as she

patted his shoulder. "See, I knew you were a smart guy."

"Natalie, stop hounding him. You're always hogging all the attention," Mayla said in a cracked, soft voice. A hint of teasing coated her words.

Natalie made a show of snorting loudly and throwing up her hands. "So needy! Who said you get to monopolize every man we meet?"

They moved back into the living room, Natalie plopping down into the overstuffed chair facing the couch with an overly dramatic sigh. She waved her arms back towards him like she was revealing a prize on a game show.

"Fine, May, you win, I'm done. He's all yours."

Mayla's chin dropped in shock. "Gods, Nat, you're the worst! That's not what I meant and you know it!"

He smiled at their sisterly antics, finding himself mesmerized by the pink flush of embarrassment in Mayla's cheeks.

Hours later, Anton dropped two cubes of ice into a rock glass with a clink, pouring a healthy dose of bourbon over top before walking back to his black leather couch and dropping onto the cushions with a sigh. He took a long sip, exhaling on the smooth burn while he kicked off his shoes, propping his feet up on the slate gray coffee table before him and crossing his feet at the ankles.

What.

A.

Fucking.

Day.

After leaving Mayla and her family - the former having fallen soundly asleep on the couch just before he'd left - he'd traveled across town to check in with his mother.

Elijah of course had already tattled, so Anton's mother was in full overprotective mode. He'd called her before he'd left the plaza and assured her he was fine, but despite his best efforts, the oldest and most distinguished Highblood healer was already suffering through tea and chit chat when Anton arrived. The poor man practically ran out of the room in his eagerness to check Anton over and eventually escape.

"It's a blessing from the gods is what it is. I've never seen anything like it. Your wings are spider-webbed with fracture lines. They must have healed themselves almost immediately for this type of residual pattern to occur. If the original fractures had split or hadn't healed so quickly, well, it would have been a very sad day for your mother, I'll leave it at that." The man talked way too much, but his quick treatment had at least been enough to eliminate any remaining aches and stiffness.

After getting the all clear from the healer and sending the poor man on his way, Anton chatted with his mother for over an hour, minimizing the details of the explosion as much as he could. He let her pack a huge meal for him to take back to his apartment, knowing she'd fret and fuss if he didn't, and promised to check in again first thing tomorrow.

He sent out a short, succinct text to his father on the way back into the city, but he neither expected nor cared for a response. He'd learned early on that Rupert Tevaris was a conceited, hateful bigot. Yes, his bloodline was one of the most pure left in existence, but that did absolutely nothing for the man's shit personality and antiquated ideologies.

His parents marriage had been arranged, and like most Highblood marriages it was more a business merger than a love match. His mother's bloodline was not quite as pure as his father's, and no one in the universe gave a shit about that fact other than his father. The man had spent years bemoaning his 'poor match' and his 'slightly diluted son.' His mother took it all in stride, ever genteel and serene, she let her husband's barbs slide over her like water over a slick rock.

At seventeen, Anton made the mistake of asking a Lowblood girl from his high school out on a date. They'd gone to the movies and then stopped for coffee and dessert after. They'd chatted, laughed, and he'd had a great time. It was all so...comfortable. Easy even. Not like the stuffy, overdressed dinner parties his father insisted on throwing, or the sly, conniving games the Highblood girls at school were always trying to play with him. For the first time in his life, Anton had met someone who wasn't interested in him because of his blood, his magic, or his father's money. And though obviously he couldn't love her, since Highbloods couldn't manage such a thing, he *had* gotten a funny, excited feeling in his stomach when she leaned over and kissed him at the end of the night. He'd already decided to take the leap and ask her out again the next time he saw her.

He'd come home excited, dying to tell his mother every detail. They were sitting in the kitchen, chatting at the table with two mugs of tea between them when his father entered. The man's jaw was clenched tight, his face purple with rage. Anton had no idea how long he'd been skulking around in the next room listening.

"Falling in love is for the weak. There's a place for Lowblood females in our world, boy. They're excellent at cleaning our floors and warming our beds, but they shouldn't have a seat at our table or access to our fortunes. Never give any woman that much power. Even Highblood females can barely handle the pressure and responsibility of running a household and raising children. Take her to your bed, that's fine, but keep her kind out of my house." The condescending smile on the man's face had been sickening.

"Sexist jackass," Anton muttered.

He'd been ignoring his father's twisted opinions and comments for years and had come to expect them. What he hadn't expected was the backhand that knocked him out of his chair, or his father's water magic suddenly filling his lungs.

Down on his hands and knees, coughing up cupfuls of water, he tried desperately to find his breath. His father knelt down, pulling Anton's head back by the hair and sneered.

"Watch how you speak to me, boy."

Anton hadn't thought about moving, hadn't even considered fighting back. At least, not until his mother tried to step in. As soon as she placed a hand upon his father's arm, Rupert Tevaris had backhanded her as well, sending her reeling into the cabinets beside them. Her face bounced off the white oak and she fell to her knees. In the next heartbeat, Anton was on his feet, pushing his father back, two giant shards of ice piercing the man's shoulders and pinning him to the wall behind him. Heavy gray clouds gathered in the kitchen, swirls of biting snow blowing in every direction.

No one touched his mother.

It was Anton's turn to grab his father by the hair, moving

in until they were nose to nose, his lip curling up off his teeth in a clear threat.

"I'm sorry, Father," Anton snarled, as the older man's eyes went wide, his breath starting to crystallize. "I must not have been clear. What I meant to say was that you are an outdated, old-fashioned, belligerent, hateful, SEXIST ASSHOLE who should be put out of his misery."

His father started to sputter, clawing at one ice shard and then the other in pure panic.

"Would you like me to help put you out of your misery, OLD MAN?!" As Anton's eyes narrowed, his father's breathing grew ragged, hunks of ice now falling out of his mouth with each exhale.

Only his mother's soft, warning squeeze to his shoulder brought him back to his senses. Anton closed his eyes for a moment, trying to breath through his fury, and pulled his ice magic slowly back.

Shame. He'd really considered killing the bastard.

His mother stepped between the two of them, one hand pressed to her swollen, reddening cheek. She informed her husband that she was filing for divorce in the same calm tone she would have used to tell him what was for dinner. She and Anton packed up and moved out that very same night, leaving his father to fester and stew in his own ignorance.

Despite his father's constant assurances that women were incapable of such feats, it had taken his mother a scant five years to become ridiculously successful in the field of finance, purchase a home that far outshone their last, and accrue a fortune that put his father's to absolute shame. At this point in their lives, Rupert Tevaris was a minor inconvenience on paper and nothing more.

Back in his apartment, Anton watched the stars outside the floor to ceiling windows glitter in the inky darkness. The image of storm-cloud eyes and soft pink lips jumped to the forefront of his mind.

Mayla.

He said her name out loud, letting his tongue caress the sound.

"May - laaa."

She'd literally exploded into his life only a few hours ago, so why couldn't he get her out of his mind? Taking another slow sip of bourbon, he let the liquid sit in his mouth for a moment, ruminating, before swallowing it down. He was home. The day was over. Everything was taken care of, at least for the moment. So why, in the name of all the gods above, was he still so worried about her? Why did he have the urge to drive over and sit in front of that house all night just to make sure she stayed safe?

He thought back to her parents home, about how the exhaustion had finally tightened its hold on her. She'd fought the heaviness of her eyelids for as long as she could before falling asleep still sitting up. Anton had watched as her father eased her over onto her side, covering her with the blanket and tucking her dark hair away from her face before they'd all left the room. When the rest of them gathered in the kitchen, Mayla's father had gripped Anton's shoulder, shaking his hand and thanking him for his help in watching over his daughter. The little white dog however, refused to be won over, continuing to glare at him on his way out the door.

Two hours later, Anton had moved from the couch to the floor, empty containers of the food his mother had sent scattered haphazardly across the coffee table amidst a stack of work files. He'd refilled his bourbon once - okay maybe twice - but it now sat to the left, half full and completely forgotten. After eating he'd finally had a chance to take a long, hot shower. He spent extra time making sure he got all the bits of glass and drywall out of his hair before drying off and throwing on a black tank top with a pair of gray sweatpants. Then he'd returned to the living room. No sense wasting time lying in bed when he knew he'd never sleep anyway. Work was about the only thing he could get his mind to focus on. The only thing other than...her.

Elijah popped by just long enough to drop off the files Anton had asked him to deliver from the office. Based on the outfit and the aftershave, Anton could tell his friend had plans of the female variety lined up for the rest of the evening. The man always seemed to have a woman or three waiting in the wings somewhere, though Anton couldn't remember his friend ever having a relationship that went past pure physical enjoyment.

Once Elijah left, the penthouse apartment had grown quiet, the darkness creeping in until Anton had been forced to turn on the recessed living room lights to still see the files.

The Anord problem was officially out of hand. Preliminary witness statements all said the same thing. A figure in a black hoodie - no one was sure if it was a male or a female - walked in and sat at a table in the far corner, head lowered and looking at their phone. Some remembered a briefcase or laptop bag. No one saw the person's face. The lab was running down countless prints, but the chances of them finding a direct match from an obliterated crime scene? Slim to none.

They desperately needed a lead. He'd take anything at this point, a tip, a suggestion, hell, even just a fragment of a possibility. He'd been leafing through every file the department thought might have an Anord connection for the last couple hours, and he'd just stumbled into another horrifying realization.

Lowblood children were disappearing.

Each of the files spread before him now represented a child that had gone missing in the last three months. Eight from this month alone. Five the previous month, three the month before that. Which begged the question, what possible use could the Anord have for Lowblood *children*?

8

When his cell phone shattered the silence a few moments later, Anton snatched it up, not bothering to look at the screen. He wasn't sure what time it was, midnight maybe? Either way, good news didn't come this late. Which meant it was either dispatch or Callan calling him with yet another problem, making this officially the longest, most brutal day ever.

"What," he barked, picking up one of the files to flip through while preparing for the worst.

"Oh. I'm…I'm sorry. I know it's late, but, is this…Anton? Anton Tevaris?"

The file slid out of his fingers, landing back on the coffee table with an audible splat. The voice on the other end of the line was *not* Callan. No, this voice was soft, feminine and slightly hesitant. Her face flashed through his mind for what must have been the hundredth time since he got home this evening. She sounded half asleep, all groggy and husky and sexy as hell.

"Mayla? Is that you? How are you? I'm sorry, I mean, did you get any sleep? Are you feeling any better?"

Great, he was rambling. Him, task force lead and top marksman of the entire department, tripping over his own damn tongue because he was talking to a girl.

A soft sigh came through the phone and licked at his ear.

"I'm okay."

He leaned back against the front of the couch, files forgotten. "You were already asleep when I left. I would have said goodbye."

When she didn't respond, he waited, content to listen to her soft breathing. She wanted to ask him about something, he could tell, but he wasn't going to push. He could wait until she was ready.

"Were you able to get some decent rest? Today was pretty rough."

"Yes, I slept for a few hours. I'll go back and rest more in a bit but first, I wanted to talk to you. About what you said earlier. What you told me about me being a...," she let the thought hang, afraid to say the word out loud.

"About you being an empath?"

"Mm-hmm. It's just, the only empaths I've ever heard of are only in history books. I've never heard of any modern empaths, I didn't think that kind of magic still existed."

Anton stretched his long legs out under the table, settling in.

"There are still a few out there with the ability, but not many. That type of magic definitely isn't manifesting as often as it used to. The few I've heard of are Highblood and they live very quiet, very private lives. I do know *one* personally, he does some undercover work for the department when he's not on active duty. I texted him earlier to see if he might be able to meet with you. I'm still waiting to hear back."

"Thank you, for doing that I mean. If he's okay with it, I think I'd like to talk to him. Maybe there's some kind of test or something I can do?" She paused, then hurried on. "It's not that I don't believe you, it's just—"

He smiled against the phone. "I get it Mayla, I really do. I should apologize, actually, for just dumping that on you the way I did. It wasn't fair, especially after the chaos of today. I should have waited until you recovered, maybe taken you for coffee or something to talk it over."

Mayla sighed again, and he imagined he could almost see her smile in that exhale of sound.

"Anton, no offense, but it's going to be a good long while

before I go anywhere near a coffee shop again."

He laughed out loud. "You're absolutely right. Probably safer for us both if we just stick to take out. My life will be over if I bring you home to your family again looking like you've been hit by a truck. That dog is already planning to kill me, I can tell. "

Her soft throaty chuckle warmed him from the inside out. "Don't take it personally. Diva thinks she's a doberman, and we're all just too afraid to try to tell her otherwise."

The next morning, Mayla tucked her feet up under her and sat back gingerly in her overstuffed ratty blue chair. The steaming mug of tea she cradled in both hands smelled like orange and vanilla, a stress relieving blend Willow had created especially for her, and now sold regularly at her shop.

Or at least she used to.

Taking a small sip, Mayla took a moment to just be, letting her mind settle. As she focused on nothing in particular, she engaged her breathing. In slowly. Out even slower. Again. Her body relaxed, wayward thoughts fleeing. These calming moments were vital. Time to be alone, to catch her breath and quiet the big, loud, obnoxious world that always seemed to be trying to keep her on edge.

When a sleek black form with two intense golden eyes leapt onto the arm of the chair, she jumped, the movement sending pain radiating through her. Climbing out of bed this morning had been tough, her back was so stiff she felt like she'd been beaten with concrete blocks. Even moving her head too far one way or another was sending shooting pains down through her shoulders.

She reached up despite the discomfort and scratched the cat's head, a low, rumbling purr beginning under her hand.

"You're not a normal cat, Pan, you know that right? You're supposed to be aloof, completely unconcerned with the rest of the world. Instead, anytime I'm sick or sore you're always right here, ready to play nursemaid."

Panther, completely undisturbed by her comment, stretched languidly across her lap, closing his golden eyes in ecstasy as she continued to stroke his onyx coat. Mayla giggled.

"What's so funny?" Natalie asked, walking into Mayla's

bedroom rubbing at her damp hair with a towel. She wore a cream colored silk robe with burgundy accents shaped like tiny foxes frolicking along the seams. Natalie was a buyer for one of the biggest department stores downtown, though Mayla secretly thought she should be modeling the clothes instead of purchasing them. Even now, fresh out of the shower, her sister was drop dead gorgeous.

"It's Pan. He does the whole cat thing wrong," Mayla answered. "I think he likes people too much."

"You mean he likes you too much. I'm pretty sure he doesn't like me at all. Last night he snuck into my closet and made tissue paper out of my favorite silk scarf." Pan slitted one cat eye open in response, and Natalie stuck out her tongue out at him.

"I had to get up at two a.m. and chase his little butt out of my room. What about you though, did you sleep okay?"

She tossed the towel over the side of a nearby hamper, and grabbed a wide toothed comb, crossing the room. Flopping down on the bed and sinking a bit into the pastel blue comforter, she began slowly pulling the comb through her damp hair.

Mayla took another slow sip of her tea. "I slept like a rock, why?"

"Yesterday was pretty intense, May," Natalie said quietly, her hazel eyes concerned.

"Intense is an understatement," Mayla agreed. "There was so much pain everywhere, I felt like I was drowning in it."

Natalie nodded. "Well to be fair, you kind of were, right?"

Mayla bit her lip, her mind flashing back to those moments yesterday, flying through the air with Anton.

"Mayla, your power was what pulled us away from that blast today. Your magic did that because you wanted it to…Mayla, you're not just a healer. You're an empath. The strongest damn empath I've ever seen."

When she woke on her parents' couch sometime around midnight the night before, she'd found her sister sound asleep in the recliner nearby. Though she was still exhausted, Anton's words had been playing on a constant loop in her head. After staring at the shadows on the ceiling for twenty minutes, she'd finally caved and looked up his number. She'd tiptoed to the bathroom and shut the door before dialing.

"Mayla? Is that you? How are you? I'm sorry, I mean, did you get any sleep? Are you feeling any better?"

Just hearing that rough, warm voice had instantly quieted the chaos in her head.

Later, when the time came, she found herself not wanting to hang up. She couldn't bring herself to admit she wanted to fall asleep with his voice in her ear, that the sound of it made her feel settled and safe.

Instead they'd hung up with whispered goodbyes and promises to get in touch soon. Her sister had opened the bathroom door thirty seconds later, hands on her hips, eyebrows raised. At that moment she'd looked so much like their mother Mayla had collapsed into a fit of giggles.

"You look like you're getting ready to ground me for something!"

Natalie's face curved into a grin and she let out a chuckle of her own. "Don't tempt me. What the hell are you doing hanging out in the bathroom? I was worried when I woke up and you weren't there." She dropped down to sit next to Mayla, their knees touching.

When their giggles subsided, Mayla gave her sister a sideways look.

"Nat, you do remember I'm the older sister here right? I mean just because you're taller than me doesn't mean you get to boss me around all the time; I am capable of taking care of myself on occasion."

Natalie snorted. "We've had this discussion a million times. I look out for you when you need it, you look out for me when I need it. We're a team. I'm just a little louder about it when it's my turn is all. I can't help it you got all the calm genes in this family and I got the feisty ones," she shrugged. "Now what's going on, did you throw up or something? You're not feeling sick are you?"

Mayla shook her head. "No, I'm tired and sore, but otherwise I'm fine. I was talking to someone." She paused, but Natalie didn't respond. "On the phone I mean." She paused again, doing her best to look completely innocent while her sister's eyes narrowed on her. After another minute of complete silence, she puffed out a breath of defeat.

"Okay, I admit it, I was talking to Anton."

Natalie's face broke into a wide grin and she wiggled her eyebrows suggestively, knocking a knee against her sister's.

"You were talking to tall, broad and blue eyed? In the middle of the night? Why? Wait, don't tell me," she held up a hand, then snapped her fingers. "I bet you're thinking of doing something mildly illegal right? You know in some states certain sexual positions are still considered—"

Mayla gasped and swatted her sisters arm, giggling. "Would you stop?! That's not it! He told me something today that I'm still trying to wrap my head around."

"What did he say?"

Mayla stood up slowly, her whole body protesting. She offered her sister a hand and pulled her to her feet.

"I'll tell you in the car, let's go home, I want to sleep in my own bed."

They left a note promising to call their parents the next day, and headed back to the apartment they shared in the city. On the way, Mayla told her sister everything. Anton's revelation that he thought she was an empath, her slowly growing belief that it might actually be possible, and finally his promise to set up a meeting with another empath to help her find out for sure. Her sister's eyes never left the dark road in front of them, but she listened with rapt attention. When Mayla finished talking, Natalie pulled the car over onto the shoulder where they sat in silence for a few minutes.

"Well shit! What kind of dumbasses are we that we didn't think of that possibility any sooner?"

"May, did you hear me? I asked how you're feeling this morning?"

"Still a little tired, but better," Mayla said, looking down at her EARTH is Just EH without ART mug.

Natalie raised an eyebrow, her don't-even-try-it-with-me going unspoken. No one knew her quite as well as her sister. Which meant it was really, really hard to keep any secrets from her. When those hazel eyes stayed leveled at her, Mayla sighed, caving under the pressure.

"Okay, fine. Emotionally? I feel a lot better. Physically? I feel awful. My back hurts so bad I want to cry. I don't know why, but every time I move it hurts."

Her sister was up and off the bed in an instant.

"Let me see."

Rising slowly from the chair, Mayla turned her back to her sister. Natalie helped slip the oversized t-shirt she'd slept in up to her shoulders.

"Fuuuuccccckk."

"What?! Is it that bad?" Mayla asked, twisting to look before wincing in pain and straightening again. "Damnit Nat, tell me. How bad is it?"

Her sister wasn't listening. When Mayla finally managed to right her shirt and turn around, Natalie was across the room, Mayla's phone in hand. Scrolling for a moment she tapped the screen, putting the device up to her ear.

"Who are you calling?" Mayla hissed.

Shit. She did not need their parents finding out about this, they'd be beside themselves with worry. But when Natalie started speaking, it was immediately clear that their parents were not the ones on the other end of the line.

"Hello yourself, you righteous, Highblood prick. You said you were looking out for Mayla all day yesterday. So how about you explain to me - as quickly as physically possible if you value keeping your man parts - why does my sister's back look like someone carved a giant spiderweb into it?!"

9

Mayla watched through her small kitchen window as a midnight black Audi R8 pulled up in front of their apartment building and her heart skittered. Returning to the living room, she felt her stomach twist. She turned on her sister.

"Why would you call him?! This is not his fault Nat, it's mine! I can't believe you did that. This is so embarrassing."

Her sister ignored her, casually touching up her makeup at the hallway mirror.

"Complain all you want, May. He knows more about this than we do, and he's got better connections to better healers. Didn't you tell me healing him was the hardest thing you did yesterday? He owes you for that."

"That's not what I meant and you know it. He doesn't owe me anything," Mayla muttered.

Of course her sister looked phenomenal in her black slacks, chunky heels and sleeveless black blouse with matching teardrop earrings. Mayla on the other hand, looked like a pile of whatever got swept up at the bar after closing on Saturday night. A sharp, heavy knock sounded at the door and her stomach spun again. This was mortifying, she hadn't even been able to shower. She'd tried, but the water felt like needles piercing her skin, and she just couldn't bear it. Her hair was messy, her t-shirt and sweats the oldest and softest ones she owned. Shit, had she even remembered to put on deodorant this morning?

When Anton strode into the room a moment later, she wanted to dig a hole and disappear. He looked amazing. His silver white hair was soft and clean, hanging in soft waves to his shoulders. He wore dark blue jeans stretched tight across powerful thighs, and a light blue v-neck sweater that made her mouth water. The V revealed the strong masculine line of his collarbone and her eyes fixated on that spot.

She and her friends had had multiple conversations about which parts of men were the most attractive, and thus the most dangerous. While those conversations usually took place in her living room surrounded by a few empty bottles of wine, the conclusions were always the same. Eyes, jawline, collarbone, shoulders. The most dangerous though, as *every* woman knew, were those stupid hip flexor muscles that made your insides go all warm and tingly whenever you saw them. She bet Anton had those.

"Show me," he said quietly.

She coughed, lowering her head to hide her blush at her random thoughts. What was she doing? Objectifying him while he stood in the middle of her living room? Especially while *she* still looked like she was coming off a three day bender? Awesome.

"Mayla, please show me."

His tone wasn't demanding, but it wasn't sympathetic either. It was simply determined. Good, she really didn't think she could handle sympathetic right now anyway. He stood a foot or so away, his soap, sandalwood and clove scent washing over her. She probably smelled like day old blood, rancid sweat and drywall dust. Heaving a sigh of resignation, she turned away from him, her hands trembling as she grabbed the fabric of her t-shirt at her shoulders, slowly pulling it up.

His sharp intake of breath and mumbled expletive she'd expected, but when his warm fingertips brushed against the marks on her spine she lost her breath on a gasp, startled at both the contact and the gentleness. Dropping the shirt, she spun around, her cheeks flaming. He'd eliminated the space between them, and his head lowered, his hands finding both of hers.

"Mayla, come with me, I can fix this, I promise."

His eyes, the same sky blue as that sweater, were intently searching her face. She dropped his gaze, shaking her head.

"Anton you don't owe me anything. If I just lay low I will be fine in a couple days. I told you my magic can be temperamental. This was my doing, not yours."

"Mayla, listen to me," he interrupted, squeezing her hands gently. "I'm sorry for everything you went through yesterday. I wish," he clenched his teeth in frustration, then started over. "I wish, more than *anything,* that I'd known what was going to happen so I could have done something to prevent it. I'm sorry that I didn't manage to do that."

Mayla's head snapped up. She ignored the spear of pain that shot through her at the motion. He couldn't possibly think the explosion yesterday was his fault, could he?

"Anton, yesterday was not your fault."

"Let's just agree to disagree on that one, shall we?" He caught her eyes again, refusing to look away. "My point is, you saved my life yesterday. If you hadn't been there, I would not be standing in front of you today."

Mayla's eyes widened, but she said nothing.

He nodded at her. "It's true. I saw a healer last night who couldn't believe his eyes. He kept reminding me how lucky I am to be alive. So this pain you're feeling right now? This pain *is* because of me, because *you* saved *my* life. No matter how much you argue, you will not convince me otherwise. So please, just put me out of my misery and let me help you."

She glanced at Natalie who shrugged and nodded, then she blew out an exasperated sigh."Fine. I guess I could use a little help this one time." She ran her hands down her faded sweatpants. "I look awful though, I'm sorry. It hurts too much to take a shower yet."

"You have nothing to be sorry for, Mayla. I'm sorry you're hurting. I promise I will make that go away very soon."

He stepped back, making a show of looking her up and down.

"And just for the record," a slow smile twitched at the corner of his lips "you look pretty damn adorable to me."

Natalie let out an undignified snort, walking over to give her sister a gentle hug.

"May, I've got a buyer's meeting I'm already late for. I'll

call you right after and check in?"

Mayla nodded. Natalie turned her attention to Anton. "You might turn out to be okay after all Tall, Broad and Blue Eyed. Just make sure you take excellent care of my sister."

Anton's eyebrows shot up, but he nodded as well.

Mayla's hands flew up to cover the heat blooming in her cheeks.

Once Natalie left, shutting the front door behind her, Anton turned to her, one eyebrow cocked.

"Tall, Broad and Blue Eyed?"

In no time at all, they were riding along in Anton's black-leather-everywhere sports car, traveling deeper into the heart of the city at a speed well above the recommended limit. He'd helped her throw some clothes in a bag, grumbled his way through putting out extra food for Pan, and then tucked her into the car as gently as if she were made of glass. He even insisted on running back inside to swipe a pillow off the bed to slip between her back and the leather seat. She tucked away a smile at all his fussing.

"I'm taking you straight to my apartment. I've called in a family friend, she's the best female healer I know. She'll meet us there."

He paused a moment, changing lanes smoothly, then picked up his thought once again. "I figured you might be more comfortable with a woman."

Mayla felt a warm heat spread slowly through her chest. That meant he must've called the healer as soon as he hung up with Natalie, *before* he'd even seen what was wrong with his own eyes. He'd even been considerate enough to call in a female. Tears of gratitude welled in her eyes, threatening to spill over. She turned quickly to look out the window, blinking rapidly and inwardly cursing her overactive emotions.

"I also contacted that empath we talked about. The man I mentioned last night?"

Mayla cleared her throat and nodded, turning back to face him. "I remember. You said you guys were in the academy together?"

Anton let out a low chuckle. "Yeah. We managed to get into some pretty serious trouble together back then. He's a good man, I trust him. He's going to swing by around noon. Hopefully he can give us a crash course in Empath 101."

The tentative hope in those light blue eyes, and the way he'd said "us" almost brought on the waterworks again. He was so determined to help her. They'd met less than a day ago, thrown together by pure chance, and she didn't even really know him at all. So why did he seem to care so much?

The healer, Adriana, was tall and willowy with sleek, straight gray bob. Her gray eyes were serene, her thin lips set in a soft, comforting smile. She was waiting patiently in the lobby when they arrived, and when she stood, the hem of her floor length gown - the exact same gray as her eyes - floated softly to the floor. She looked effortless, stunning. Anton greeted her with a warm hug and she ruffled his hair in return. Once the three of them were in the elevator, she finally spoke, her words clipped.

"You've not been by to see me in more than a month, Antoni."

"My apologies, Teta, my duties at the task force have kept me very busy." He cleared his throat, shifting his weight a little bit, reminding her of a child uncomfortable with being scolded.

"Too busy for my pork roast and zeli? You love my zeli more than my own husband does, yet you can't be bothered to join your godparents for dinner once in a while?" The affectionate tease in her voice was crystal clear.

Anton caught Mayla watching him and playfully rolled his eyes behind the woman's back. Then he leaned in, giving Adriana an apologetic kiss on the cheek.

"I'm so very sorry, my sweet, beautiful, Auntie. I am the laziest, most good for nothing godson an amazing lady such as yourself could *ever* have."

Mayla couldn't hide her giggle, and Adriana's smile grew. She nodded at him.

"It's a chore, I will admit. Still, you'll be at dinner next Tuesday to make it up to me. Six p.m., *sharp*."

Anton placed a hand over his heart and nodded solemnly, his eyes dancing with mischief. "I so solemnly swear."

His godmother playfully swatted his shoulder as the

elevator doors opened on the penthouse level.

Once inside the massive apartment, Adriana sent Anton to the kitchen with instructions to make tea, before ushering Mayla down the hall and into the master bedroom. Massive windows in the main living area took Mayla's breath away, but they were nothing compared to the floor to ceiling ones in the bedroom. All of Miradea spread out below them, going on for miles. Anton's apartment building was one of the tallest in the city, so there was nothing to block the amazing view. His king sized bed was neatly made, everything in the room done in varying shades of gray or black.

It was stunning. Classy. And clearly cost way more than what she was used to. She thought of her own bedroom, with its second hand furniture, mismatched color scheme and thrift store pictures on the wall.

"Anton gave me very strict instructions to help with anything you might need my dear." She tsked. "As if I wouldn't already do that without the boy's nagging. Are you ready to begin? I'll need to know where the worst problems are before we get started."

Mayla nodded. She liked Adriana, the woman's playful manner with her godson had put her instantly at ease.

"The biggest problem is my back. And yes ma'am, I'm ready, thank you so much for doing this."

"Psshhaww," Adriana waved her hand in a dismissive gesture. "Ma'am is for stuffy old ladies that smell like mothballs. You may call me Auntie or Teta, as Anton does. Now, let's go ahead and get this shirt off of you and take a look, shall we?"

She helped Mayla gently ease the shirt off and instructed her to lay diagonally across the bed on her stomach. Mayla did as she was instructed, resting her cheek on her folded hands and staring out at the city.

The sheets we deliciously soft beneath her, and she pictured Anton laying here in this bed, watching the massive TV on the opposite wall. If he was alone he'd probably be shirtless, maybe a pair of sweatpants riding low on his hips, those damn hip flexors in full view. The thought sent a sweet flutter through her belly. Since it was just a silly daydream anyway, she pictured herself wearing one of his t-shirts, crawling up the bed to snuggle in against his side.

A clatter in the kitchen snapped her back to reality, and she turned, burying her face in the fabric. She really needed to get a grip. She appreciated a good looking man as much as the next woman, but she wasn't some silly teenager. She wasn't the type to daydream about men she'd just met. There was just something about Anton that felt...*different,* but she couldn't put her finger on exactly what it was.

When the soothing warmth of healing magic slid slowly across her back, the tension in her muscles released bit by bit and she let out a soft sigh of relief. With each pass of warm magic, the pain faded more and more.

Adriana's words behind her were soft, but firm. "This injury, how did it happen? Are you in some kind of trouble, my dear?" The woman's breath sucked in on a hiss as if a thought had just occurred to her. "Did someone do this to you deliberately? If someone did this to you because you're working for my godson, I swear I'll knock that boy straight into next week."

Mayla shook her head, sending a soft smile over her shoulder to ease the woman's worries. She sounded like she might march out the bedroom door and take Anton over her knee right then and there.

"No ma'am, I mean, no *Auntie,* this wasn't Anton's fault. I don't work for his department, I actually just work for an insurance company."

The furrow between Adriana's brows eased, so Mayla turned back once more, easing the strain in her shoulders and resting her chin on her fist.

"It's my fault actually. My magic has always been a little...off," she admitted with a sigh. As Adriana's magic moved up into her shoulders, she felt her heart rate level, slow and even.

"Your magic isn't off my dear. But it is very, very strong. And a bit confused I think. I can feel it within you and it has a very positive aura. I think maybe you don't understand each other very well yet, but you will. Your magic just wants to help, you see."

Could have fooled me, Mayla thought, but she kept her words to herself, letting Adriana continue to work. The slow, gentle waves of warmth made her drowsy, and her eyes drifted closed. She must have drifted off, because the next thing she knew Adriana was gently nudging her awake.

"Sit up slowly now sweetheart, and try to stretch."

When Mayla did so, her movements were smooth, easy, and pain free. Yanking her shirt quickly back over her head and shoving her arms into it, she bounded off the bed, wrapping Adriana in a huge hug.

"Thank you, Auntie! That feels so much better, and it would have taken me *days* to recover without you. Thank you, really. Thank you so much!"

The older woman smiled broadly, returning the hug. "You are quite welcome my dear, I'm happy to help. Anton tells me you're quite the healer yourself. Perhaps one day our roles will be reversed and it will be I who needs your help." Adriana wrapped a slender arm around her shoulders as she spoke, turning them towards the bedroom door.

"Now, let's go see what kind of disaster my good for nothing godson has made of that tea, shall we?"

10

Out in the kitchen, three steaming mugs of tea waited for them on the table, sugar, honey and milk all within reach. When Anton's eyes met hers, he blushed, waving a hand towards one of the chairs before turning away. Mayla was stunned, and momentarily fascinated. What could possibly make the stern, serious, take-charge detective blush like a schoolboy after his first kiss?

"Well done, Antoni, there is hope for you yet, little one." Adriana said, taking her seat and spooning a dollop of honey into her tea.

As Mayla took a seat across from the healer, Anton sat to her left, still avoiding her gaze. Why was he acting so strangely?

"Anton calls you Teta, you're his aunt then?" She asked Adriana.

Adriana smiled, taking a graceful sip of tea. "In word and relationship, yes, though there is no blood relation between Anton's mother and I. We've simply been dear friends since childhood. I have been blessed to be Antoni's god mother and Auntie since he was born." She set her cup down, holding a slender hand to the side of her mouth conspiratorially. "Not that he can be bothered to come see me now that he is such a big, fancy detective."

"Teta *please,* it's only been two months. You are still my favorite girl, you know that," Anton insisted, his voice laced with affection.

Adriana reached over and patted his hand, mischief dancing in her eyes. "Well, we'll just have to see what happens next Tuesday, won't we?"

An hour later, Mayla was luxuriating in Anton's huge black marble shower, the hot water and sudsy lather clearing away the last bits of dust and fatigue still clinging to her from yesterday's ordeal. She still struggled to understand why anyone would want to blow up a coffee shop full of people. What could possibly be the motive for such a thing? Her heart ached for everyone who'd been injured, even more for the families of the lost. She prayed Anton's team would find those responsible.

Closing her eyes under the hot, steady spray, Mayla relaxed into the sensation of the hot water sliding across her skin. Uninvited, Anton came to mind. Him carrying her into her parents living room, him teasing her over the phone last night, his flirty little smile this morning when he told her she looked adorable in her ratty sweats. Then there was that blush earlier in the kitchen. Was he just being nice or could he actually be interested in her?

She'd only ever had two real relationships, and neither had been anything worth bragging about, so her instincts when it came to love weren't all that reliable. She knew she was decent looking, but she certainly didn't hold a candle to Highblood women. They reminded her of fashion models, all perfect proportions, stunning eyes and sculpted cheekbones.

So why would Anton bother flirting with her when he probably had plenty of those kind of women eating out of his hand? She had to be overthinking. Yesterday had been intense. He was just doing his job, making sure she was safe after the chaos of yesterday. She tried to push his image from her mind and failed, opening her eyes to look around the expansive black marble shower instead. It was *huge.* She felt tiny, the space big enough for six more people, easy. It was certainly big enough for her and Anton if they were ever in here together.

Nope. She chopped that thought off at the knees. Was the man insanely good looking? Yes. Was his body all hard ridges and smooth skin that made her fingers itch to reach out and touch Absofrickinlutely. Was she going to make a move and embarrass herself for the rest of eternity? Not a chance in hell. She had more important things to think about anyway.

She'd been so exhausted last night, she'd completely forgotten about filing the missing persons report for Willow. Which meant she'd officially earned the title of worst best friend *ever*. She'd completely forgotten about her best friend since elementary school. Willow, who was always there whenever she needed someone, who had always supported her, no matter how crazy her mood swings or how frantic her anxiety. Willow who had seen her at her worst and never batted an eye. The person she giggled with, got drunk with, even cried over boys with. No matter what, her friend had always been like the sunshine - warm, bright and welcoming. And she'd been that way ever since the first the day they met.

Mayla could still smell the chocolate, still feel the cold thickness of the milk as it slid down the front of her brand new shirt, coating her new book and dribbling onto the crotch of her jean shorts. In the middle of the fourth grade lunchroom, she was now the center of attention. Her face was so hot with humiliation she wondered how her hair didn't catch on fire.

Allegra Hines stood in front of her, emptied chocolate milk carton in hand, smug smile of satisfaction on her face, and not a hair out of place on her perfectly blonde, Barbie doll head.

"You shouldn't be sitting here. This is strictly a NO WEIRDOS table."

Allegra was by far the most popular girl in school. She was blonde and perfect in every way that Mayla was dark and peculiar. Allegra wore name brand clothes, and was president of their class - mostly because no one had the nerve to actually run against her - and she was always bragging about the places she'd been or the amazing concerts she'd seen. Her dad was some kind of Highblood tech guru with metal magic, and her house - not that Mayla had ever been invited there of course - was not only huge, it had a pool, a hot tub, AND a full time staff. Which naturally made Allegra instafamous with the entire school.

Unfortunately for Mayla, anytime Allegra approached her, a dark brown ooze of anxiety would climb up Mayla's throat and choke her with invisible hands. The first time Allegra ever spoke to her, Mayla ended up in a full blown panic attack. That time she'd thankfully managed to escape, hiding in the bathroom for half an hour until she could get her breathing and trembling back under control. But the second encounter, that one had happened in the lunchroom, and ended with Mayla curled up on the floor, hugging her knees to her chest and rocking back and forth. She didn't remember much about that day, just her dad showing up and carrying her out to the car, all of her classmates snickering behind their hands.

The next day when she returned to school, she was a certified freak. Everyone whispered, laughed and pointed when she walked by, chatting about her panic attack like they were talking about the weather. She'd been mortified. Her anxiety was a living, tangible thing and she hated it. She didn't understand why her mind sometimes pictured people in colors, or why she sometimes saw things that weren't even there. All of it only served to prove that she really was the weirdo everyone wanted to make fun of.

And no one more so than Allegra. The girl now bullied Mayla every time she got the chance. Mayla tried her best to avoid her, volunteering to stay after each class and help put away chairs or clean up. She even asked the librarian if she could spend her lunch time putting away books, but that had been a no go.

Her desperation must have set off some red flags, because before she knew it she was sitting in the guidance counselor's office being asked questions like "is everything okay?" and "is there anything you would like to talk about?" Mayla'd had two options. Tell the counselor and be bullied by all of Allegra's friends for getting her in trouble, or pretend everything was fine and just try to keep her head down. Her choice had been clear.

Three days later, here she was, gulping down her peanut butter and jelly as fast as possible, keeping her face buried in Tuck Everlasting and trying desperately to avoid being noticed.

It hadn't worked.

Allegra spotted her as soon as she exited the lunch line with her entourage, and Mayla hadn't had time to escape. Now, looking down at her lap, Mayla prayed the dark ooze of ugliness that was spreading up her chest wouldn't reach into her throat and suffocate her. Chocolate milk was embarrassing enough, but another panic attack would be the ultimate nightmare. Everyone in the cafeteria was now watching, many of them already laughing at her. The chocolate milk was cold, and it was now soaking through her jean shorts.

Gross.

Her skin started to tingle, and her heart began to pound.

"Look at me, weirdo."

Mayla kept her chin tucked into her chest, watching one brown splatter soak into the page of her book. Right over Winnie Foster's insistent claim - 'I need a new name. One that's not all worn out from being called so much'.

I get it Winnie, she thought. I really do.

"Buzz off, Allegra. Nobody likes a bully."

The girl that slid into the seat next to Mayla had short, bouncy brown hair and friendly, bright green eyes. Mayla peeked at her, astounded.

"Hi, I'm Willow," the girl said with a smile. She sat close enough for their arms to press together, and Mayla immediately felt a soothing green mist wrap around her.

"M...Ma...Mayla," she whispered back.

A second girl, this one with a long blonde braid and warm brown eyes plopped down on her opposite side and Mayla jumped. The girl held a cell phone pointed at Allegra, clearly recording. In Mayla's mind she wore a full suit of golden armor, but in the lunchroom she wore black jeans with a plain green hoodie.

"I'm Eliana. It's nice to meet you Mayla."

Mayla looked between the two. She blinked rapidly, the mist and the armor in her mind finally disappearing. They were just two normal girls, suddenly sitting on either side of her almost like...bodyguards. Even better, they both seemed completely unimpressed with Allegra.

Eliana spoke up, her expression cocky."Hasn't your rich techno daddy explained the trouble you'll get into if you get caught bullying someone, Allegra?"

Mayla pulled in a breath, her trembling leveling out. Where had these two come from? Didn't they know this could be a popularity death sentence?

Willow stood then, helping Mayla to her feet."Eliana, I wonder what would happen if this video got posted online?!" She asked with mock horror.

Eliana nodded, wrapping one arm around Mayla's waist, the other still aiming her phone at Allegra. The rest of the cafeteria had stopped laughing, watching now with rapt attention.

"We're going to go help Mayla get cleaned up," Eliana spoke with a syrupy sweetness, the threat in her next words obvious. "Unless you

want me to send this to my dad, wait...did I mention he happens to be the chief of police? Anyway, unless you want him AND the principal to get a copy of our little video, you're going to clean this up." She nodded at the chocolate milk splattered across the table and pooling on the ground beneath. "You're also going to stay away from Mayla from now on, got it?"

Allegra fumed.

Eliana waited, then cleared her throat loudly.

"I SAID, you're going to stay away from Mayla, AREN'T YOU?!!"

Allegra's blonde head finally nodded, fury blazing in her expression, her cheeks a bright, fire engine red.

The three of them moved towards the cafeteria doors, Willow calling back over her shoulder.

"Doesn't matter how pretty you are on the outside, Allegra. The ugliness inside will always shine through."

11

Out of the shower and rubbing vigorously at her hair with a plush white towel, Mayla had to smile at the memory of that first day they'd met. She and Willow were inseparable after that, and more often than not they were a foursome, Natalie, Eliana, Willow and herself. Over the years giggly sleepovers and late night calls turned into girls nights out and texts about their latest romantic failures. They knew each others deepest, darkest secrets and most embarrassing moments, and no matter what, they were always there whenever they were needed. When bad things happened, Willow was always the first to show up, and she always brought one of three things with her. A carton of ice cream, a bottle of wine, or a shovel. Depending on which one she thought was needed most.

That was typical Willow, she was the ultimate caretaker. Her nature magic gave her an amazing talent for growing things, a true affinity with animals, and an uncanny sixth sense about a person's real nature. It's what made her plant nursery and herbal tea shop the perfect undertaking.

Mayla still remembered the four of them cleaning out the moldy old building in the weeks after Willow bought it. One Saturday in particular the four of them bought cheap wine coolers and set to work scrubbing the walls and repainting. That night they'd devolved to flinging paint at each other, drinking much stronger wine, and laughing so hard they'd all been sore for days. Thanks to their paint fight, the stockroom still looked like an abstract art piece to this day.

The front of the store had eventually come together perfectly though. These days it was covered in ivy that bloomed with purple flowers, with windows bright and gleaming, the amazing smell of fresh brewed herbal tea always floating in the air.

Or at least, that's how it had been before her friend disappeared.

Throwing on clean clothes and winding her damp hair into a bun, Mayla headed out of the bathroom. It would be another hour or so before the empath friend of Anton's showed up, plenty of time to get the missing persons report filed.

She needed Anton and all his connections out there looking for Willow, now.

Anton sat across from her at the kitchen table a few minutes later, black laptop open and ready, his expression all business.

"Full name of the missing?"

"Willow Elise Sloane."

"Time and place she was last seen?"

"Her boyfriend Tyler said they had dinner and drinks the Saturday before last and he told me he dropped her off at home around 1 a.m. Sunday morning. She lives in an apartment above her shop, Green Tease over on Smithfield Parkway."

"The plant place? The one with all the flowers?"

"Yes. She makes her own herbal teas too, that's how she came up with the name. They're amazing, by the way. If you haven't tried them you really should. Willow's crazy talented, she can grow just about anything. She puts flowers and herbs together in a way I never would have thought—," she broke off. "Sorry, I think I'm rambling."

Anton leaned back in his chair, offering her a small smile. "Sounds like she's a pretty good friend."

"The absolute best," Mayla admitted.

"Can you tell me why you think she's missing? I mean, I do believe you," he hurried to add, "But I still have to ask. Sometimes people just decide to take a break, get out of the city for a couple days."

Mayla shook her head. "She'd never leave the shop without someone set up to look after things. That place is everything to her. She would have said something to one of us."

"One of us?"

"Oh, uh, myself, my sister, or Eliana. The four of us are really close, we basically grew up together. Natalie hasn't seen or heard from her and neither have I. Eliana was deployed to Greece last month so we keep in touch over text. I double checked with her yesterday before calling the station. Willow never mentioned going anywhere to *any* of us."

Anton was nodding. "Okay. You mentioned she has a boyfriend?"

"Tyler Atlas. They've only been dating a few months. I thought that's why I hadn't heard from her. I figured she and Tyler were spending all their time together. I can give you his number. I'm guessing you"ll want to have someone talk to him?"

"I will, yes. Does Willow have any other family nearby?"

"No family, at least not anymore. It was always just her and her mom growing up, but her mom passed a few years ago. She's never spoken a word about her dad, I got the impression she didn't know who he was."

Anton lowered his head, typing for a moment before looking back up. "Got it, thanks. Do you happen to have a current photo you could send me? I'd like to get this in the system right away."

Mayla grabbed her phone, texting him a photo she'd taken two months ago, on the day Natalie had treated them all to mani/pedis. She stared at the image of her sister and her friend, side by side and grinning, fingers and toes on full display. Tears welled in her eyes.

"Mayla." Anton reached across the table, grabbing one of her hands in his and squeezing hard. "I promise you I'm going to do everything I can to help you find her."

A sharp knock at the front door made her jump and he dropped her hand. Anton rose to answer it while Mayla retreated to the bathroom, swiping at her tears with her sleeve. She threw some cold water on her face and dabbed herself dry with the hand towel hanging nearby.

Anton would find Willow. He had to.

The man sitting on the couch sipping a Diet Coke and chatting with Anton certainly didn't look like an empath, but come to think of it, Mayla wasn't exactly sure what an empath was supposed to look like. He had short black hair, a neatly trimmed black goatee, and a small silver hoop in one ear. He wore a tight black t-shirt, military style black cargo pants with boots, and black gloves, every inch the standard Miradean soldier. His twinkling dark brown eyes, caramel skin and easy smile offset the intimidating military attire though, making him look friendly and approachable. Before she could lose her nerve, Mayla walked into the room, hand already outstretched. He stood as soon as he saw her, setting his soda down quickly before taking her hand in both of his.

He was still wearing the gloves.

"It's so nice to meet you, Mayla, I'm Skyler. Anton has told me a lot about you and what you're going through. Hopefully I can help answer any questions you might have?" His smile was big and genuine, his deep dimples giving him a hint of little boy charm. Mayla liked him instantly.

"Gods, I sure hope so. And if I don't live up to your expectations, I only just found out I might be an empath yesterday, so don't expect me to be able to tell yet if you're disappointed.

Skyler threw back his dark head and laughed. It was a deep, rich belly laugh, and before she knew it, Mayla was giggling right alongside him.

"I think we're going to get along just fine," he said, motioning for her to sit as he returned to his chair. "I guess I'll just start at the beginning, yeah?"

Mayla nodded eagerly.

"So the ancient empaths, the most powerful, could not only read other people's thoughts and emotions, they could influence them as well. The few of us that exist nowadays don't have that much power, but we do still have some of those capabilities. We can read emotions easily and gain access to other people's minds when we need to. The level of capability is different for each empath."

Skyler raised his hands in front of him and wiggled his gloved fingers at her.

"That's why I wear these. In my case, I have immediate access to someone's mind when I am skin to skin with them. We empaths call it 'mind walking' or 'reading' someone. Touch can also magnify my ability for most of us. My magic is a bit stronger than most, so the gloves are another way for me to shield against unwanted emotions and unintentional readings. They don't take away the information completely, but they do at least help to mute it a little." He leaned in closer, studying her.

"With your permission, Mayla, I'd like to take these gloves off and see if I can get a reading on you. Completing a mind walk will tell me immediately if you're truly an empath."

Goosebumps rose on Mayla's arms. He wanted free access to her absolute mess of a mind?

"It's a huge ask, I know, but it's also the fastest way to get the answers you're looking for. Now, if I were you, I would tell me exactly where to go and how fast to get there. But if you *are* an empath - and I've never known Anton to be wrong when it comes to identifying skill magics - if you are an empath this might be the safest way for us to find out."

Mayla raised her eyes to meet Anton's, still unsure. He nodded once.

"Skyler knows I will decapitate him if he tries anything that might harm you." The words were spoken in jest, but the warning in them was clear.

Skyler nodded emphatically. "I do know that. And if this could hurt you in any way I wouldn't even attempt it, I swear." The dark eyed man placed a hand to his heart and waited.

Mayla took a deep breath, looking pointedly between both of the men. "Alright then, if this is what I have to do, let's get it done."

Skyler began pulling off his gloves. "Now Mayla, do you have some kind of token from home? Something you can hold that will help ground you? A necklace maybe, a favorite trinket of some sort?"

Mayla shook her head. Her favorite trinket would probably be her FoxI.Ny plush keychain, but it was back at her apartment, attached to the strap of her laptop bag like always.

"She can hold on to me."

The words were low and calm, but they sent a small thrill

through her. Anton stepped closer to her side, his face completely blank. She wished she could tell what he was thinking. Did he just want an excuse to touch her? Or was this still him looking out for her?

Ugh. Men were so confusing.

Skyler looked at Anton with a smirk.

"You're a little bit bigger than what I had in mind, Anton. I was thinking something she could hold in her hand."

"It's better if it's him," Mayla blurted. She felt her cheeks heat, but she didn't hide from Skyler's curious expression. "I don't know a lot about this, at least not yet, but I do know when my magic is making me crazy," she took a beat, knowing her next words were going to make her sound needy at best and codependent at worst. "Being near him helps. I don't know why, but I felt it multiple times yesterday. Maybe his magic helps mine or something?"

Skyler gripped her shoulder so fast she jumped. A low noise came out of Anton's throat, and Skyler immediately let go.

"I'm so sorry, I didn't mean to startle you. What you said just now was extremely important. Mayla, are you telling me that being around Anton helps settle you? Helps you keep a better hold on your magic? This is important, Mayla. It's very, VERY important."

She suddenly felt as if she were standing under a gigantic spotlight. If she said yes, was she confessing to her growing feelings for Anton? Or was she simply admitting her Lowblood magic was still too much for her to handle? Did needing Anton around to calm her mean she *wasn't* an empath, she was just an over anxious disaster? If she said no when she really meant yes, would the test still be accurate?

"I...I mean…I don't know, I guess…maybe…I just…," Mayla's stomach started somersaulting as she stood between the two men. She had absolutely no idea what to say. Her nerves jangled and tightened, and her mouth went dry. She could feel her skin prickling, her heart pounding in her ears. No. Not now.

She could not do this now. Not here. Not in front of them. Her gut was tying into knots that kept getting tighter and tighter. She shouldn't be here. Her hands went ice cold and she trembled, fighting back a shiver. She needed to leave, make some kind of excuse before this got bad. Her breathing shortened, coming in fast little gasps. Skyler had come all this way. He was going to look into her mind for two seconds and tell her she was a complete fraud, just a Lowblood with little magic and even less control.

She was no one. Useless. Just that same weirdo from the

lunchroom so many years ago.

A warm calloused hand wrapped around hers, and then she was being turned into a pair of strong arms, her face pressing against a warm, hard chest. She felt herself shudder, her trembling hands coming around to lock together around Anton's waist, tears leaking out of her eyes.

"Skyler, can you give us a minute?"

Mayla felt the words rumble through the chest she was pressed so tightly against, but she didn't move. She closed her eyes, mortified to be falling apart for no reason whatsoever.

Anxiety sucked balls.

"Sure thing."

She heard Skyler's footfalls moving away from them, then a click as one of the bedroom doors shut. She burrowed her face even deeper into Anton, her heartbeat pounding in her ears. She didn't know what to do with the sensations steam rolling through her. All of it rushed back, the fear and horror from yesterday, the pain and embarrassment of this morning, the uncertainty and confusion of right now. It threatened to choke her completely. She gulped at the air, feeling like a fish out of water.

Anton's hand slid gently into her hair, cradling her head against him, his other arm wrapping tightly around her waist, and his chin resting slowly on the top of her head.

"Breathe, Mayla.

Just.

Breathe."

The words were strong but soft, and they managed to cut through the chaos spinning in her mind. She pulled in a slow, shuddering breath. His hand shifted to rub slow circles across her back. She tried to focus on that feeling, to let go of everything else. Her body relaxed a little with each rotation of his palm. Heavens bless him, he didn't ask her what was wrong, and he didn't tell her to calm down. He just held on, giving her mind and body time to do whatever they needed.

Gods why did this feel so right? How could a man with ice magic be so incredibly warm, so naturally comforting?

She didn't know how much time had passed when her stomach finally stopped churning and heat returned to her fingers. Her heart rate settled and her trembling finally stopped. She let out a long sigh, opening her eyes, but her arms didn't loosen from around his waist.

Anton's next words were soft, simple, and held no judgement. "The last twenty-four hours have been intense. Sometimes we just need to catch our breath and give our minds a chance to process it all."

She wanted to kiss him for the understanding and blind acceptance he was offering. Tears continued to trail quietly down her face. Panic attacks and big emotions were a part of who she was, but for the very first time, she didn't feel less than because of them.

Anton leaned back just enough to put a hand to her cheek, tilting her face up until she looked him in the eye.

"Can I let you in on a little secret?"

She nodded.

"The first time I saw a violent crime scene I wanted to drive straight to my mother's house, climb into her lap and have her rock me to sleep. I was twenty."

Mayla smiled at the mental image but remained silent.

Anton was nodding. "Yep. I was an officer of the law, top tier in my class, and the first crime scene I entered and saw blood, I wanted to run screaming in the other direction. When I got home that evening, I curled up in my bed with a gallon of mint chocolate chip ice cream and watched cheesy Hallmark movies until I finally passed out."

Mayla giggled. "You just made that up," she whispered.

He shook his head, utterly serious. "Nope, it's the truth. Never told a soul about it until right now. If I have to work a particularly bad scene, I still come home and go straight for the freezer to this day." He held her gaze for another long moment before speaking again.

"My point is Mayla, the way you react to certain things is just a part of who you are. It's a part of what makes you, you. There are no perfect people in the world, no matter how hard some of them might like to pretend. Everyone is battling something. So whenever it's too much, whenever you need a break, whenever you want everything to stop, *you're allowed to stop.* Take a step back, catch your breath. Screw the world, the world can wait. And if you can't, if you're not sure how, just find me.

If you need me to, I will stop the world for you."

12

"If you need me to, I will stop the world for you."

Mayla let out a giant breath she hadn't realized she'd been holding, and felt everything around her settle. The way he'd said those words to her, like they were the only two people on the entire planet, and then he'd gone and actually *done* it. He'd stopped the world…for her.

He grabbed her an ice water from the kitchen, then settled her onto the couch with a blanket before settling in right beside her. He chatted with her quietly for a while, unhurried. He acted as if Skyler wasn't waiting in the other room, as if he wasn't supposed to be running a task force right now and she didn't need to eventually get back to her own life. There was nothing and no one else to worry about, just the two of them, here in this moment.

She learned his parents had split when he was younger, and that his relationship with his dad was strained. He found out she did insurance work from home and that her favorite color was blue. They talked about their parents, the city, their favorite books, even the weather for a bit. Throughout it all, he never pushed, never rushed her. He let her simply relax and be in the moment.

It was the single nicest thing anyone had ever done for her.

When her mind finally felt like her own and her body was calm and relaxed once more, Mayla set her water down on the end table and threw back the blanket, scooting to the edge of the couch so she could put both feet on the floor.

"I'm ready. Let's get Skyler out here and find out if I'm really an empath."

"Are you sure? We can always do this next week. Or next month. Maybe even next year?"

She grinned. "You think you could put up with me for an entire year?"

His answering grin was wickedly flirtatious. "I could think of worse ways to spend my time."

This time when her stomach flip-flopped, it was a soft, fluttery feeling that she thoroughly enjoyed. Fulfilling an obligation didn't involve comforting and patience, followed by small talk and flirting. When he stood, she caught his hand in hers and squeezed. He turned back, eyes wide in question.

"Thank you. No one has ever done *anything* like that for me before."

He smiled broadly, bringing her hand up to brush his lips across her knuckles once before letting go and striding down the hallway to retrieve his friend.

Skyler apologized profusely when he returned to the living room, and she did as well, grateful when he brushed off the incident with no further questions. She sat on the plush gray sofa, Anton's big body tucked behind her, her back resting comfortably against his broad chest. He held both her hands, wrapping their clasped hands around her waist.

Well. This was certainly cozy.

Everywhere she and Anton touched was deliciously warm. She wanted to turn in his arms so they could be face to face. Wanted to wrap her arms around those broad shoulders and trace his jaw with feather light kisses. Maybe let her hands slide up under that blue sweater and...

Anton cleared his throat, shifting a bit behind her.

Giving herself a mental shake, she focused on Skyler's fingers against her temples and closed her eyes. Immediately she saw him, pacing back and forth along the edge of her mind. It was a bizarre feeling, knowing someone else was in your head. At least his aura was a warm golden color, and soft around the edges. But why was he pacing? Is that what empaths were supposed to do in these situations? More importantly, did being where he was give him access to all of her thoughts? Surely he couldn't tell that the more she felt Anton against her back the more she wanted to slide her hands up those strong thighs? Or that she could picture herself trailing her lips across his bare chest every time she closed her eyes? Anton shifted behind her once again, coughing softly.

Oh gods, what if Skyler could see all that? Stop thinking! Stop thinking right now! She yelled the command deep into her own mind, pushing out only thoughts of a spring meadow, a playful puppy and a tennis ball instead.

Skyler inhaled, his body drawing back, but his hands never moved.

What happened? Had he found something awful? She reached her own mind outwards toward him. Maybe, if she really was an empath, she could somehow see what he was seeing.

Between one instant and the next, she found herself inside a sterile looking hallway, standing in front of a black metal door. Is this what the inside of her mind looked like? The door looked heavy and immovable, but Mayla knew the answers she sought were somewhere behind it. Still, this place felt foreign to her. Was this even her own mind, or was Skyler somehow testing her?

She tried the knob. Locked. There was no keyhole. She pushed her hands against the cool metal and gave it a good shove just in case, but it didn't budge. Looking around for a tool to perhaps pry it open, Mayla realized the hallway she was standing in just kept going. Door after door continued in both directions, going on and on as far as she could see.

Leaning back on her hips, she crossed her arms in front of her. Okay, if she took a beat, she could figure this out. She loved puzzles, and this was just a bigger, slightly imaginary puzzle, wasn't it?

Mayla placed her hand back on the cool steel knob and focused. She imagined the knob turning under her hand and the door opening, pictured it behind her eyes. She sent calm, soothing feelings before her as if she could somehow convince this hulking piece of metal that she wasn't a threat, that she belonged here. This was her hallway, her doorway, in her mind after all. It was supposed to do what she told it to.

The knob began to slowly turn under her hand, squeaking in protest, and the door swung inward slowly. Mayla's eyes went wide.

Well then. That was more like it.

Inside sat a lone metal table with a single metal chair. A large two way mirror took up half the wall behind the table and she wondered who or what might be on the other side. Maybe it was Skyler, watching to see what she would do?

The room still felt foreign. It reminded her of the interrogation room she'd seen in one of her favorite police dramas. But why was it here? She'd never interrogated anyone. She didn't spend time in places like this, so why would Skyler be testing her this way? The only residual emotions she felt here were dark, ugly and secretive, and she didn't like them at all.

If Skyler was powerful enough to create this in her mind and convince her to somehow interact with it, he could probably keep her here if he really wanted to. That idea made her skin crawl. It was time to leave. Now.

Mayla left the bare room, moving back into the hallway and searching anxiously for an exit. There had to be a way out, she just needed to find it. The door to her right opened without a sound. Maybe Skyler was showing her the way out?

But this door wasn't metal like the last one. It was barely a door at all. It was just scrap pieces of wood haphazardly nailed together. Stepping inside, she gave the rickety door a wide berth and looked around. Mayla yelped in surprise when she saw a small boy with ebony hair tucked far back in the corner, watching her with wide, ebony eyes. His looked terrified. His bruised, gangly arms were wrapped around knobby knees that he had tucked up tightly against his chest. What in the hell was this? How had a child gotten in here, imagined or otherwise? Mayla made a mental note to give Skyler a major tongue lashing when all of this was over. His testing methods needed a serious overhaul.

She approached the boy slowly, pushing feelings of warmth and safety towards him with her mind, but she didn't speak. She lowered herself to sit on the floor next to him, his big dark eyes and small tense body reminding her of a rabbit ready to bolt. So gradually she could barely feel herself moving, she offered him her hand, palm up. He stared at it a moment, measuring it to decide if it was a threat before tentatively putting his smaller one inside. His little fingers gripped hers so hard she winced. Was he lost? How had he even gotten here? Maybe her test was helping him leave this place.

"I'm Mayla," she whispered to him, "I'm here to help you, I promise."

The offer was barely out of her mouth before the boy had launched himself into her lap, scrawny arms and legs coming around her to cling like a newborn monkey. She wrapped her arms loosely around him and patted his back gently.

"I didn't mean to hurt her," he whispered.

"Hurt who, sweetheart?"

"Mama. Daddy says I hurt her on purpose because I can't control myself. But I didn't, I swear! I didn't mean to hurt her!"

The last came out on a wail, and he buried his face against her. Mayla tightened her hug and began rocking him just a bit.

"It's okay, hey, it's okay. Of course you didn't mean to hurt anybody. You're a good boy, I can tell. You'd never hurt anyone on purpose would you?"

The small dark head shook violently back and forth.

"See? There you go. You didn't mean to hurt your mama. I'm sure she knows that."

"She doesn't know it. She can't. She's dead...I killed her."

Mayla's blood turned to ice in her veins. Surely he didn't mean?

"Daddy says I can mind walk. He always says 'that boy's magic is too strong for his own damn good' and the only safe thing is to beat it out of me. Mama yells at him though, every time he hits me. She says all I need is someone who can help me learn to control it. She says I'm you…you," he slowed down, sounding out the word, "you… neek?"

She felt the little body tremble under her hands as he continued. A pit was forming in her stomach.

"I got bad sick. I got fevers and I couldn't eat. Mama said I had ammonia." Mayla's mind jumped. Ammonia? What was he—? Wait, did he mean pneumonia?

"I was on fire in my sleep. My skin was burning so I started screaming. Daddy says Mama tried to wake me up, but I burnt her mind up and killed her. He says I can't be trusted, so that's why I have to live here in the shed, so he can keep the rest of the family safe."

Mayla started to tremble. She had to ask, but she was terrified to hear the answer. Leaning in close and keeping her voice low she asked, "What's your name sweetheart?"

"Mama calls me CB. It's from when I was a baby, cause she used to call me her little cinnamon bun. It's silly, but I like it. But that's not my real name.

My real name is Skyler."

In the next breath, Mayla was back on the couch, Anton's arms wrapped firmly around her middle, her mouth hanging open and her face draining of color.

Skyler stood all the way across the room, utterly rigid. His skin was pale and he trembled just the slightest bit as he hurried to yank his gloves back on. Mayla jumped up, giving him a chagrined, apologetic look. Anton unfolded his large frame from the couch behind her, but for once she ignored him completely.

"I'm so sorry Skyler. I didn't realize. I would never have...I thought it was some kind of test. I would never intentionally..." She raised her hands in a placating gesture, but dropped them again to her sides as her words trailed off. She'd overstepped in a huge way and she didn't even know how she'd done it. She had no business wandering around anyone's mind without their permission.

Wait.

She had been *in* Skyler's mind. The small terrified child hiding in that cold, tiny room had been him, reliving one of his most horrible memories.

Holy shit.

She really was an empath.

Skyler puffed out a breath and cleared his throat, nodding. "Yes, you really are an empath." He started to pace.

Mayla jerked. "Skyler…I didn't say that out loud."

Skyler turned on a dime and stared at her, his goateed mouth dropping open. His dark eyes were round as saucers, his expression stunned.

Mayla swallowed hard. Was he reading her mind now? And if he was, how was he doing it without touching her?

"You're right, I shouldn't be able to without physical contact, but I am. But this isn't normal mind walking. I can hear your thoughts in my head, not see them. Right now you're wondering how this is even possible."

Mayla gasped, her hand flying up to cover her mouth.

"Wait just a minute," Anton interjected. "You're reading her mind? From over there? How? Why? And fucking STOP IT."

Skyler was shaking his head. "It's not like that. I'm not doing anything. My magic is completely dormant right now. It's," he looked over at Mayla, eyes growing wide, "it's her magic doing this, not mine."

It was Mayla's turn to pace. No. No. *No.* Her magic was a mess, okay fine, she could live with that. She was an empath. Totally wild, but okay. But this? This mind reading from across the room…She couldn't have a complete stranger reading her mind. Yes, Skyler was a very nice man, but—

"Thanks for that," he said under his breath.

Mayla spun to face him, narrowing her eyes in warning. This could not be happening. She had too many thoughts she didn't want anyone knowing. Like how she was still a little afraid of the dark, even at her age. Or how she still watched Disney movies for fun and knew all of the songs by heart.

Sweet gods, what if he saw how attracted she was to Anton?!

Skyler choked but quickly smothered it. He stared at the floor, refusing to look at her, his cheeks flushing.

Mayla groaned. He'd heard that! Oh gods, she could die right here and now!!

"Mayla?" Anton stepped up, grabbing her shoulders and giving her a little shake. "What is it? What's the matter?"

She just shook her head weakly at him.

Anton's glacial gaze turned to Skyler, the temperature in the room beginning to cool considerably. His tone when he spoke was low and dangerous.

"Skyler, whatever twisted mess you've managed to create, fix it. *RIGHT FUCKING NOW.*"

Skyler stared at the two of them. His eyes dropped to where Anton's hands still gripped Mayla's shoulders.

"Anton, please trust me and don't move an inch. Mayla," Skyler's voice was slow and deliberate. "I need you to think about your favorite color."

Mayla raised an eyebrow at him. Her every thought was currently open to him like a friggin' library book and he wanted parlor tricks? What did her favorite color have to do with anything right now? Still, without really willing it, a soft light blue came to mind. It reminded her of the early morning sky, and the photos of tropical oceans that she'd only seen in magazines. It also just happened to be the same color as Anton's eyes. Keeping those thoughts front and center, she nodded at Skyler.

"You're thinking of it right now? Your favorite color? You're sure?"

She couldn't help the slight eye roll of annoyance at his insistence, but nodded again. "Yes. I'm thinking of it right now."

The tension in Skyler fled, and he deflated like a balloon that had been blown up but never tied. The lean, muscular male flopped into the chair, heaving a giant sigh.

"I can't hear anything. I can't read your mind anymore."

Mayla blew out a huge breath herself and her body sagged. Anton's arm slid around her back and her heart gave a little flutter at the contact before settling back into a calm, steady beat.

"Someone start talking," Anton growled.

Taking a long swig from the soda he'd set down earlier, Skyler scooted forward in the chair and braced his elbows on his knees. "Honestly, so much happened in all that I'm not even sure where to start."

"I messed it up," Mayla admitted, staring hard at the other empath. She needed to know for sure. "I think I was in Skyler's mind while he was in mine. And then when I left his mind, he could still read my thoughts."

Skyler nodded, watching them both. "I think you should both sit down."

Mayla was completely on board with that idea, her knees were still wobbling from what had just happened. Moving to the couch, she turned, realizing Anton hadn't budged. He stood, watching Skyler intently, his body tense as if he was prepared to launch himself at the empath if necessary.

Skyler motioned to the sofa. "I can't hear her thoughts anymore, I swear it. All connection has been severed. Please Anton, just sit down."

Anton finally unlocked, moving to one end of the couch,

then thought better of it and shifted closer to Mayla, their legs touching from hip to knee. Skyler watched, his lips curving in a strange, knowing smile.

"I've got a lot to tell you both, and some of this is going to sound pretty crazy."

"Finally, something I'm used to," Mayla joked.

Skyler sketched her a quick, appreciative smile. "First, the elephant in the room. Mayla, you are absolutely an empath. You are not only an empath, you're the strongest empath I have ever come in contact with."

Oh.

Okay wow. That was *not* what she'd been expecting at all. She shot a slightly panicked look at Anton, but he just raised his eyebrows once and turned his attention back to Skyler.

"I've never met someone I couldn't gain immediate access to up here," he tapped the side of his head with a finger, "especially when I'm touching them. But Mayla, with you, I couldn't even get a glimpse."

Her brows furrowed. That couldn't be right. She'd sensed him there, seen his aura pacing back and forth. "But I saw you. You were right there, right at the edge of my mind."

"Exactly. The outside edge. That's as far as I got. Also, just for your reference, people with no empathic power would have had no idea I was even there."

"Wait, but if you couldn't get into my mind, then how did we connect enough that you knew what I was thinking?"

"I could only read your thoughts after I let go, and I let go after you got into my mind instead. Mayla, you not only got into my mind, you got through every trap and every protection I have in place, and trust me, I have plenty."

"I didn't see any traps," she admitted on a whisper.

"I know. You wouldn't still be conscious if you had. My traps pack enough kick that most people pass out if they trigger one."

She felt Anton stiffen next to her at that, but Skyler kept talking.

"Mayla, you got into the deepest parts of my mind and you didn't even know you were doing it. It was almost like an afterthought for you. I've been training my empath magic for the past twenty years and no matter how hard I tried, I couldn't find an entrance to your mind. It's not that it was secure, it was like it simply didn't exist. Like you didn't exist."

"The power it would take to do something like that?" The soft mutter was under Anton's breath, but the awe in it was clear.

"My thoughts exactly," Skyler agreed. "I have safeguards in place. I started intensive training when I was still a kid," his dark eyes found hers, darting quickly to Anton, then back to her.

She understood immediately. Anton didn't know about his childhood, and Skyler was begging her to keep it that way. She dropped her chin in a tiny nod.

"By the time I was a teenager the top empaths I met in training could only see a locked metal door in my mind, they could never go any farther. After a while they started to pass out whenever they even attempted it. It's what makes me perfect for working black ops. If I can get my bare hands on a suspect, I can gain entry into their mind and find out everything I need to. For the few that have magics that might help them escape, I can not only pull them in, I can lock them into my own mind to interrogate them. It's usually foolproof."

He paused, and gripping the armrests of the chair, he let out a low chuckle of disbelief.

"But Mayla, I wasn't pulling you in. My mind was fully guarded. I was trying to get into your mind, not the other way around. I was looking for an entrance and the next thing I know I'm in a meadow, with a tennis ball in my hand, a little yellow puppy in my lap." His tone was incredulous.

"I'm violently allergic to dogs. I would never have thought of such a thing. You put that thought in my head, that image. Once I realized it wasn't real, I could suddenly feel you in mine instead. I saw when you reached the door, watched as you made it want to open on its own. I tried to push back, to keep that door locked tight, but it didn't work."

Skyler dropped his face into his hands and the words that came out were ragged with disbelief. "Mayla when you left that room, you went off exploring into areas of my subconscious that I didn't even know existed. Are you hearing what I'm saying? It took you all of two minutes to get into parts of my mind that I've never accessed before. You took over completely. I was a spectator. I could see you, watch what you were doing, but I had absolutely no control.

Mayla, your magic is so strong it not only gives you access to people's minds, it also gives you total control as well."

13

Mayla opened her mouth, then snapped it shut once more. Skyler's words bounced around in her head like balloons she couldn't quite catch. She'd gotten into his head and found things even he, an incredibly strong empath himself, hadn't known were there. What? Just…no. *WTF*?

Anton took her hand in his and she looked down at their intertwined fingers, blinking slowly. He gave a tiny squeeze, and she realized Skyler was still talking.

"—to ask, because everyone with our type of magic is a little different. When you physically touch people who are in distress, do you *sense* what they need, or do you actually feel what they are feeling?"

"I see images first, before I touch anything. Colors too, sometimes. If someone is sad I see a dark blue or a gray color surrounding them. If they're angry its red or orange. After that I usually get an image of why; they fought with someone, or got bad news from a doctor, those sorts of things."

Skyler was nodding, entirely focused on her.

"Then when I touch them, I can feel the sadness they're feeling. I feel like I was the one who got into a disagreement, or I was the one who got scary medical news."

"And does the same thing happen when you use your healing magic?" Skyler asked gently.

Mayla nodded. "Yes. If they're injured, once I put my hands on them I can sense where the pain is and I send the magic there. Sometimes, if it's not as clear, I can focus my magic to go look for where the damage really is. When I do it that way, my body starts to physically hurt wherever theirs needs the most help. I try not to do that too often though. It takes a long time for that kind of pain to turn off again when I do. "

An anguished croak came out of Anton. "Mayla, yesterday, when you helped me, you *felt* all that?" His question came out harsh and insistent, his body tensing beside her.

She nodded, lowering her eyes to her lap. Anton dropped her hand, shooting to his feet to begin pacing like a caged tiger. His jaw clenched so tightly Mayla worried it might crack.

"After the explosion yesterday," he told Skyler through gritted teeth, "she used her magic to heal me. I didn't know it at the time, but my wings were close to shredded."

Skyler's dark eyes went wide and he looked at Mayla, stunned.

Anton spun to face her, his voice rising. "Why would you do that? What were you thinking? If you knew you were inviting in all that pain," he ran a frustrated hand through his hair. "When I came to you were there, already touching me and I felt—," he stopped, staring at her hard. "I felt like I'd been ripped apart, Mayla. Every part of my body hurt and my wings felt like they were on fire. I thought I was dying. Damnit, Mayla, why would you do something so foolish?!"

"Because you *WERE* dying, Anton!!"

He froze.

"I knew, okay? I *knew* you were dying. My magic told me."

Horror spread across his face.

Mayla threw up her hands in frustration. "What was I supposed to do? Sit there and watch that happen? Just wait for your last breath like I was watching some sort of damn television show?"

Anton rocked back, his brows furrowing, but he said nothing

"I was just coming into the plaza when I saw the image of the bomb in my head. Everything in me started to panic. I was going to turn around, to run away, but then I saw you. You were facing all that glass and you had no idea what was coming. I screamed, I tried to warn you away, but you didn't move. And then the next thing I knew I was running. I don't remember telling myself to do it; my body just decided for me. I had to get to you.

After the explosion, you were lying there and you were so still. I just…I did what I *had* to do. I didn't have a choice." Her voice faded with the confession, and she gripped the edges of the couch cushion tightly, her knuckles going white.

Skyler coughed, drawing Anton's gaze. He widened his eyes once, then narrowed them again in silent scolding. Anton sent him a grimace, looked at Mayla, back at Skyler, and then shrugged. Skyler pursed his lips, jerking his head towards the couch, his silent *get-over-there-and-fix-this-dumbass* perfectly clear.

Anton scrubbed a hand down his face, blowing out a heavy sigh before moving over to kneel in front of her.

"Mayla, I'm sorry. I shouldn't have yelled like that. I overreacted. Of course you helped me, you would help anyone in that situation because you're a good person. I just…the idea of you being in pain like that because of me? It just makes me a little crazy. I'm used to protecting people, that's my job. I guess I'm just not used to anyone protecting me. I'm sorry. Please don't be mad."

She raised an eyebrow, a small smirk tucking her lips up at the edges. "Has anyone ever told you you're a domineering ass sometimes?"

Anton's ears reddened, but he nodded. "I get that quite often, I'm afraid." He lifted his eyebrows, fixing her with a remorseful expression.

Mayla side-eyed Skyler and rolled her eyes, but nodded her forgiveness. Anton gave her a dazzling grin, then quickly resumed his seat next to her on the couch, turning back to Skyler.

"After what happened yesterday, she woke up this morning injured in a similar way. It was a step or two down in severity, but it was still very, very bad. Can you tell us why that happened?"

Mayla felt her cheeks burning and rushed to answer before Skyler could. "It's because I get too tired too fast. Sometimes, if it's just a minor injury, I can fight it off. But for bigger problems, my magic is too weak and I'm just not strong enough. Lowblood, remember?"

"It has NOTHING to do with how strong you are, Mayla. You might be the strongest person I've ever met." The response came out on a snap, so forceful it stole her breath for a moment. It hung in the air, then seemed to settle, dropping to wrap around her shoulders in a comforting swirl.

"Anton is right," Skyler said, his eyes locking with hers. His expression intensified as if he could somehow push the truth into her with a look. "You're not weak, Mayla. I understand where you could misunderstand it; the emotions, the physical pain, having to process all of that at the same time would be overwhelming for anyone. Even the strongest Highblood couldn't tolerate that much sensory input on a regular basis. The fact that you've not only tolerated it, but found ways to work around it for this long? That tells me Anton is right. You're far more powerful than you give yourself credit for. The physical manifestation of the injuries is puzzling, but my best guess is it's happening because your two magics are mixing."

Mayla couldn't tamp down the swell of hope building within her. Neither of these men, Highblood men no less, thought that she was weak. What if her constant anxiety wasn't because she was too weak, but because she was actually too strong? She had *two*, distinctly different kinds of magic. Even the most powerful Highbloods she'd seen on TV or read about in magazines, only ever had one type of magic. Though if she was going to be an overachiever and have two, she should probably learn how to handle them both correctly.

"What do I need to do to separate them?"

Skyler's smile was placating, as if he could sense her urgency. Which, come to think of it, he probably could. "I think your magics have been mixing since you were a child. No one ever realized you had empath magic on top of your healing capabilities, so no one thought to teach you how to separate them.

Your healing magic uses your empath magic as a conduit to determine where it's needed. Your empath magic turns around and feeds off your healing magic like a battery, giving itself a boost in stressful situations. Since they're so accustomed to being used together, when you heal someone and start to feel any pain, your empath magic comes barreling back from its target thinking it needs to protect you. Your healing magic is doing its job, but it's along for the ride, so when your empath magic rushes back, it's drawing some of that residual injury into you along the way."

Mayla blinked at him.

"Think of it like this. If you were a surgeon, your right hand would be your empath magic, and your left would be your healing magic. You're supposed to be operating with just your left hand, but your right hand keeps getting in the way. Then, as soon as your empath hand feels the pain from your patient, it's pulling back into your mind to protect you. The problem is, it's still got a grip on some of that pain and injury, so it drags both back with it when it comes. It's why I could read your thoughts even though your power is so much stronger than mine. You opened that channel into my mind, grabbed onto it, and pulled me back with you by accident."

Mayla rolled this new information around for a moment before responding.

"Okay, I think I get what you're saying. But then, how do I stop them from mixing? I can't just stop healing people. I mean, when I see someone who needs help I can't just ignore them," she sent Anton a pointed look, but he pretended not to notice.

Skyler leaned back in his chair, crossing an ankle over his opposite knee.

"I wouldn't expect an empath of your strength to be able to ignore anyone in need without years and years of training. When the empath in you reaches out and feels that someone needs help, your healing magic is already on board to do its thing."

He steepled his fingers under his chin for a minute, thinking.

"Now that I'm thinking about it, I doubt there's a physical way for you to rein in your empath magic. It's way too strong. What we can do though, is work on building a mental barrier between the two. Once you have that in place, you can start trying to use each one independently. Even if it doesn't work and we aren't able to fully separate them, the barrier should at least help prevent some of the bad side effects you've been experiencing."

"A barrier? Something like your metal door you mean?" Anton asked.

Skyler nodded again. "Exactly." He chuckled a little and shrugged his shoulders. "I'll be honest. I have no idea how hard or how easy it might end up being for you, Mayla. Your magics have been blended your entire life. They might separate easily, or they might fight it like crazy. We can't know until we try it out."

Anton was nodding beside her. "She can do it. She's tough, I've seen her in action."

The she in question wasn't quite as certain. Empath. Crazy strong. Mixed magics. Side effects. Mental barriers. This was suddenly…a lot.

"There's one more thing," Skyler added.

Of course there was. Mayla rubbed tiny circles against her temples, trying to massage away her growing headache. She felt a warm hand come to rest on her knee, and looking up she found Anton watching her. When those light blue eyes met and held hers, an instant sense of calm passed through her. He made a point of raising his shoulders in a deep breath, and she matched her own breathing to his, feeling the calm settle even deeper. When his eyebrows raised, she nodded.

His gaze never leaving hers, he spoke to Skyler. "Tell us."

"The pure fae empaths of historical times could enter a person's mind and take over their body completely. Now, there's no documentation to validate this, but there are rumors that they could even have them turn weapons on themselves, things like that."

At Mayla's visible cringe, Skyler's voice softened a bit.

"It's dark I know, but it's important. The empaths back then could go so deeply into someone's mind that they needed an anchor, something that could keep a piece of them tethered to their own body. If they went too deep without an anchor, they ran the risk of not returning. For most, the anchor was a talisman, like a necklace or a special weapon of some sort. The tradition continues to this day."

Skyler tugged a leather cord out from underneath his shirt collar, a small circular golden pendant dangling from it.

"All empaths keep an anchor with them, just to be safe. None of us are strong enough to really need one, but it's still a safety net, as well as a badge of honor. We aren't really strong enough that it will be put to use, but you?" He broke off, looking at the pair of them with a completely mystified expression and shaking his head.

"Skyler," Mayla's voice was weary, "you've just completed the most massive info dump in history, so forgive me if I have NO idea what you're trying to tell me right now." She wrapped both arms around her middle and leaned forward, confused. "Ancient fae and anchors? Are you telling me I need to find a special necklace? Or are you trying to say I'm going to kill someone?"

Anton pressed his left leg against hers and leaned

forward, effectively blocking her from Skyler's view.

"Skyler, I think you're starting to scare her. Get to the point."

The soldier rubbed his palms together quickly, putting both feet back on the ground.

"I don't think you're going to kill anyone, Mayla. What I'm trying - and failing miserably - to tell you, is that you don't have to worry about any of that. You don't have to worry because you already found your anchor."

Mayla raised her head, fixing him with an incredulous look.

"I did?"

"I don't have the slightest clue how, or why," Skyler admitted, "but yes, you did. I've been watching you today. I kept telling myself I was crazy, but I saw it happen over and over again. You don't need to find an anchor. You already have one. *It's Anton. He's your anchor.*"

14

She couldn't have heard that right.

Anton's cell phone began buzzing in his pocket, but he made no move to answer it. Instead he sat motionless, staring at Skyler. When a full minute passed and he still hadn't moved, Mayla dared to place a soft hand on his knee. The phone in his pocket vibrated again, then went silent.

"Skyler," Mayla said softly, turning her attention back to the dark-haired empath sitting across from them, "did you just say Anton is my anchor?"

Skyler nodded, jumping out of the chair to come stand before them both, rubbing his now re-gloved hands together. Mayla could feel the waves of excitement rolling off him.

"Yes! I know, it sounds crazy, but hear me out. Earlier when you needed some time to process and I left the room; I assumed you two were close because of the stress of yesterday's events. But then, when I was getting those echoes of your thoughts and we couldn't break the connection? It broke as soon as he touched you. It clicked off instantly, like a light switch. A minute ago you were starting to get a headache. You were rubbing your temples, remember?"

Mayla nodded slowly.

"And then he touched your leg?"

Her eyes widened.

"And how is your head now? Still hurting?"

She took a moment, mentally checking in with her own body.

"No, my headache is completely gone."

Skyler started pacing. "And just a minute ago, when you were starting to feel overwhelmed, he leaned his leg against yours. As soon as he did, the furrow between your brows disappeared. Think about it. When you're close to him, what happens with your emotions?"

Mayla couldn't speak, staring instead at the corner of the end table as the light dawned.

"You two haven't known each other very long, but somehow he calms you down, right?"

Mayla cleared her throat, suddenly awkward, and slid her hand away from where it had still been resting on Anton's knee. She took a breath, then jumped in with both feet.

"When I'm around him I feel…settled. It's like everything else pauses and takes a step back. I can breathe again. The colors and the emotions and the overload just…disappears."

Skyler clapped his hands together. "Exactly! That's what an anchor is supposed to do. They mute the demand of the magic, in order to keep the empath tethered to the here and now." He studied the two of them, still sitting hip to hip on the couch, Anton's larger masculine frame dwarfing Mayla's slender one.

"I mean if you really want I can separate the two of you for a day or two and we can test it, but I really don't think there's a need at this point. *You're* an empath. *He's* your anchor. Those are just the facts."

Mayla shot to her feet, mumbled something about the bathroom, and then hurried down the hall to disappear into Anton's bedroom. They heard the distant click of the bathroom door.

Skyler's gaze traveled to Anton, who still sat on the couch, looking for all the world like someone had just smacked him upside the head with a shovel.

"Hey man, you okay? Sorry to dump all this on you, but it's important that you know."

Anton's eyes finally focused and he nodded, standing.

"Yeah. Look, I think that's enough for today, Skyler," he said. "We're going to need a little time to process. Thanks though, for coming by today, and for your help with," he made a halfhearted motion with his arm, "with all this."

"Not a problem. I wish I could tell you more, but this is totally new territory. Anton, she's at a power level I've never experienced before. Eventually she's probably going to need some professional training."

Anton's head shot up, his glare sending Skyler back a step, hands up in immediate surrender.

"Hey, hey, calm down. I said she'll need it eventually, just for her own peace of mind, man. I'm not trying to recruit her or anything, ease out."

Anton's shoulders relaxed, but his fists remained clenched at his sides.

Skyler sent him a sideways look. "Damn Iceman, I've never seen anything get you this worked up. What is going on with you? That explosion yesterday rattle your cage or something?" He placed a comforting hand on his friend's shoulder.

Anton blew out a long, slow sigh and shook his head. "I don't know, Sky, maybe. I'm just…not quite myself lately."

They heard the soft sound of Mayla's sock feet coming back down the hallway.

"I'll figure it out though, I promise," Anton said under his breath.

Skyler nodded, his I hope so going unsaid.

When Mayla entered the living room, the tendrils of hair around her face were wet, her cheeks ruddy as if she'd been scrubbing at them. Anton's expression immediately softened. He wasn't stupid enough to ask if she was okay. He didn't know anyone who would be okay after hearing all of that.

"Hanging in there?"

She nodded, giving him a tremulous smile.

"Look, I really got to get back to headquarters, guys. Sorry for setting off an information bomb in the middle of your lives and all." Skyler shrugged, looking sheepish. "Once I get back on base, I'll put some feelers out and see if I can dig up any more information for you."

The phone in Anton's pocket buzzed, and he snatched it out to accept the call, impatient.

"This better be life or death," he growled into the device.

A moment passed as he listened to whoever was on the other end, and his lips pressed into a thin hard line.

"We'll be right there."

When they approached the entrance to Magnolia Park, it was blocked by three of the biggest, blackest, most tactical looking vehicles Mayla had ever seen. An MTF jacketed officer hopped into one immediately, and shifted it out of the way as they approached in the Audi. Anton nodded his thanks as they passed, Mayla watching in the side view mirror as the vehicle moved immediately back in place behind them.

After Asher's call demanding Anton get to the park immediately, they'd made their goodbyes to Skyler, the latter promising to call if he was able to find out anything more about her situation.

Her situation. It made it sound like she had a terminal disease or something. She was still turning over everything she'd learned today in her head, but the most important at the moment was the final note of advice Skyler had offered before they parted ways.

"Mayla, don't try to build your mental barrier from scratch. Start by imagining a door that's already there. Your healing magic can pass through the door freely, but your empath magic cannot. Keep that thought in your head, always. When you need your healing magic, don't open it at all unless you absolutely have to, and if you do, only a crack. For your empath magic, open it gradually, grab the information you need, and close it back as soon as you can. Never open it completely unless you're with Anton, okay? Better safe than sorry."

As they drove further into the park, they could make out a large white medical tent set up in the middle of one of the currently deserted baseball fields. Her gut started churning. They wouldn't put up a tent unless there was something the police really didn't want people to see, right?

She rubbed her suddenly clammy hands down her jeans and wondered yet again how Anton did this job every day. As they pulled in, parking next to an older, light blue square-body Chevy pickup truck, a cherry red Jeep roared into the spot on their other side.

Coming around the back of Anton's car, Mayla had to smother a giggle at the *My Other Ride Is Your Mom* sticker on the bumper of the jeep. Somehow, she wasn't the least bit surprised when Elijah's strong, masculine frame exited the drivers seat. She was completely shocked however, when her sister Natalie emerged from the passenger side.

"Nat? What are you doing here? I thought you had work?" She rushed over to embrace her sister, pulling in a deep breath when those familiar arms squeezed her back. She could use a little family comfort after all the chaos of this morning.

"May! How's your back, all better I hope? I wrapped up my meetings early today. Was getting ready to dial your number as I left, but Prince Not-So-Charming," she looked pointedly over at Elijah and rolled her eyes, "was waiting for me beside my car. He said he worked with Anton and promised to bring me straight to you."

Elijah stood just behind her, but spoke up. "That's when she promised to castrate me and feed me my own bits if I was lying," he told Anton with a cocky grin. He wiggled his eyebrows. "I think I like this one, she's got fire."

Mayla hugged her sister again, laughing. "Oh Nat, you didn't, did you?"

As soon as Mayla released her, Natalie planted both hands on her hips.

"You're damn right I did. I've never seen this cretin before in my life! For all I know he could have been trying to kidnap me. I just made sure he knew exactly what he was signing up for if he planned to try anything shady."

Elijah, looked over at Anton. What's a cretin? He mouthed.

Mayla snorted, then hooked an arm with her sibling. "Nobody would ever dream of messing with you Nat, not if they wanted to keep all their parts in working order. And my back is much better. I saw a healer this morning and she was wonderful. She's actually Anton's godmother, and she's so beautiful, Nat. I can't wait to tell you about the outfit she was wearing, you'll lose your mind!"

Asher emerged from the tent, approaching quickly, his

faded brown work boots making no sound at all in the soft grass. Mayla remembered seeing him during the clean up after the explosion, but they'd never officially been introduced. She vaguely remembered thinking he was handsome yesterday, but standing this close she realized that handsome didn't do him justice. He was absolutely gorgeous. His hair was straight and black as midnight onyx, and long enough to fall straight over his forehead, almost into his eyes. And those eyes. They were sharp and intense, a warm honey brown that instantly grabbed your attention and locked in, refusing to let go. His features, along with perfectly sculpted cheekbones, hinted at the possibility of Asiatic heritage somewhere in his bloodline.

Natalie nudged her in the ribs, leaning close to her ear and whispering, "Who is that and where can I get one?"

Asher cut his eyes in their direction and Mayla shook her head, shushing her. There was no way he could have heard that, but still.

He wore a plain gray t-shirt, stretched snug across well defined shoulders, and his faded jeans looked almost worn through in places. He was all lean muscle and corded arms, tendons flexing as he shoved his hands deep into his pockets. He locked eyes with Anton for a long moment before shaking his head.

"This one is ugly, chief."

"How ugly, exactly?"

"The ugliest. This thing," he waved a hand haphazardly towards the tent, "shows up out of nowhere and starts attacking citizens, in the middle of a gods damn little league game of all things. Witnesses say a white van pulled into the lot, the back opened and this…this *whatever* comes barreling onto the field. Pure chaos after that, screaming kids, panicked parents, all of it." Asher pulled in a hard breath and then released a low, menacing growl. Mayla felt the tiny hairs on her arms stand up. She suddenly remembered why his eyes seemed so predatory and why he seemed to lope when he walked. Elijah said something yesterday about him being a wolf-shifter. There were a lot of shifters in Miradea, both Highblood and Lowblood alike. But the predatory shifters, the tigers, wolves, hawks and such, those were always Highblood.

"The thing killed three people before a lion shifter finally took it out. The man is on his way to the hospital now, he was having seizures when we arrived. There might be a poisoning agent on this thing's skin, it smells…off, sick somehow. So do yourself a favor and don't touch it with your bare hands. I've got officers heading to the hospital to question the shifter if he stabilizes."

Asher tilted his head back, sniffing the air once before shaking his head vigorously like he was trying to clear his nose. "Gods, it smells awful. It's like nothing I've ever smelled before."

Natalie wrinkled her nose and nodded her agreement. "Rotten, like rancid meat."

Mayla sniffed, but she didn't smell anything except the clover at her feet and the very faint, coppery scent of blood.

Asher took his hands out of his pockets, running them both haphazardly through his hair. "We've got two more witnesses we're finishing up with. I had Briggs and Matheson take them to the farthest squad cars to sit, figured it was better than keeping them around to eyeball the cleanup. Victims have already been processed and transported. We're just waiting on you to give the okay to get this thing wrapped up and sent back to the lab, but I knew you'd want to check it out first," he paused for another long moment.

"There's one more thing."

Anton searched the shifter's face, then nodded firmly. "Tell me the rest of it, Ash."

When Asher spoke again, his voice was dark and thick with emotion. His caramel eyes haunted.

"I don't understand it, but it didn't touch a single Highblood. Not one. Apparently it walked right past them like they didn't exist. Just kept going for Lowbloods like the others weren't even there. That's the only reason the lion shifter was able to finally take it down. How the hell could it even tell the difference?" Asher's fists clenched and unclenched at his sides, his anguish more than evident.

Mayla didn't want to think about the chaos the shifter must have seen when he'd arrived earlier. She knew that the worst of it had already been cleaned up. If not, there was no way Anton would have let her and Natalie come.

But Asher's anguish was a heavy gray weight that pressed on her heart. Maybe if she tried she could just…stepping forward, she placed a hand gently on the shifter's forearm.

Asher jerked at the unexpected contact, looking down at her quizzically, his dark eyebrows raised.

"I'm sorry," Mayla said softly, "we haven't officially met yet, my name is Mayla. I don't mean to bother you, or to interrupt, I just wanted to say thank you. For what you do, I mean."

The tension in his shoulders gradually eased, the haunted look in those caramel eyes slowly dissolving.

Mayla let her hand drop from his arm before turning away, her own face now gray and her eyes tormented. She looked up and met Anton's eyes, her hand reaching out for him.

Closing the distance between them quickly, Anton grabbed it, his eyes watching her face. Moments later, the pink began returning to her cheeks, her eyes brightening. She gave him a small nod and a grateful smile.

Asher watched them intently, but didn't say a word.

Without releasing Mayla's hand, Anton turned back to him. "Go on and head back to the office, Ash. E and I will handle the rest here. It's been a rough couple of days, take your time on the way back. Go grab a meal or something."

The black-haired man nodded, turning towards the square-bodied Chevy. After a few steps he paused, turning back.

"Mayla." He said quietly.

His tone was so flat Mayla was immediately nervous. Had she upset him with what she'd done? "Um, y-yes?"

"Whatever that was that you just did? When you touched my arm and then…well, *whatever* it was? Thanks for that. I," he blew out a long, easy breath before continuing, "yeah, I needed that, so, thank you."

"You're welcome," Mayla answered softly.

Once the man was in his truck and headed out of the parking lot, Anton and Mayla looked at each other.

"I thought he might be mad at me for helping," Mayla admitted.

Anton shook his head. "No, it would take a lot more than that to get Asher upset. He's pretty even keel most of the time." He squeezed her hand. "You sure you're okay though?"

Mayla nodded. "I just helped smooth some of the sharper edges a bit. Once you held my hand I felt better almost immediately but—."

Suddenly realizing they were being watched, Anton and Mayla turned to find both Elijah and Natalie only inches away.

They both started speaking at once.

"May what the hell was—"

"Dude! How did you—"

"Did you somehow remove—"

"Her eyes were all—"

Anton held up and hand and silence fell. "We'll explain it all at length, I promise. But for now all you need to know is Mayla is an empath."

"Are you shitting me?" Elijah blurted, clamming up again when Anton shot him a warning glare.

Natalie crossed her arms over her chest, sending Elijah a condescending look. "I already *knew* that part."

Elijah rolled his eyes and stuck his tongue out at her.

"Mayla is an empath," Anton repeated, raising his voice for attention. "And I am her anchor. So we're just going to have to—"

"Whoa, whoa, whoa big guy," Natalie interrupted, completely ignoring the way Anton clenched his jaw in irritation.

"You're her *what* now?"

15

Anton blew out an exasperated sigh, and Mayla burst out laughing, breaking the tension. He looked at her, purposefully ignoring the other two, and smiled.

"I'm glad one of us is enjoying this."

She grinned back. "Oh come on! You have to admit it's kind of funny. They're so alike they're practically bookends!"

The objections began instantaneously.

"She and I are nothing—," Elijah blurted.

"Me and THIS guy? Are you kidding?" Natalie interrupted, adamant.

Anton and Mayla laughed, turning and walking towards the tent as they shook their heads, leaving the other two sputtering and staring at each other in disbelief.

When Elijah and Natalie caught back up to them, E was already talking.

"Hey A, when we're done here can I call it a day? I got a six-pack at home with my name on it."

Anton looked at his watch, then looked pointedly at his second-in-command.

"It's barely noon, E, not a chance. There's a stack of overdue incident reports sitting on your desk that you've been avoiding for weeks. You got a hot date with those when we're done here."

"Aww, man! You know I hate all that paperwork bullshit," Elijah whined.

Anton held the flap of the tent open and ushered the rest of them inside.

"I do know. I also know that if you don't get those incident reports turned in, I don't have to pay you. No paycheck means no beer and no nightlife my friend, so zip it. Plus, we both know Asher got the worst of it these past two days. His team completed all the death notifications after the explosion yesterday, and then he pulls the short straw as lead on this mess?" Anton waved his arm around. "The least we can do is get a jumpstart on the damn paperwork and assign notification duties elsewhere."

The heavy tent flap dropped behind them, and it took a moment for their eyes to adjust. The interior was sparsely lit by small electric lanterns sitting in a large circle on the ground. They were spaced every five feet or so, and they encircled a large gray green… something.

"Yeah, I guess you're right," Elijah was saying. "All those families wanting answers, all those images of the victims in your head. That kind of stuff blows. Wait, what. In the hell. Is that thing?" He asked, his lip curling in distaste.

The grotesque creature on the ground before them was obviously deceased, huge claw marks criss-crossing its torso. But the claw marks were the only normal part of what they were looking at. Whatever it was, it was reptilian in nature, with bulging muscles covered in dark, slime covered scales. It was larger than Anton by at least a foot or two, which meant standing it would tower over anyone here. The head was elongated, coming to a point in the front with two longer - good gods they were fangs - on either side of its mouth. A long, muscular tail covered with jagged spikes of bone curled behind it and a gray, foul-smelling mucous covered its entire body.

Mayla now knew exactly what Asher and her sister had been talking about, her nose crinkling at the sudden stench of sulfur and rot. It seemed to be coming from the puddle of green liquid pooled on the tarp beneath the creature. Was that its blood?

"It's a *Kobold*. An *ancient*." Natalie said on a terrified whisper.

Mayla, Anton and Elijah turned to stare at her, but the normally defensive red head ignored them, her eyes never leaving the lizard creature lying on the ground. She'd gone white as a sheet.

Mayla dug through her memory, recalling the ancient fae stories her parents used to read to them when they were children. They were awful stories, most of them dark and twisted, but they certainly got the intended results. Hard to argue about eating your broccoli when you were worried the Sluagh would find out and come feast on your flesh. She remembered scrambling to clean her room as a child before the Gremlins discovered she hadn't and showed up to burn all of her toys. The Kobold though…she thought back, remembering a big, leather-bound book her parents would read from, and she could almost hear her mother's voice.

"Centuries ago, before Miradea was divided by high or low blood, there were only the pureblood fae of the city and the horrible fantastical beasts that called the badlands home. The sluagh, the kobolds and the banshees roamed there, free to consume any who wandered into their territory. Back in those times, the mightiest warriors would hunt the beasts, processing the corpses for important medicines and magics. The formidable Kobold was the most fiercely hunted, the mucous they secreted prized above all others. It had the power to make women stunningly beautiful, and men extremely powerful."

Mayla blinked. "I think she's right. Our parents used to read us the stories." She huffed out a heavy breath, a wayward lock of ebony hair on her forehead jumping at the exhalation. "I just, never thought they might actually be true."

"But…but," Elijah spluttered, utter disbelief riding his features, "Kobolds are myths. They're made up. We all heard those stories when we were kids, but they were just stories to make us eat our vegetables and behave in front of the neighbors. And, if by some tiny, minuscule, damn near invisible chance they did exist, that was over a millennia ago. Right?"

He'd directed his question at Anton, but the male in question remained stone-faced, staring at the creature before them with a deeply furrowed brow.

Mayla could feel a mixture of both curiosity and concern

swirling around his shoulders. The image of an ancient book, one much older than the one on her parents' bookshelf, flashed in her mind. Detailed drawings and diagrams resembling the Kobold decorated the pages. Then images faded, a wave of orange guilt suddenly rising to bring a lump to her throat.

Guilt? Why would he be feeling guilty about this?

She placed a hand on his bicep, squeezing a little and pushing a soft feeling of peace through her fingertips. Anton took on too much responsibility when bad things happened, as if Miradea were his to protect and his alone. He was entirely too hard on himself. As he continued to stare intently at creature, she studied his profile.

He was entirely too attractive as well.

As soon as the thought flashed in her mind he turned, giving her a half smile and looking pointedly down at her hand. She raised her eyebrows in challenge and left her hand where it was. Was he telling her not to help him when he needed it? He leaned his head down, whispering in her ear.

"You might want to check that doorway, Mayla. You're wide open to me right now."

If it was meant as a warning, an instruction for her to practice what Skyler had taught her, why he have to say it in the most husky, sensual tone she'd ever heard?

Oh wait. Oh gods.

She felt the heat of embarrassment creep up her neck, and she dropped her hand, taking a quick step to the side.

Anton turned back to the beast. "It is a Kobold. I've seen them before, though only in the ancient books and manuscripts in my father's library. I just have no damned idea how it still exists anywhere, or how the hell it got here. They've been extinct for the last thousand years."

Mayla watched Elijah step in close to the creature, two of his knives palmed and his shoulders tense. When the tent flap fluttered in the breeze behind them, he moved so fast Mayla almost didn't catch it. His knives sliced a wide and brutal X across the creature's throat, the massive lizard-like head separating completely and rolling off the tarp into the grass.

Anton snorted. "I think you won, E," he said sarcastically.

Elijah blushed, looking only slightly sheepish. He holstered his knives before turning away.

"I *hate* monsters."

The flap to the tent lifted, and two uniformed officers worked to secure it high overhead, waving towards an MTF van backing up in their direction. More officers were swarming in to help when Anton suddenly held up a hand. They all froze on a dime, watching him. He dropped to one knee, peering into the now splayed open neck.

"E, what the hell is *that*?!"

Elijah stepped in behind him, peering over Anton's shoulder, his eyes narrowing and his brow furrowing deep.

"Yeah I see it. It doesn't make any sense, but I see it." Elijah took a big step back as Anton lurched to his feet, his face white as a sheet.

"Get this thing loaded up and back to headquarters *RIGHT NOW.*"

Less than an hour later, standing in the forensic lab at MTF headquarters, Elijah leaned as far back from the metal table as he could manage, staring at the severed head as if it might reanimate and decide to attack him.

Looking down at the mechanical gears and rods attached to the bone and gray tissue beneath, Anton supposed it really wasn't that far out of the realm of possibility.

Fucking wonderful. He already had an unsolved explosion in the middle of downtown to deal with, Lowblood children that were going missing on a regular basis, and now the gods decide to dump some kind of robo-lizard in his lap?

"Enwyn, can you please tell me what the hell I'm looking at?" He pointed at the kobold head, looking expectantly at their Chief Medical Officer.

Enwyn MacIntosh had pixie blood, so they stood only three feet tall. With a sharp, military style trim to their white blonde hair and a naturally stocky build, no one at headquarters dared to mock Enwyn for their height. It was a known fact that the step stools and ladders spread throughout the medical office were never to be commented on, unless you wanted one of your appendages surgically removed.

Enwyn shifted the side-lighted medical glasses to their forehead and focused their light purple eyes on Anton.

"It looks to be some type of bio-mechanical modification. The spine and extremities are authentic, the skin, muscle and soft tissue as well. The poison glands that run along the spinal ridge and those in the mouth, those are all genetically normal. But the rest of this?"

They used a pen to point at a pair of metal gears in the location of the jaw, now clearly visible thanks to Elijah's earlier knife work.

"None of this is genetically normal. Someone deliberately PUT this here, someone ridiculously talented in biomechanics from the looks of it. This gives increased strength and power to the jaw, so much so that the pounds of pressure added to any bite would be astronomical."

Enwyn directed them over to a second table where the rest of the kobold's body lay, and indicated the front claws, which now lay severed from the creature at the wrists. Metallic parts gleamed inside those joints as well.

"These are the same. They increase the strength at the joints to the point where this creature would be able to crush bone with a simple squeeze. Based off the minimal scarring I can find, these modifications were most likely done through a combination of bio-mechanical engineering and very strong magic work. You say this creature was attacking people at random?"

Anton ground his teeth together at the reminder, but nodded his affirmation. "It was attacking people at a little league game in the park this afternoon. For some reason, it focused only on attacking Lowblood citizens."

Enwyn's naturally light-colored eyes went crimson with anger and they let out a long sigh. "I'm very sorry to hear that. Though that information certainly explains the modifications I found to the olfactory system. The alterations would make it so the creature could detect subtle differences in blood purity through scent alone - though why they would need such a thing I simply cannot fathom. Someone spent a great deal of money to breed and modify this thing. It was created to be a killing machine, and from a mechanical standpoint, a damned efficient one. I don't know who is behind this Chief Tevaris, but I suggest you find this person and put an end to their experimentation," Enwyn practically spit the word, "as quickly as possible."

Next to them, Elijah started bouncing on the balls of his

feet, all pent up energy and excess testosterone. "Oh we're going to find them. We'll hunt them down like the dogs they are and when we locate them I'll finally get cut loose a little." He continued to bounce, his movements getting bigger by the moment.

Enwyn's voice was low and matter fact when they spoke. "If you break anything in my exam room, Rambo, I will cut loose your legs."

Elijah stopped moving on a lurch, and Anton tucked away a smile before the pixie's next words hit him right in the gut.

"Chief? If there are more of these creatures out there? You're going to need more than just one over-caffeinated killer on your team. You're going to need an army…or you're going to have more dead bodies on your hands than you can count."

16

Mayla wasn't sure what had gone on in the medical examiner's office, but when Anton emerged into the hallway where she and Natalie were waiting, the tense set of his shoulders told her it hadn't been good. Even Elijah was uncharacteristically quiet, and that never happened.

At Anton's clipped, "Let's go," the foursome passed through a short breezeway and into the building next door. The entrance was marked simply MTF with a single deadbolt lock. When they entered, and she saw no security checkpoint or guard, Mayla was momentarily taken aback. Then again, she wondered, how many criminals were really itching to break into the police department?

"You guys are awfully comfortable with security around here," Natalie commented from just behind her.

Elijah snickered, pointing towards the ceiling. A small camera tracked their group as they passed, then returned to its original position facing the door.

"We have an all female security team of five, two bear shifters, two tigers, and one falcon. They have a running competition to see who gets to maul the most people per month. Last month's winner got a spa day and a date with yours truly."

Natalie made a loud gagging noise.

Anton looked back over his shoulder. "Trust me, you're safe here. No one uninvited has ever gotten more than ten feet into this building."

Miradea Task Force headquarters was not at all what Mayla had expected. It was a large, open industrial space, with desks positioned haphazardly around the outer edges of the room. Some desks sat alone, others were clustered together in groups of three or four. Farther down one wall was a door marked with a black and white sign. "Everyone Poops" was printed in large block letters. Underneath, the phrase "Except Vampires!" Had been scrawled in large, red, handwritten script.

Mayla looked pointedly at the door and raised her eyebrows at Anton.

He sighed, shaking his head. "It's the restroom. Vampires, ours in particular, aren't nearly as funny as they'd like to think."

"Perfect timing though," Natalie muttered, and breezed through the restroom door.

Mayla snorted.

They skirted a large, round table sitting in the middle of the space, and continued on towards a huge U shaped bank of computers in the center of the room. The gaming chair that sat in the middle was a horrendous pepto-bismol pink. A fair haired man faced the computer screens, his ears covered with kitty cat headphones in the exact same awful shade. They stopped about ten feet away, but, as if he had somehow sensed their arrival, the man was already sliding his headphones down to his neck and spinning around.

He was so lean he was almost scrawny, and considerably shorter than Anton or Elijah, with close cropped strawberry blonde hair. He wore a black t-shirt with the phrase Currently Unsupervised But The Possibilities Are Endless emblazoned across the front, a designer pair of bedazzled jeans, and black and white Vans. The young man had a small patch of freckles across his hawk-like nose, and when he finally smiled at her, his elongated, sharply pointed canines were evident. Vampire. That explained why he looked so much like a teenager, she supposed.

"Callan, this is Mayla. She's an empath," Anton paused, then added, "and a friend, so play nice. Mayla, this is Callan."

The vampire grinned wider before kicking his feet out,

sending his pink chair spinning in circles. He waved pageant style each time he faced her.

Mayla giggled.

Anton looked skyward in annoyance. "He's our eyes and ears-"

"Don't forget mouth," Asher mumbled from a desk across the room. He didn't bother to lift his dark head from his monitor, clearly used to all the theatrics.

Callan continued waving, but lifted his other hand in a one fingered salute when his seat revolved in Asher's direction. Asher blew him a kiss back and Mayla laughed out loud.

Anton shook his head. "Callan is our overwatch. He has access to every video camera in the city, most of them legally. He runs twenty-four hour scans across all media platforms for any potential threats. He also directs us in the field, gives us case status updates daily, and keeps all of us very up to date on the latest additions to the Kung Fu Tea menu."

"He's an addict," Elijah muttered, walking past them to take a seat at what must be - judging from the massive stack of paperwork sitting upon it - his own desk.

Callan smoothly redirected his middle finger to his new target without missing a beat.

"He has questionable fashion sense, an absolutely terrifying Spotify playlist, and we'd be completely dead in the water without him," Anton admitted.

Callan nodded solemnly before standing and coming forward, sketching Mayla a deep, aristocratic bow. "Now that's more like it. Finally I am afforded the appreciation I am clearly due. A true pleasure to meet you, Mayla."

Mayla gave him her best imitation of a curtsey in response. "The pleasure is all mine."

"And mine. I love your jeans by the way, did you do those modifications yourself? I'm Natalie." Her sister appeared on her left, offering Callan her hand.

Up close, Mayla realized belatedly that Callan's bedazzled jeans were actually covered in tiny yellow smiley faces. How adorable.

Callan's eyes glowed with excitement at the compliment, and he grabbed Natalie's hand in both of his own, his smile growing.

"I sure did. Took me over a month to get it right. Fashion is a bit of a hobby, though I really wish I was good enough to work in the industry full-time. Aren't these just the most?" He spun, jutting out one hip supermodel style, then the other. "Be yourself or why be at all, that's my motto," he placed a hand over his heart for emphasis.

"Don't we all know it," Anton muttered, but his lips quirked up in an affectionate smile.

"Ignore him," Callan insisted. "He's all bluster and blow, and not even the really fun kind of blow, if you know what I mean?" He waggled his eyebrows suggestively.

Anton's face went red while Natalie and Mayla laughed, blushing.

Callan laughed as well, throwing a lanky arm over each of the women's shoulders and pulling them into his sides. Strangely enough, when he touched her Mayla's empath powers felt...

Nothing. Absolutely nothing.

How gloriously peaceful.

Callan looked pointedly at Anton, who now stood, arms crossed and frowning at the threesome, then over to Elijah who was trying his best to spin one of his knives on a fingertip and failing completely. After a moment, he froze when he realized they were all staring in his direction.

"What?"

The three of them laughed again, Callan dropping the volume of his voice to a clearly heard conspiratorial whisper. "Honestly ladies, I have no idea what you see in these two other than the obvious physique factor, but the heart wants what the heart wants I suppose. As your brand-new GBF, I've totally got your back."

Natalie waved a hand at Elijah dismissively.

"Nope, not me. That one is definitely not my type."

Elijah rolled his eyes at her and turned his attention back to his knife.

"What's a GBF?" Mayla asked.

"Gay Best Friend, of course! Girl, don't you worry, I've got loads of practice so you're in the best hands, I promise."

Natalie sighed loudly. "Well it's about time. I can finally take down that damn Craigslist ad! You wouldn't believe the crazies that are out there these days."

When the three dissolved into giggles once again, Callan beamed. "O-M-G ladies, you are both so adorable! You clearly have phenomenal taste in new friends and fashion. Unfortunately, duty calls me away at the moment, but prepare yourselves, the three of us will be getting together for happy-hour karaoke ASAP!"

Natalie and Mayla were sitting at the round table sipping on sodas and nibbling on chips from the vending machine a short time later, when a young, blonde officer hurried through the door, heading straight for Anton. Elijah, who'd been making more progress on his third bag of Cheez-Its than the stack of paperwork in front of him, stood from his chair, listening.

"Latest update on the Well Grounded explosion, Chief," the blonde man said, handing Anton a thick manila folder.

"Thanks, Eric. Hey, how's that newest addition to the Fredricks clan doing?"

The officer's face split into a huge smile, his clean shaven cheeks pink with delight. "Sophie's wonderful, sir. Barely a month old and almost sleeping through the night already. When she's not happy though, man she's got a set of lungs on her, let me tell you!"

Anton chuckled. "I have no doubt. Give my love to Samantha, and make sure she brings that new little one of yours in sometime soon to see us all, okay?"

The officer grinned. "Yes sir! I absolutely will!"

"Fredricks, while I've got you here, I put in a missing persons report earlier today. Can you make sure everyone in the department gets a copy of that right away? It's for a Willow Elise Sloane. I've already flagged it top priority and I want people working on it immediately. All eyes on this one, all the time. I'd like you to pick a couple other officers and head out to her place of business, get a good look around. I'm taking point on this one, so anything you find, any interviews, absolutely everything comes back through me, you got it?"

Fredericks nodded, all business. "Yes sir. I'll grab a team and head out right away."

"Good man, thank you."

As Fredricks left, Callan moved over to take a seat at the table, popping open a lime green laptop and typing away with ridiculous speed.

Elijah dumped the rest of his Cheez-Its in his mouth, balling up the wrapper and draining a trashcan shot before coming over to sit at the table as well. "Hit me with some good news, A," he mumbled around a mouthful of cheese flavored crackers.

Anton's eyes scanned the interior of the folder. A few moments later he snapped it shut, tossing it onto the table in disgust. "Nothing concrete to tie the explosion to the Anord. Just more signs pointing to that possibility. They used a high end, military grade explosive and detonator. A handful of witnesses saw what they assume was a small framed man in a dark hoodie come in with a briefcase and leave a few moments later. Most thought he was going up to the counter to order coffee. None can positively identify any facial features. And once again, there are no gods damned prints." Anton spat the words out as if they had soured on his tongue.

Asher leaned back in his desk chair and sighed. "No video footage from the security cameras next door either. The system was offline and awaiting repair." Weaving his fingers together behind his dark head, he thunked his boots up on the corner of his desk.

"Why is it so hard to catch a break with these assholes?"

"How about we settle for a little circumstantial evidence instead?" Callan said, grinning as he turned the laptop around to face the rest of them.

On the screen a middle aged couple smiled broadly for the camera as they prepared to cut a Now Open ribbon in front of Well Grounded.

"The owners of Well Grounded are Martin and Teresa Carrino. Martin and Teresa just happen to be the aunt and uncle of congresswoman Susan Carrino."

"Susan Carrino? As in Chairman of the Lowblood Equality Party, Susan Carrino?" Anton asked.

Callan was already nodding. "One and the same. Carrino's legal team successfully defeated the motion to outlaw Highblood/Lowblood marriage that was put before the Senate just a few years back." Callan's smile continued to grow, and he looked downright predatory with both of his fangs exposed. "Anyone want to take a wild guess where Susan gets the majority of her campaign donations from?"

"Her aunt and uncle," Elijah said flatly.

"Bingo."

"That sure sounds like motive to me," Asher growled.

"Wait, I'm sorry, *why* would that be a motive exactly?" Natalie asked. "You said Anord earlier, are you talking about the same Anord I keep seeing in the newspaper? The Highblood purity propaganda group?"

"That's the one," Callan said. "They also happen to be the most annoyingly professional group of shithead extremists we've ever had the opportunity to hunt."

"They're the reason this task force exists." Anton's words held an undercurrent of frustration. "The brass asked me to put together a team to try and shut them down about three years ago. We've been chasing them nonstop ever since."

Mayla's eyes widened, and she raised her arms, indicating the entire space. "You mean you've grown from a couple officers to all this in just three years?"

Anton nodded. "The Anord have gotten bigger, bolder, and unfortunately much, much deadlier in that time frame. Right now I've got teams working kidnappings, robberies, murders, cybercrimes, trafficking, you name it. These creeps are neck deep in all of it."

"These guys are really that bad?" Natalie asked, her features skeptical. "I see articles about them on occasion, but if they're that extreme why aren't we hearing more about them in the news?"

Asher fielded the question.

"Because everyday citizens have a tendency to panic, and that's the last thing we need right now. The Anord are focused on pushing a Highblood agenda by eliminating Lowbloods. How they choose to do so seems to be up to the individual members, but they've got some very powerful backers hiding in the shadows. Every time we get a confirmed sighting we somehow end up with little to no physical evidence. The handful of times we've been able to get far enough to bring someone in for questioning, a million dollar lawyer is standing here waiting for us when we walk through the door. Three years, and all we've got to show for it is a pile of ridiculous skull masks and a trail of bloodshed." He tsked in disgust.

Natalie looked at the wolf-shifter quizzically. "But, you're Highblood. Why would you even care what happens to Lowbloods like us?"

Asher's lip suddenly curled, revealing a stark white canine that slowly lengthened. His eyes shifted from their warm honey brown to a bright, crisp yellow and a low, menacing growl rumbled deep within his chest.

Natalie took a startled step backwards, bumping right into Elijah's chest.

Stepping around her, Elijah put himself between the two,

giving Asher his back.

"Look, I don't know what you're thinking, but we aren't some kind of macho elitist assholes just because we have extra fae blood, Cherry."

Natalie's eyebrow jumped at the nickname, but she remained quiet, waiting for him to continue.

"Most of the people you see here have spent their lives working against the ridiculous class division here in Miradea." He nodded towards Asher, who was now stalking stiffly back to his desk. "Asher's adoptive parents are Lowbloods. He's here to protect his family. These Anord jack-offs killed mine. I owe them some serious payback. Callan is discriminated against constantly because of his vampirism. Most Highbloods think vampirism is a mutation and therefore beneath them. Though let's be real, most of them have much bigger vices than having to get dinner from a bag of blood in the fridge."

Callan began typing furiously on the laptop, head lowered, his cheeks flaming. Elijah waved a hand haphazardly at Anton, as if the head of the department were simply an afterthought.

"Anton's just a decent guy all around, he insists on taking care of everybody. It's kind of nauseating. Bottom line? We don't believe in Highblood or Lowblood around here. We're not here for politics, we're here for people. Every so called Highblood person in this room has been in a life or death situation where it was a Lowblood that had our back, and vice versa. We aren't any better than them, and they aren't any less than we are. So if these Anord assholes want to target them for some kind of twisted our-blood-is-better-than-yours bullshit?"

Elijah flicked his wrist, his eyes never leaving Natalie's, and one of his black handled knives flying across the room to bury itself in the far wall. It vibrated there for a moment, right between the eyes of a round, smiling man on a poster that read Only YOU Can Prevent Workplace Accidents.

"That's just not happening on our watch."

Natalie swallowed. The rest of the room was dead silent now, even Callan had stopped typing, all eyes focused on Elijah.

The angry shrill of the phone ringing shattered the tense quiet, and Asher leaned over, snatching it up off its cradle.

"MTF headquarters, Officer Ezhno speaking. Yep... okay...wait, are you serious?! At the elementary school?" He grabbed a pen and began scribbling notes quickly. "Fucking A, that's awesome man! Where is he now? Hell yeah we want a crack at him! Hey, thanks. Seriously, tell the guys in vice the next Miradea Marauders game? Tickets are on me, right behind home plate. You guys are beast mode, for real." Asher hung up, those intense caramel eyes sparking with excitement, a wolfish grin spreading slowly across his face.

"Our friends over in vice are bringing us a little present. They were doing surveillance on a suspected enhancement dealer over at the elementary school this afternoon. They didn't catch the dealer in the act, but they did interrupt an attempted kidnapping in the school parking lot. The perp had a red skull mask and a black hoodie in his possession, so they figured we just might be interested in talking to him. They ran his ID, and surprise, surprise he's on record as having been questioned in connection with the kidnapping of a Lowblood child last year. He ended up with a really expensive lawyer that managed to get him off on a technicality and the child was never found. They'll be dropping him off in five minutes."

Elijah let out a whoop, jumping up and punching a fist in the air.

"I got dibs!"

17

A disheveled man with a patchy brown beard stumbled through the main door, dirty hands cuffed together in front of him and heavy work boots stuttering on the linoleum as he struggled to keep his balance. Elijah entered just behind, giving him another forceful shove.

"Everyone, meet Carl Richards. Carl is a Highblood firebug with a nasty little side habit of abducting Lowblood children." Elijah handed a manila folder over to Asher, deliberately shoulder checking Carl as he did so.

"Carl's had no convictions so far because his lawyer is one of the most expensive attorneys in the nation. What I'm wondering Carl, is where the two of you met? Somehow you just don't strike me as the type that attends a lot of dinner parties."

Carl, ash brown hair hanging in limp oily strands around his face, didn't answer. He wore stained jeans, a faded blue work shirt with Miradea Motors emblazoned across the front pocket, and dark brown work boots with the laces untied and fraying at the edges. He smelled like an ashtray that hadn't been emptied in months. When he finally decided to speak, the voice that came out of the man was harsh and a bit whiny, with the heavy rasp of a chronic smoker.

"This is harassment. I was helping that kid get back up after she fell down. I wasn't trying to kidnap nobody."

"See, I'd like to believe you Carl, I really would," Elijah said, "but that's just not what the guys from vice are telling us, and they saw the whole thing. They even have it on video, Carl."

Asher stepped in closer, sending a boot into the back of the Carl's leg so he dropped to his knees. The wolf shifter squatted, his teeth elongating and his eyes shifting to yellow as he leaned in, bringing them nose to nose.

"The guys from vice told us that little girl was screaming, Carl. They said you were running across the parking lot, carrying her towards a beat up Plymouth when they caught you. When they ran the plates on that car, guess who it came back registered to? I'll help you out, because you don't seem all that bright. It's registered to you, Carl."

Elijah moved over to the table, setting down a brown paper bag and motioning for Anton to take a look.

"What else did they find in that Plymouth, Carl?" Asher snarled, his fury barely constrained.

Anton pulled a red skull mask and a black hooded sweatshirt out of the bag, setting them both down on the table with slow precision, before fixing a dangerous glare on the mechanic. Goosebumps rose on Mayla's arms as small white flecks appeared in Anton's blue eyes.

Anton's voice echoed in the cavernous room. "If you'd like to keep all your teeth, Carl, I suggest you start talking."

Asher rose from where he'd been crouched nose to nose with man, moving instead to pace a short distance behind him. Mayla caught Natalie's worried, questioning look, but shook her head. These guys knew what they were doing, and from the sound of it, Carl clearly deserved whatever punishment they might decide to inflict.

The man on his knees remained silent, staring blankly ahead with his thin lips pressed tightly together in a white line.

"Take him to one of the interrogation rooms and make him comfortable," Anton ordered.

Elijah nodded, yanking Carl up by one arm and marching him towards an unmarked door just past Asher's desk.

When Asher and Anton moved to follow, Mayla blurted, "Wait! The little girl? Is she okay?"

Asher looked back with a wolfish grin and nodded. "She's

just fine. Vice said Carl dropped her when he saw them coming. She turned around and nailed him in the nuts with her fist and he dropped like a stone. They made the arrest while he was still puking on the pavement."

Mayla beamed.

"Atta girl," Natalie added, nodding in appreciation.

As Elijah pushed Carl towards the interrogation room and the others followed, Anton spoke up.

"Sounds like she might be MTF material when she grows up. Let's go ahead and get her name added to the potential recruitment log." His comment was met with an enthusiastic round of applause.

Two hours had passed, and Mayla swore she could actually hear Asher's molars grinding together in frustration. The shifter was well past agitated, moving in a loping pace back and forth in front of his desk. So far their questioning had gotten them absolutely nowhere, with Carl remaining steadfastly silent no matter how hard they tried to bait him. As they approached the third hour, the entire team was on edge, their frustration sky high.

Fredericks had returned half an hour ago with even more bad news. The back door to Green Tease had been broken into. They found signs of quite a struggle throughout the store, with a lot of items inside broken or damaged. Forensics was going through the store right now, but the icing on the cake had been the torn piece of red skull mask they'd found tucked up under a large overturned plant. It confirmed what many of them had suspected already.

The Anord had Willow.

Mayla and Natalie had been sitting on the couch ever since they'd heard the news, arms wrapped tightly around each other. They were shell shocked, half numb with disbelief and fully terrified for their friend.

"How long do we just sit here putting up with this?" The gravel in Asher's voice kept deepening. "Just let me in there with him for ten minutes unaccompanied, and unplug the cameras. I guarantee my wolf will get him talking."

Elijah, currently kicked back in a chair with his tactical

boots propped up on the meeting table, nodded his agreement. He tapped a black throwing knife lazily against one temple as he stared at the interrogation room door.

"I'm completely on board with that idea Ash, but you know as well as I do a coerced confession isn't going to help us. We need something concrete. The location of a safe-house, plans for another attack, anything that will get us actual evidence and put one or more of these assholes in the same place." His amber eyes narrowed in fury. "Is Pin the Knife on the Child Abductor considered coercement? Because that sure sounds like fun."

Callan, who'd been uncharacteristically quiet for the past hour, cleared his throat and everyone turned.

"I uh, just wanted to give everyone an update. I checked in with our uni stationed at the hospital. Two more passed today due to injuries sustained from the Well Grounded explosion. Magdalena Herrera, 74, mother of four and grandmother to seven. She did volunteer work at both the library and the public gardens, and grew prize winning tomatoes every year. The other was Kim Min-jun, 27, recently married and expecting his first child. He was a middle school math teacher. His students were invited to attend a state math competition in Atlanta later this year and he'd been downtown putting up fliers to advertise the fundraiser."

Heaviness laid across the room like a weighted blanket.

"One small bit of good news though, all remaining patients are stable and expected to recover, thank the gods."

Anton emerged from the interrogation room, his face hard. He sat down at the round table with a heavy thud, leaning back and running his hands through his hair. When he realized all eyes had turned to watch him, he shook his head.

"Nothing. This asshole isn't talking."

Asher stopped his pacing. "What happens if we can't get this guy to roll over? He gets a couple years inside for attempted kidnapping, if his lawyer doesn't get him off again, and we're right back at square one? This is what we've been waiting for, this is the opportunity we needed. There has to be a way to get the information out him."

"Asher's right, a couple years inside for attempted kidnapping isn't enough. We've got to get this guy to talk. Whatever it takes," Elijah agreed.

Mayla rubbed her sleeve across bleary eyes and stood on wobbly legs. Natalie bounced immediately to her feet beside her.

"What are you doing?" Her sister hissed.

Mayla ignored her. The Anord were out of hand. They'd kidnapped her best friend. They could be torturing Willow right now, or worse, she might already be…Mayla sucked a deep, slightly shaky breath between her teeth and stepped forward.

Natalie tugged at her arm. "May! Whatever you're thinking about doing? Don't."

Shrugging her arm out of her sister's grasp, Mayla approached the table, looking at each of the men gathered there before finally speaking.

"What if you could get the information you need, without him having to talk at all?"

The room went deathly silent, all eyes locking on her.

"Mayla," Anton stood abruptly, approaching her and shaking his head, "no."

Mayla ignored him, focusing instead on Elijah and Asher.

"What I mean is, I'm an empath, right? If I try, I might be able to get into Carl's mind and get us the information you…we need." A nervous giggle of apprehension slipped out of her mouth. "I can't really promise anything. I'm still pretty new, and I've had exactly one lesson so far on how to control it, but I could at least give it a shot."

"That wasn't a real lesson, Mayla, and this guy is a criminal," Anton said sharply. The temperature in the room cooled.

Mayla turned to him, eyebrows lifting. "If I can to get into his mind like I did—," her gaze shifted quickly to the other faces fixated on the two of them. She stopped, pulling in a deep breath. Probably best not to mention that she'd entered Skyler's mind if she could help it.

"I've already done it once, Anton. I can do it again. If I succeed, it just might help you get the lead you really need." Her chin lifted, and her shoulders stiffened defensively.

Anton gripped the back of a chair with one hand, ice crystals forming on the plastic. "What did I tell you about not putting yourself at risk? This man is evil, there's no telling what kind of horrors are in his head. We have no idea what could happen, and that means it's not safe. Besides, you're not ready, you haven't even had the chance to start training."

Out of the corner of her eye, Mayla saw Callan pull on a purple hoodie. Elijah blew hot breath into his cupped hands, and Asher stood eerily still, eyes locked on the two of them.

Her chin ratcheted up another notch. "I'm the strongest Skyler has ever seen, Anton. I should at least give it a shot."

Natalie spoke up, "Mayla, maybe you should—"

Mayla's eyes shot to her sister. "Nat, NOT the time," she snapped.

Natalie's mouth popped shut and she nodded, taking a step back.

"I. Said. No."

Anton's blue eyes had gone fully white, a gray cloud forming quickly over their heads. He'd moved to stand right in front of her, his irritation clear.

Another chill went through her. Followed quickly by a flicker of irate fire.

"I don't remember asking for your permission."

"Fuck, is it actually snowing right now?" Callan whispered theatrically.

"Damnit, Mayla, I said it's TOO DANGEROUS!" Anton thundered.

Mayla reached over, bracing her hands on his biceps, and rising up to her tiptoes. When she spoke, her words were soft and dripped with sugary sweetness.

"Anton, you aren't my daddy, my brother or my man, so respectfully? BACK OFF. This isn't your call to make, it's mine. And it's theirs." She motioned to everyone else in the room, then placed a quick kiss against his cheek before dropping back down flat-footed and giving him her back.

His eyes went saucer wide, the white dissipating quickly. The snow ceased and the gray cloud above them disappeared.

Mayla glanced around to find stunned expressions on all but one of the faces focused on them. Elijah, of course, was grinning.

"It's up to you," Mayla told them. "If I can get into Carl's mind I might be able to get you the information you need. Again, I can't promise anything, but I am willing to give it a try. It's your call."

Elijah's boots were a sudden thunderclap of sound pounding across the floor. He wrapped Mayla up in a bear hug and spun her around, placing a loud smacking kiss to her forehead.

"Yes! I say YES! That big, beautiful brain of yours just might be the answer to our prayers!"

A low, menacing sound came from behind them, and Elijah quickly set her back on her feet, clearing his throat and stepping back. He sent Anton a wary look.

"I mean, you know, as long as everyone else is cool with it."

Asher stepped closer, those honey eyes still incredibly intense, but now holding a trace of curiosity as well. "That's how you knew. How you made things easier for me, at the park."

It wasn't phrased as a question, but Mayla nodded anyway.

"Sort of. I mean, I didn't go into your mind or anything. I just took some of the bad stuff around the edges away."

Asher's voice softened, and for the first time in hours she heard no hint of a growl when he spoke. "You would be willing to do this? For us?" He stole a careful glance over her shoulder at Anton. "Even though it could clearly put you at some kind of risk?"

Mayla nodded. "As long as Anton will still help anchor me, there is very little risk. And it's not just for you. The Anord has my friend. This guy works for them. I'll be looking for my own answers while I'm in there too. Maybe he's seen her, or maybe he knows where she is. I want to do both, help you find a lead and help find my friend."

Asher considered her a moment, then nodded decisively and placed a hand over his heart.

"I'll make you a deal. You find something we can use, and I swear to you, I'll find your friend."

Mayla stared at the man strapped down to the chair across the table from her. His brown hair looked even more dirty up close, hanging in greasy, uncombed clumps across his forehead. The air around him was overpowering, a toxic mix of stale cigarette smoke and body odor. Under the patchy beard she could see a puckered scar running the length of his left cheek. His muddy brown eyes were dull and uninterested, staring back at her with a defiant sort of boredom.

Anton stood behind her chair, his large frame so close she

could almost feel his body heat through her clothes.

Behind them, Asher was pacing again. She was starting to realize the shifter paced any time he wasn't fully comfortable, which, as it turned out, was pretty often. No wonder his physique was all lean muscle.

Callan sat to her right, doing gods knew what on yet another laptop, this one yellow with a lime green keyboard, and a TMNT sticker emblazoned across the back. When he glanced up and caught her watching him, he gave her a saucy wink and a cock-eyed, fang exposing grin. She smiled back, despite her clattering nerves.

After realizing she had no intention of listening to him and abandoning this idea, and after being summarily outvoted by the rest of them, Anton had finally conceded. His one requirement was that he remain in physical contact with Mayla the entire time.

She had to admit, his presence right now was probably the only thing keeping her from backing out altogether. Talking about doing this and actually doing it were two totally different things, and she was starting to wonder if she'd bit off a little more than she could chew.

No. This was not the time for doubts. She took a deep breath. She could do this. She knew she could do this. Okay realistically? She knew she could *maybe* do this.

Skyler's instructions echoed in her head once more.

Keep your magics separated. Pry open the door slowly, and only wide enough for yourself to slip out. Take it slow.

Anton had warned her - a few too many times for her liking - that this man's mind would most likely be a terrifying place. And if she took a moment to be honest, she wasn't sure what opening herself up to evil in someone else's mind would really do. Would she fail to keep her magics apart and end up absorbing some of that darkness? Was something like that even possible?

She had no idea.

There were so many what ifs floating around, but if walking around in this horrible man's mind could potentially help them find Willow? She owed it to her friend to at least try.

Plus, Elijah had said this creep hunted Lowblood kids. Who knew how many of them he'd successfully captured? And for what? Some kind of twisted, distorted fun? Or worse a demented, sexual thrill? The idea made her sick to her stomach. If she could help stop him, she would.

Stop thinking, she thought to herself, start doing.

Rising from her chair, she came around the table to stand in front of Carl, her hands clenched into fists at her sides. The idea of touching him was revolting, but she forced her hands open and raised them. She trembled there a moment, watching him. His eyes blazed with sudden anger, as if just now realizing what she intended, what her magic must be.

He struggled against his restraints, but he was going nowhere. Asher had delighted in shackling Carl's feet to the chair legs and his hands to the armrests. He'd even gone so far as to bungee cord the man to the back of the chair, duct taping his chin and forehead back against a wooden board they'd found in the storage closet. When she'd sent Anton a glare at the obvious overkill, he hadn't batted an eyelash.

"That's nothing. If this guy so much as breathes sideways I'll freeze every drop of blood in his veins," he promised. Somehow she knew he wasn't kidding.

He stepped in behind her now, leaning close to her ear, "I need to know you're sure about this." The deep rumbling whisper traveled in a delicious trail down her back. It tickled the tiny hairs on her neck, and raised goosebumps on her skin. She gave herself a firm mental command not to shiver in front of the entire team.

"If you prefer, I can just let Asher shift and have a go at him. It'll be messy, and it'll mean a lot more paperwork, but it'll be worth it." His tone was soft, husky, and only partially joking.

She gave him a sideways look and a half hearted grin, wiping her clammy palms down her jeans and trying to focus on taking deep steadying breaths.

"Mayla, seriously, you don't have to—"

She held up a hand, effectively silencing his protest, and heard Callan snicker.

"I can do this," she said firmly.

She wouldn't turn and look at him again. If she did, she knew she'd want to just crawl into his arms and hide there until all this evil was gone and everyone she cared about was safe.

"I can do this," she insisted again. "You just make sure you don't let go." She said the last on a whisper, feeling him step into her so tightly their bodies were flush from knee to shoulder.

He wrapped a powerful arm around her waist and leaned down once more.

"Never," he whispered.

Mental command or no, she couldn't prevent the shudder that traveled down her spine. Puffing out a frustrated breath at the distraction, she rubbed her palms together.

Okay. Here we go.

Reaching out, she placed her palms on either side of Carl Richard's head, studiously ignoring the greasy feel of his dirty hair against her palms. She closed her eyes, reaching inside her mind to picture a door, exactly as Skyler had suggested.

When she opened her eyes once more, she stood in a bright, open courtyard, sunshine streaming down to warm her cheeks. Turning in a small circle, she found a door, big and wooden with iron hinges. It reminded her of something you might see in a castle. She crossed the courtyard and placed both hands flat against the wood, pretending not to notice that her fingers were trembling.

She took a slow, deep breath.

This was her magic, and she was in control. She would find what she needed, and would ignore the rest. She didn't want this scumbag coming back into her mind, so he wasn't getting in, it was as simple as that.

She leaned her weight against the door, and it opened smoothly. On the other side, the sky was black as pitch, ominous storm clouds hovering above and flaring with intermittent lightning. A cold, biting wind whipped her hair across her face, and a dark, putrid smell assaulted her nose. Her stomach hollowed.

Of course his mind would make her feel like she was marching to her death. What had she expected? Cartoons? She sighed, taking a big step out into the darkness, then turning to make sure the door was shut firmly behind her. She would protect her courtyard at all costs.

As the door creaked closed and the sunlight from within completely disappeared, her nerves went on high alert. Her skin tingled and her heart raced, panic flooding her system.

No.

Absolutely not.

She could not have a panic attack.

Not right here. Not right now.

"Something you can see, something you can smell,

something you can feel, something you can hear," she whispered to herself, using a trick one of her old therapists had taught her.

She could see her hand…barely.

She could smell something rotten, like old meat.

She could feel her cotton t-shirt between her fingers.

She could hear the wind whistling past her ears.

She could see the door she'd just closed, a darker void in the dim light.

She could smell something sour, like old milk.

She could feel the rough texture of her jeans beneath her palm.

She could hear the rumble of thunder in the dark clouds overhead.

She fought down the panic with a few more long, deep breaths. Then she straightened her spine…and started walking.

18

It took less than five minutes for Mayla to decide that Carl Richards' mind was the coldest, darkest, most terrifying place she'd ever been. One that she wanted to get the hell out of as soon as possible. She hadn't been expecting kittens and rainbows, but something a little less on point with Stephen King's nightmares would have been nice.

When she moved away from her door, she'd quickly lost sight of it in the darkness. Going on pure instinct, she turned left, moving slowly and keeping her hands straight out in front to feel for any obstacles. When her foot stepped out into pure air, she screamed, pinwheeling backward and landing on her ass in the dirt. A flash of lighting revealed a sheer drop down into…nothing.

Okaayyy, maybe her instincts weren't quite as good at this as they really needed to be. If she survived this, she was going to force Skyler into regular practice sessions as soon as she had the chance. Crab walking back away from the ledge, she slowly rose to her feet, deciding that going right was definitely the safer option. She raised her hands in front of her once more, the darkness an inky black curtain over her eyesight.

A few steps later, she smacked face first into a small tree, the barren black shape suddenly looming up out of the darkness. Stumbling back a few steps, she rubbed gingerly at her stinging forehead wondering if she'd end up a black eye. If she did, Natalie and Anton would be up to here with the I-told-you-so's. She and her sister had argued over her doing this in the first place, Natalie and Anton the only ones that had voted against the idea. Her sister had gotten so loud about the whole thing that Mayla basically had to kick her out of the MTF office to go cool down. Which meant she really didn't need to come back with a black eye and prove that Natalie might have been right.

She clenched her fists at her sides. She would *not* have a black eye. When she got out of this hellhole, and she would get out once she found what she was looking for, then she would be perfectly fine. The door between her magics was firmly closed, she'd made sure of it. Though she could feel the pain while she was here, it wasn't real. Her body was perfectly safe back with Anton.

When the next streak of lightning illuminated the dark for a few seconds, she spotted a huge cliffside looming behind the tree, the middle opening down into the mouth of a large cave. Everything in her told her that the cave held the answers she was looking for. Determined not to run into another tree or step off another ledge, Mayla took a few steps and paused, waiting for lightning to streak across the sky once more before running in short bursts to the cave entrance.

The cave opening was a dense void of cold air. Insects of all shapes and sizes, crawled over the ledge and out into the night, including - she bit the inside of her cheek - spiders. Gods, she *really hated* spiders. The air coming out of the cave was frigid, and it bit at her face. She really didn't want to go in there. The chill had her teeth chattering and her heart rate jumping, panic trying desperately to seep into her mind and shut this all down.

She shook her head forcefully. They all needed this. The task force was stuck, and she was the only one who could help. Willow needed her to do this. If there was even the tiniest chance that Carl knew something about where her friend was, Mayla wasn't leaving until she found out one way or another.

Giving herself a quick mental slap, she ground her teeth together in determination. She couldn't very well go back and tell everyone she gave up because she saw spiders and spiders gave her the heebie-jeebies. She was going in there, no matter how much it made her skin crawl. Taking a slow, deep breath she closed her eyes and focused inward. Skyler said she was the strongest empath he'd ever known. She'd gotten past all his defenses, despite his years of training. If she could get into Skyler's well protected mind, she could certainly get what they needed from this sketchy, unwashed, waste of space child abductor.

Mayla tamped down her fear, squared her shoulders, and walked into dark void of the cave.

Once inside, it took a few minutes for her eyes to adjust. She could feel the insects climbing across her Adidas and a shiver of revulsion went through her. Nope, not thinking about it. She kept walking, saying it like a mantra in her head. Not thinking about it. Not thinking about it. NOT thinking about it.

The cave suddenly opened up into a huge cavern and the activity going on inside had her momentarily stunned. The vast space was filled with images. Some looked like still photos, just memories caught in time. Others were choppy, flickering scenes playing over and over, stuttering like old home movies from decades ago. Still more were crystal clear, flowing easily, filled with bright color and clear details. Her mind raced to process what she was seeing. The crystal clear scenes were definitely the most violent, all of them bloody and horrifying. She covered her mouth and tried not to be sick.

She felt the added weight as more insects climbed over her shoes and up the bottom of her jeans, but she ignored it, transfixed. The cave was bathed in red and gray light, fear and anger woven together in a gruesome tapestry of sheer anguish. These were Carl's memories. The things he'd seen. Worse, the things he'd done.

She tried to skim the memories flashing before her, searching frantically for anything showing a red mask or a black hoodie. Instead, her eyes were drawn back over and over to one stuttering scene in particular. It was of a young boy, happily eating ice cream next to a woman with matching golden hair.

Carl loved when his mom took him for ice cream. The sweet dessert on his tongue always made him forget the yelling and arguing his parents did at home. His mother and father fought often, but all Highblood families had their difficulties. Carl realized it wasn't ideal, but he knew his mother was always there for him, always protecting him. He was her only child, the"light of her life" as she liked to say.

She protected him from his abusive, alcoholic father, always taking the brunt of his yelling, hitting and spitting whenever she could. His father didn't like him much because according to him, Carl was a complete disappointment. His minimal fire magic wasn't strong enough to raise them any higher in society, so in his father's eyes, he was useless, just another mouth to feed. Still and all, the three of them were a family nonetheless.

Or at least they HAD been, before that stupid gardener started working next door. Carl knew the man was Lowblood the first time they met, his only magic making flowers appear when he snapped his fingers. What a stupid, useless kind of magic that was. It was irritating how often he used it, too. Whenever he saw Carl's mother outside, he'd give her a daisy here, or a rose there. Carl didn't know why his mother smiled softly and always took them, they both knew she'd have to throw them away before his father got home. It was silly to take them in the first place.

Then it happened.

He'd come home from school one day and his mother was gone. His father didn't seem bothered by her absence at all that first week, he simply stayed drunk, almost forgetting Carl was even there.

Until he found the letter. Carl wasn't sure how long it had been sitting on the kitchen table, mixed in with the rest of the mail they hadn't bothered to open. Maybe his father had recognized the handwriting, or maybe he'd actually been motivated to clean off the table, who knew. Either way, that letter brought Carl's former life to a brutal and screeching halt.

That stupid, AWFUL letter.

The one saying his mother had run off with the Lowblood gardener, and she wouldn't be coming back. The one that made his father go ballistic, kicking the kitchen table over in a rage. Carl had hidden in hallways and around corners, watching as his father threw all of his mother's belongings out onto the back lawn. He'd set fire to them while polishing off an entire bottle of whiskey, and then he'd turned his attention to his son.

That night his father had taken him to the basement and beaten him so badly his eyes had swollen shut and it hurt to breathe. After that, Carl spent every night trapped in that dark, cold basement, nursing welts from his father's belt, burns from his cigarettes, and bruises from his pounding fists.

He barely remembered what his room looked like anymore, and he'd forgotten what it felt like to sleep on an actual bed. Despite all the pain, Carl didn't blame his mother. She had been a protected and cherished Highblood woman and that Lowblood scum had preyed upon her vulnerability. She was too naive, too innocent, and she had CLEARLY been taken advantage of by that dirt blooded jackass. The only thing Carl knew for certain was that if Lowbloods didn't exist in Miradea, his family would be whole and none of THIS would have ever happened.

Carl killed his father on his fourteenth birthday. Though he certainly hadn't realized what day it was until much later. By that time he'd spent six years in that gods damned basement, constantly being battered and beaten. It had taken him six years of practicing, of focusing on his magic hard enough and long enough to finally be able to escape. That night, he could hear his father's rafter-shaking snores as he slept off yet another bender. Carl had finally managed to sustain his magic long enough to melt the deadbolt lock off the basement door.

Once upstairs it wasn't a choice really, it was a simple necessity. He grabbed the biggest knife he could find and put a quick end to his father's miserable life.

He left home that same night, tossing some of his father's clothes, the knife that had finally ended his torture, and a stack of money in a backpack. He walked to the closest bus stop, ignoring the disgusted looks he received from the other passengers as he rode into downtown. He was sure he smelled, couldn't even remember the last time his father had let him bathe, but he honestly didn't care. His life wasn't about impressing anyone, it was about SURVIVING, plain and simple.

He'd gotten a hotel room and sat up that whole first night, watching the door with the knife in his hands, waiting for his father, the police, or SOMEONE to come for him.

But they never did.

When the money ran out a month later, he started sleeping on the street, picking up odd jobs or resorting to theft to keep himself fed. It was on one of those freezing, miserable nights when his stomach was so hungry that he felt hollowed out, that he'd realized something. A Lowblood had stolen his entire life. The Lowbloods needed to pay, and pay dearly.

That was when he'd decided to start hunting their children. They'd stolen HIS childhood. The very least he could do was return the favor.

At eighteen, Carl found the Anord. He'd gone to the first meeting only because someone at the soup kitchen mentioned there would free food and beer for everyone. A few minutes in though, and he knew he'd found his place.

He'd finally found Highbloods who felt exactly as he did.

They didn't just sit around sipping mojitos out of crystal goblets and performing parlor tricks to show off their magics at dinner parties. THESE people had a mission, a plan, and plenty of money to back it up. They had lawyers, business men, hell they even had a few senators on their side. And they were determined to eradicate the Lowbloods from Miradea through any means necessary. Killing, trafficking, bombing, intimidation, anything and everything was not only allowed, it was encouraged. Whatever it took to get rid of the dirt bloods permanently. This wasn't just A cause, it was HIS cause.

When he'd approached the leadership after the meeting and told them about his talent for snatching Lowblood kids and making them disappear for good, he'd gotten nothing but smiles and support in return. THEY were impressed by his dedication and cleverness. They put him up in his own little studio apartment, bought him the Plymouth, even gave him the address to the abandoned property where he could take his trophies for fun after he caught them. It was perfect. Sure, it was a bit annoying that for every three kids he snatched they wanted one dropped off unharmed to that creepy old building, but if it meant he always had a warm place to sleep and food in his belly? Yeah, he could deal. Give and take was the basis of every successful partnership - he was pretty sure he'd heard that somewhere. Now, after little Samuel, his latest grab, he still had one more he could snatch before another delivery was due.

He just had to sit back and wait for their lawyers to get him out of this stupid place, just like they'd done before, and then he'd be paying little Samuel a visit. That kid was a fighter, and DAMN but Carl loved a good fight.

19

"Do you think your giant white haired boss is in love with my sister?"

Elijah took one look at the beautiful redhead sitting across from him at Della's Pizzeria, and realized something very important.

The woman had lost her entire damn mind.

He looked down at his soda and tried to smother his laugh. He wasn't sure exactly what she might do with those blood red nails if he insulted her, but he was pretty certain it would be painful. Blissful perhaps...but still painful.

After Mayla had offered to jump inside Carl Richards' head and grab any evidence she could, they'd all taken a vote.

Three for, two against. Anton and Natalie had made up the nays of course, and when she realized her sister had every intention of playing around in the gray matter of a potential serial kidnapper, Natalie had kicked up one hell of a temper tantrum. There'd been a lot of yelling going on between the two women, things getting so heated that Elijah was actually sweating by the time they calmed down.

Mayla had finally ordered her sister out of the office, demanding she go eat or take a walk somewhere to calm down. Lucky him, he'd somehow been auto-selected to accompany her. But hey, at least now he had an excuse to eat the best pizza on the planet. Not only that, the MTF was paying for this little lunch date. He was going to make sure of that.

Normally, in any other accidentally-thrown-together-with-a-beautiful-woman scenario, he'd be taking full advantage. He'd be turning on the sweet talk, charming his date right out of her clothes and at least half of her inhibitions by the time happy hour ended. Unfortunately for him, Natalie just wasn't his type. She was way too demanding, as well as being too passionate, too fiery, too…everything.

For the gods sake, two minutes ago she'd ordered a salad.

A salad at Della's. Who did such a thing? It was a shame her personality was so abrasive though. She really was beautiful, a total stunner in that porcelain goddess kind of way. As it was, every time he got near her, he felt a weird, breathtaking sort of…something. It reminded him of standing too close to a fire, the type of heat that just stole your breath.

Natalie glanced casually around the pizzeria, taking a sip from her Diet Coke before looking at him expectantly, her tongue darting out to moisten those red lips. His jeans tightened until he had to shift in his seat in order to catch his breath.

Mentally, he sent a no, stop it to his downstairs friend. She's high maintenance, hateful, and we don't need that kind of drama, he ordered. The way she was just downright rude to him for no reason, like he was somehow not worth her time. He was a full grown Highblood male, an actual assassin, and not to pad his own ego or anything, but a damn good looking one at that. Women fell at his feet, they didn't sneer at him and treat him like some kind of cabana boy.

When she snapped her fingers in front of his face a moment later, he only just barely kept himself from launching a knife out of sheer reaction.

"You still with me, Pretty Boy?" she asked, her eyebrows raised.

He snorted. He was second-in-command to the entire Miradea Task Force and this woman spoke to him as if he was her plaything. A Friday night fun and done hookup. Gods help the man she actually ended up with, he thought.

"Yeah, I'm with you Cherry, but you're completely off your rocker. To answer your question, no, Anton is not in love with your sister. Highbloods don't fall in love."

"What, like ever? Highbloods get married and have kids just like Lowbloods do, I've seen it," she argued.

"Of course they do. People aren't going to just stop reproducing because fated mates ceased to exist."

"Wait. What? What do you mean fated mates?"

He sighed. She was like a dog with a bone when she wanted answers. And not a cute, cuddly puppy either. More like a gorgeous Rottweiler with an attitude problem. Taking a deep breath, he mulled over his answer. He could recite the histories he'd learned in school, or all the details his mother had shared with him when he was young. But the fact that fated mates had died out centuries ago was, to be brutally honest, seriously depressing. Talking about it only served to remind him and other Highbloods of what they'd never have, what they saw Lowbloods find day in and day out.

Love.

"Hello? Earth to Pretty Boy, fated mates? Spill it." Natalie pushed.

He glared at her for a long moment before speaking, just to prove to himself that he could.

"Centuries ago, every fae had a fated mate. They were, in all ways, the perfect pairing. Everything about them was predestined to mesh perfectly, likes and dislikes, strengths and weaknesses, even temperaments."

"Wait, so a fated mate was like a carbon copy? So the fae idea of love was finding a carbon copy of yourself? Seems a little self-centered to me." The disdain in her voice was obvious.

He bristled. "No actually, it's not. It's not as simple as your pitiful little human idea of love at first sight," he let the words dribble out of his mouth slowly, like candy abandoned by a child. "Fated mates weren't copies, they were counterparts. Almost perfect opposites."

A massive extra cheese and pepperoni pizza was set down on the table between them and Elijah's face lit up. No one could make a pie like Joe Della. No one. The cheese to dough ratio was guaranteed to set off all the pleasure receptors in your brain.

And Elijah should know, he'd been coming here ever since they'd opened the place ten years ago. He focused on sliding two of the perfect slices onto his plate before he continued.

"If the fae was extremely strong, their fated mate would be slight, less prone to brute strength and more likely to use wit or wisdom to accomplish what they needed. Their wit would counteract their mate's brutish tendencies, while the strength of their partner would in turn give them a sense of fearlessness…and so on. They were supposed to be the perfect balance. If he's usually calm, his mate is more feisty. If he's hotheaded," he purposely ignored her sarcastic snort, "his mate is calmer and slow to anger."

"So, if he likes dogs, she likes cats sort of thing?"

"Well in the simplest, most dumbed down terms, yes. But a fated pair didn't have to be a he and a she you know. Destiny is destiny, no matter your sexuality," he chided.

She set her drink down with a thud and rolled her eyes. "Obviously. Don't be obtuse, you know that's not what I meant."

"Just making sure those Lowblood ideas of yours aren't too antiquated."

She huffed at him, shifting in her seat and crossing her legs at the knee. The snug black slacks she wore clung to the curve of her hip and his mouth suddenly watered. He snapped his gaze away.

It was for pizza. His mouth was watering for this amazing pizza, and nothing else. He picked up a slice, preparing to take a bite, but froze when she interrupted, *again*.

"So, what happened to them? Did you big, brawny, more-fae-than-human guys manage to piss off all your potential mates? Because that sounds like a definite possibility."

He raised an eyebrow. Gods did this woman live only to taunt him?

"Funny, but that's not how it worked. Every fae had one fated mate, not a group of potential ones," he clarified, finally taking a giant bite. He closed his eyes and let out a moan of ecstasy at the creamy mouthful of cheesy perfection.

Natalie's forkful of salad froze in mid-air. "Wait, so if a super energetic lady might need a handful of you guys to keep her happy, she would just be out of luck? Now who's ideas are antiquated?"

Elijah snorted, but didn't respond, choosing instead to take another huge bite of pizza and following it up with a sip of his drink. Across from him, Natalie set down her fork, crossing her arms over the black sleeveless blouse that dipped between her breasts in a dangerous V.

Sitting this close, he could see the creamy perfection of her skin and the tiny smattering of freckles that danced across her nose. He could lean forward if he really wanted to, just reach over and pretend to straighten one of those black teardrop earrings, leave just the glance of a touch at her throat…move around the table to follow that up with the softest kiss just below her ear. Maybe even slide his lips down to meet hers and then pull her into his lap—

He jolted, soda sloshing across his fingers. Wiping his hands with the nearby napkin, he took in a slow breath, lowering his eyes and pretending to be fascinated with the wooden surface of the table.

What was *wrong* with him? He was acting like a preteen watching porn and it was ridiculous. He had thirty different numbers in his phone at this very moment, any of which would lead to guaranteed one-on-one, more than willing erotic entertainment with a quick push of the send button. And not a single number belonged to a sarcastic, overly opinionated, infinitely annoying redhead.

When he realized those huge, gorgeous hazel eyes were fixed on him expectantly, he hurried to cover his wayward thoughts, taking another huge bite and talking around the mouthful."Sorry, but this is the best pizza in the universe, so it really deserves my complete attention. Were you still talking?"

"You Highbloods sure have short," she deliberately paused with a little smirk, "attention spans."

He refused to rise to the bait, setting the pizza down instead and crossing his arms over his broad chest. He watched her intently, and when he caught her fleeting look of disappointment, it gave him pause. Wait a minute…did she actually want him to argue with her?

Gods above, Natalie thought, how did a simple navy t-shirt stretch like that without tearing in half? That chest of his was no joke, and when he crossed those arms like he was some kind of drill sergeant dealing with an errant soldier, it made her feel flushed all over. She couldn't even hide the flicker of disappointment that snaked through her when he didn't respond to her jab about being short.

"I said," she deliberately made her tone as condescending as possible, "if you could only have one fated mate - instead of three or four, which in my personal opinion should definitely be allowed - how could you know when you found the right one? Wait…let me guess, magic serial numbers?"

He actually chuckled at her joke, and Natalie felt her stomach flutter at the rich, mellow sound. His amber eyes sparkled. Damn he really was sinfully hot. It wasn't fair he was such an absolute ass.

"Close, but no, no serial numbers. Back then, when a fae met their fated mate, a symbol would appear on their body."

At Natalie's confused expression, Elijah sighed.

"The Lowblood equivalent would be similar to a tattoo. The symbol showed up most often on the chest," he patted one rock hard pectoral in emphasis, "but according to the histories, they might appear anywhere on the body. So if the fated mates met, the symbol would show itself once, then fade. If they chose to acknowledge the bond, the symbols would reappear and become permanent. Don't ask me how they do that, it was some kind of speech or something by one mate, and then the other would either accept or deny I think? No one really remembers the specific details anymore.

But the belief was, fated mates were gifted by the gods, and the markings were a symbol of that gift. The pairs were said to have some sort of undeniable, instinctual attraction to each other, so denials were pretty uncommon. I also read somewhere that once bonded, fated mates had all these weird habits. Like they couldn't be separated for long periods of time, or if one was in danger the other would sense it and go off the deep end, if one was hurt the other could share their own health to help them heal, all kinds of wild stuff. It's hard to know fact from fiction anymore."

"You *read* it? No one has ever seen it happen?"

"You're not listening, Cherry. Fated mates disappeared centuries ago. I've never seen or even heard of a mated pair in my lifetime. Highblood children are still told about them, but it's usually in bedtime stories or useless trivia. None of us have ever actually *seen* it. It's just a story from fae history."

Elijah glanced over to find Natalie utterly enthralled. Her cheeks were flushed a soft pink. She was leaning forward in her chair, chin resting in her hands, Diet Coke and salad completely forgotten.

"So what happened to make them disappear? Does anyone know? If they all went away where did they go?"

He took his time loading another cheesy slice onto his

plate and deliberately drawing out the suspense.

"No one knows. Some say the gods were angered that the humans were allowed to find the cities, so they punished the fae by no longer creating them. Others say it was because the bloodlines were no longer pure enough. As the existing mates aged and died, there just weren't any new pairs. There are tons of theories still floating around in the histories, but no concrete reason was ever discovered. My mother worked at the university and did studies on the concept before…," he trailed off.

Natalie sucked in a quick breath.

Shit. He shouldn't have said that. Her pity was already spreading all over her face and it turned his stomach. He'd almost rather she be mean to him.

"I'm very sorry. For your loss I mean. I didn't get a chance to tell you that earlier, but I am sorry."

He swallowed, the pizza turning to sawdust in his mouth. Her voice was soft, and sounded way too close to tender for his liking. And her words opened a wide yawning pit in his gut.

Anton and Elijah had both been children that humid summer night Elijah had shown up at his best friend's door, bloody, sobbing, and stumbling on a badly broken leg.

Someone called the authorities. Adriana arrived and Elijah was moved into one of the massive guest rooms. For the next two days the healer worked on healing his leg in repeated slow sessions, determined to help him avoid a residual limp. The police came and went, asking him weird questions and scribbling notes or whispering into cell phones. Through it all, Anton's mother refused to leave his side. She kept Elijah's smaller hand tucked tightly into hers, even while he slept, and to this day he'd never forgotten that kindness.

Her determined, constant comfort during that awful time was half the reason he'd decided to dedicate his life to keeping her son safe. On the third night, when she'd finally decided it was safe enough to sleep in her own bed, Anton had managed to sneak into the room to check on him.

Elijah told him everything.

"We were on our way home from that stupid awards dinner my dad made us go to? The one where I HAD to wear a tie?"

Anton had nodded solemnly. Of course he remembered, they both HATED ties.

"We were on our way home. Isabella was asleep on my mom's,"

he had to bite back a sob, "on my mom's lap in the backseat. Izzy's wings were out. She's so little, sometimes she's not good at keeping them hidden, you know? Especially when she's tired. Something hit us I think. The car went all sideways and then it started to roll. Izzy was screaming. Everything was crunching and squealing, and then the windshield exploded. When it stopped we were upside down. It was dark so I couldn't see, but I could smell gas... and blood."

He'd broken down then, huge, breath stealing sobs rocking his small body.

Anton patted his back gently.

"Izzy. Mom got her out of the car, but...she wouldn't wake up. Then we saw all the gold...her wings," he hiccuped, then swallowed hard, fighting back another wave of tears. "They got torn off somehow. She was covered in so much gold she looked like a little statue. She was dead, A."

Elijah felt his voice go weirdly flat then, so much so that he almost didn't realize he was the one talking. "I never saw anybody dead before. I just sat down on the ground, and I cried like a little kid. Mom started screaming. Dad tried to comfort her, but she wouldn't let him. She smacked him, right in the face, hard."

Anton's eyes filled with tears and he hurried to rub them on his sleeve, but Elijah still saw.

"A bunch of guys in black clothes showed up. I thought they were there to help, but my dad kept yelling at them. My mom was still screaming, holding onto Izzy and rocking her like a baby.

When one of the guys reached for me, I punched him in the stomach. It made him mad so he stomped my leg. I heard the snap and then it hurt so much!! I couldn't even stand up. I screamed. Every time I tried to stand up I'd just fall over." He rubbed aggressively at a the limb in question.

"My mom kind of went crazy after that. She laid Izzy down and then she was yelling and running at the guy that hurt me. She used her air magic, he was grabbing his neck and turning blue, but then," his voice dropped to a barely a whisper, "one of them pulled out a gun. They shot her right in the head.

I SAW it. I saw it ALL.

My mom just fell to the ground like someone had turned off all her lights at the same time." He'd stopped talking for a moment, his breathing quick and jerky.

"A bunch of them were still watching me, so I tried to be really quiet. I tried Anton, I swear I tried! But I, I couldn't stop crying. I just watched them kill my mom!" He'd rubbed his small fist furiously across his

tear stained cheeks. "Next thing I knew one of them hit me in the head with something." Elijah absentmindedly rubbed at a spot on his temple.

"I think it knocked me out, because I don't remember anything else until I woke up later. My head hurt, I was on the ground, and the bad guys were gone. My dad too. I tried to look for him. I did Anton, I promise I did!"

Anton scooted closer, putting an arm around Elijah's shoulders.

"You did great, E. You made it all the way here on a broken leg! I don't even know any grown ups that could do that."

Elijah took a few deep breaths. His friend's support helped. It didn't do anything to ease the pain in his chest that made him want to curl into a ball and die though.

"The police said they must've taken my dad somewhere else and killed him too, no reason to leave any witnesses. They must have thought I was dead too."

Elijah felt something building inside his chest. His whole body coiled up tight, like a snake. When he spoke, he knew what he had to say was going to shock his best friend, but it didn't matter."I'm going to find them Anton. I'm going to find the guys that did this." He sucked in another long, deep breath and squared his shoulders.

"And one day, when I'm old enough...I'm going to find them, and I'm going to KILL THEM ALL."

Elijah's brain came back online with a snap. Natalie was still seated across the table from him at Della's, her eyes and mouth softened in concern.

"I really am sorry," she repeated.

He cursed inwardly. Letting his own history slip yesterday had been a definite screw up on his part. He pointedly ignored her words of comfort, focusing instead on answering a question she hadn't even asked.

"With the fated mates gone, Highbloods just weren't able to fall in love with anyone the way they could with their mates. Lots of us have tried, but for us it's just not the same as what you Lowbloods do. Lust and attraction? Sure. Affection on occasion? Maybe. Real, honest to goodness love? No way.

Highblood families began arranging marriages to try and purify certain bloodlines. The hope was, if they were successful, fated mate bonds might return. But it never worked. Most long term relationships were about sex, money, or increasing magics, never anything deeper. They're more of a business transaction than anything else.

There are a few out there who have claimed they've fallen in love with a Lowblood, but the intensity is different. It's mostly infatuation and desire, nothing deeper. It's been this way for so long now, most people are starting to believe the whole fated mates idea was just a myth anyway."

Natalie was shaking her head, that gorgeous fire-red hair swaying around her shoulders.

"No way." She said emphatically.

"No way…what?"

"No way it's all just a myth. The idea had to originate somehow. Don't you know all myths are rooted in truth and history somewhere up the line? Plus, why would there be so much research and history if they didn't have some kind of proof somewhere?"

She nodded at him, leaning back and grabbing her fork once again."Besides I think it's kind of sweet. Miradea could use a little more love and magic, don't you think? Love or not love, whatever is going on between your boss and my sister, I guess I'm okay with it as long as he treats her well. If he breaks her heart though, I'll break his legs off at the knees," she warned, then looked down, tucking into her salad in earnest.

Elijah's mouth hung open, a folded slice of pizza dangling in one hand.

"Miradea could use a little more love and magic, don't you think?…If he hurts her though, I'll have to break his legs off at the knees."

The way she saw no issue whatsoever with combining those two thoughts took his breath away. Which meant he was in seriously deep shit.

20

Mayla wasn't sure any more how long she'd been in the cave. She walked in sweeping circles, ducking into other caverns, watching scenes play out, and storing away information from the images that flickered past. She was starting to get sleepy and was having a hard time remembering exactly what she was here for. Her fingers were icy, so cold they felt like they were burning. She wanted to leave this place, but no matter how far she walked, she couldn't find the entrance. Besides, wasn't she supposed to stay for some reason? Wasn't there something else she was supposed to be doing here?

Her feet eventually stopped carrying her forward, and she leaned back against the cold stone wall, sliding down into a sit so she could pull her knees in close. She no longer noticed the spiders climbing up her legs and crawling across her arms.

She was so *very* tired. Her eyelids drooped.

Maybe, if she closed her eyes for just a few minutes...she could get some of her energy back.

"MAYLA!"

The sound of her name made her lift her head wearily, glancing around. No one was there.

"That's *enough,* Mayla, *come back.*"

The rich timbre of the voice reached into her chest and struck a match. She liked that voice, it made her feel safe. It pushed away the ugly pictures and the bloody images still flickering around her, and blew warmth straight into her soul. She knew that voice, knew that she was supposed to listen to that voice.

"Let go and come back, Mayla. It's Anton. I'm right here, I've got you. *LET GO RIGHT NOW*!"

Mayla slowly opened her eyes, her thoughts sluggish. The smell of cold air and sandalwood enveloped her, and she felt heat start to seep back into her fingers and toes. She glanced around, recognizing the interrogation room at MTF headquarters. She was sitting sideways in Anton's lap, his strong arms wrapped tightly around her, and his lips pressed gently against her temple.

"Come back, Mayla. I'm right here. You've been gone too long, come back," he murmured against her skin, then pressed the softest kiss to her temple.

Her cheeks flushed at the intimacy, and her eyes darted around the room, checking for witnesses. Carl was nowhere in sight, thank the gods, and neither was anyone else. The room was empty except for the two of them.

She should get up, but suddenly she didn't want to move. She wanted to stay right here, wrapped in these arms, cradled against this hard chest, those lips against her forehead for eternity.

She'd never felt this safe before. Well actually, that wasn't entirely true. She'd felt it when she'd been in his arms once before, back at his apartment when he'd saved her from nosediving into a full-blown panic attack. She snuck her arms around his waist and held on tight, tucking her head into his shoulder.

He let out a relieved sigh, and those muscled arms gave her a soft squeeze.

"You're back. Are you okay?"

She nodded against the soft fabric of his blue sweater, still not ready for words. The heaviness of what she'd seen in Carl's mind weighed her down, bringing the sting of tears to her eyes and a lump to her throat.

What an *awful*, horrible man. What terrible, brutal things he'd done in his lifetime. And what unbelievable torture he'd endured as a child.

Thinking about the images of him in that basement, and then the images of him with his victims, she couldn't stop the tears from spilling over. She wasn't sure if she was crying for Carl or for the people he'd hurt, probably both. It was all so dark, and so...heavy. Her heart ached in her chest.

Anton put a hand to the back of her neck, tilting her head up until they were face to face. His ice blue eyes searched her darker ones, his other hand coming up to cradle the side of her face as his thumb slowly wiped away her tears. She rested her cheek against his warm palm, closing her eyes. The despair that had been twisting in her gut dissolved ever so slowly, like early morning mist in the light of the rising sun.

What was it about this man? How was he so damn good at making her feel safe and strong? And how was she ever going to go back to her old life without him?

"Mayla. Look at me," he whispered, his voice tender but insistent.

She opened her eyes, drinking him in. Those soul piercing eyes framed with dark lashes. The aquiline nose and the strong line of that sculpted jaw. Her eyes followed that line down to his chin and then back up, just a bit, to those enticing, slightly parted lips. When the hand cupping her cheek slowly pulled her closer, her pulse quickened and her own lips parted on a soft exhale. Their noses brushed once, then his forehead lowered to press against hers. When he spoke again, his voice was ragged with the remnants of his fear.

"I wanted to dive in there after you, I just couldn't figure out how. You were fine one minute, then suddenly your whole body went so cold it felt like you were freezing to death in my arms. I panicked. Even your breathing was—," he swallowed hard, and shook his head as if he were trying to expel the memory altogether.

"I was terrified I'd lost you."

Mayla shook her head gently against his, her heart clenching. "Anton, you did come in there after me. I got so tired. I'm not sure when it happened, but suddenly I felt like I'd been in there for days. I couldn't remember how to get out. All I wanted to do was sleep. It was so, so cold."

He tightened his arm around her back, pressing her body in closer against his, sharing his heat.

"But that's when I heard you. As soon as I heard your

voice I knew I was supposed to follow it." She didn't take time to think about her next words, just shoved them out into the world, heedless of the consequences.

"As long as I can hear YOU, Anton, I don't think I will ever be lost."

His eyes flared with heat at her confession, then dropped slowly to her mouth. When his head turned and angled inward, his lips brushing ever so slightly against her own, she froze, a lightning bolt of sensation shooting down her spine. He pulled back at her startled reaction, his expression unsure.

"I'm sorry, I just—"

"Anton?"

"Yes?"

"Do that again."

His eyes darkened, his hand sliding from her cheek around to the back of her neck. He was exquisitely gentle, so slow as he bent his head back down to hers. But this time, when their lips met, she didn't hesitate, opening instantly for him. His tongue felt like silk against hers and her body reacted, a wisp of paper touched by a lit match. Every nerve ending came alive, a tingling sensation moving down her arms and out of her fingertips. She felt a pure blue fire roll through her and she reveled in it. Her stomach tightened and her arms twined around his neck so she could press even closer. She wanted...more.

When Mayla's arms tightened around his neck, Anton felt like letting out a roar of victory. Considered it in fact, before realizing he'd have to pull his mouth away from hers in order to do so. And really what kind of dumbass would do something like that? Instead, he pulled her closer, angling his head to take the kiss even deeper. She tasted like a cool water on a hot summer day, and suddenly he was a man dying of thirst.

He didn't remember where they were, couldn't bring himself to care. His mind could only feel the velvet caress of her mouth, and delight in the bolts of pure desire that shot through him everywhere they touched. His hands slid around to her back, his fingers splaying wide as they glided upward, pressing her even tighter against him. He could feel the soft swells of her breasts through their clothes and wondered what they would look like, unbound and waiting for his attention. He wanted to peel off her clothes piece by piece and spend hours tasting every inch of her. Lay her across the interrogation table and…

His mind screeched to a halt.
The *interrogation* table.

He jerked back, coming back down to earth with a skull crushing smack of reality. Mother of gods, what was he doing? They were ten feet away from a camera that was constantly recording, on a feed intermittently monitored by headquarters. They were also less than a hundred feet away from her sister and the rest of his team.

He closed his eyes for a moment, breathing heavily through his teeth as his mind spun. He had no business kissing her at all. She was Lowblood. She should be kissing a Lowblood man who could fall in love with her, one who would give her his entire heart and soul, and treasure her the way she deserved. Not a Highblood like him, whose extra fae blood made him arguably great at sex, mediocre at commitment, and absolute shit at love.

When he opened his eyes, he dared a glance at Mayla, ridiculously pleased to see her lips parted and slightly swollen, those amazing eyes wide and her face flushed. Not for the first time in his life, he wished he'd been born Lowblood. He was absolutely sure he could love this woman if he had just been given the right genetics for it. But Highbloods didn't do that, his parents were a clear enough example of that. If they started something together, he could only ever give her half of what she really wanted.

He sighed. Mayla deserved better than halfway.

"I can't believe I'm going to say this, but we should probably get out there." Anton nodded his head towards the door. "Your sister is back and she's demanding to see you. She got into a nice little growling match with Asher when he wouldn't let her in here earlier."

Mayla jerked upright, her eyes going wide. "Seriously?"

Anton nodded, helping her stand. She took a few steps away from him, smoothing down her rumpled shirt and running her hands through her tousled hair. He smothered a sigh of regret, already missing the feel of her soft, heated curves pressing against him.

"It was very exciting, they even bared their teeth at each

other. Elijah and Callan managed to divide and conquer to prevent bloodshed. Your sister's pretty hotheaded, I'll give her that."

Mayla snorted, smiling. "You don't know the half of it."

He grabbed her hand, giving her a look. "We should probably stay in contact for just a little longer, just to be safe."

She blushed, but nodded. Just as he reached for the door knob however, she froze.

"Wait, Anton, before we go out there...please tell me...I don't have a black eye, do I?"

When they emerged from the interrogation room, Natalie ran to her, pulling Mayla into a big hug. With Mayla's hand still clasped tightly in Anton's, the embrace was awkward, but Natalie didn't seem to notice, pulling back instead to apologize.

"I'm sorry, I lost my cool earlier. I know you're a capable, completely independent bad ass woman, I swear I do. And I admit I can maybe, sometimes get a little too overprotective."

When Elijah snorted, Natalie spun, shooting him a scathing look. "Nobody asked for your input, Pretty Boy," she sniped.

Mayla ignored their standoff. "Nat, you know I love you. You're my sister and I wouldn't want you any other way. I just need you to know I've got this, okay? And before you even ask, yes, I'm fine. I promise."

Natalie turned back, fixing her sister with an intense gaze. "So? Did you do it? Were you able to find out anything?"

"I was. I went in, got the information and then came out. No big deal." Mayla sent Anton a sideways look. It wasn't the complete truth, but it still made pride swell in her chest, regardless. She'd actually done it. She'd not only mind walked, she'd managed to keep her magics separated the whole time. There was no black eye, her face was absolutely fine. She'd gone in, gotten what she needed, and Anton had pulled her out before disaster struck.

Simple.

Okay, so yes, she was definitely going to need to work with Skyler on learning how to pull herself out when needed, but overall, today was a big win.

She took a quick moment to do an internal scan.

She felt…great.

Energized. Comfortable and relaxed in her own skin. There was no shakiness, no throbbing head, no stomachache, no nerves whatsoever.

Well, until she thought about that kiss.

Elijah sidestepped Natalie and leaned in close to Mayla, grabbing her attention. He wiggled his eyebrows at her.

"Okay spill it. Did you get the name of his barber? Cause you know I'm dying to get in on that action."

The comment lifted the mood, and Mayla laughed out loud. A round of chuckles went through the room as Asher came to stand nearby, his eyes glancing warily at Natalie every few minutes. Callan, gods bless him, appeared in front of them with a bottled water, clucking and waving his arms like a protective mother hen.

"Give my girl some space you heathens! And somebody bring her a damn chair. She's been exhausting herself, risking soul and sanity for you ingrates, and you can't even be bothered to let her sit down."

Asher darted over and snagged a desk chair, wheeling it back so she could sit. When she tried to pull her hand from Anton's to open the water, his fingers didn't budge. She looked at him expectantly, but he just shook his head.

"Not yet. I need to make sure you're safely anchored back here with us. I'll let go soon, but not yet."

Callan rolled his eyes, but he grabbed the water bottle and unscrewed the cap before handing it back to her. Mayla took a few long, blissfully cool swallows before leaning back into the chair and looking around at all of them.

"Well, you guys were right. Carl Richards is a very, very bad guy. There was…a LOT of darkness in there. His mind is full of hate, ugliness, and violence."

Anton's fingers tightened around hers and she returned the squeeze.

"I was honestly relieved that I didn't have to see him when I came back out."

"Asher put him in a holding cell in the back as soon as your hands let go. No sense being around that stench any longer than absolutely necessary, right?" Callan asked.

Mayla nodded. "Exactly." She sent Asher an appreciative smile. "Still, thanks for that."

He nodded solemnly.

"So what was it like digging around in his cottage cheese?" Elijah demanded, rubbing his hands together excitedly.

Mayla smiled, but her smile faded when she started to speak. "His mind is a dark place, very cold and very dirty. He went through a lot as a child, and that definitely set him on this path, but he also made the choice to be evil. He actually enjoys hurting others," her voice went cold and raw, "especially children. He *really* likes hurting kids the same way," she swallowed hard, "the same way he was hurt as a kid."

Anton's hand finally left hers only to slide around her shoulders instead.

"It was so dark in there I ran into a tree. It was embarrassing, but it helped me locate the cave where he kept all his memories. It was cold, and there were a lot of bugs," a quick shiver went through her and her complexion paled, "especially spiders."

"Spiders?" Natalie squeaked, repulsed.

Elijah, on the other hand, grabbed his own chair and scooted in close, hanging on to Mayla's every word.

"Spiders were *in* that dude's brain? Were they like crawling all over you and stuff? That's so friggin cool. Did any of them bite you? You know like in Spider-Man? Or did you have to fight them off? Like in a video game or something? Were they big and creepy?" He crowded closer and Mayla recoiled.

Anton stepped between them. "E, *for fucks sake*, do you ever consider your words before they fly out of your mouth?"

Elijah's looked up at him, his face pure innocence. "What? What'd I say? That shit is *cool*! She actually went INTO this dude's head." He paused, thinking. "I wonder if you could actually touch them? Did you try to touch them?"

The question was directed at Mayla, but Anton took another warning step forward.

Asher hurried to interrupt. "Mayla, did you find out anything about the Anord? Anything you think we could use?"

"I think so, though I'm not sure if—," she suddenly froze, everything she'd seen finally cementing into place. Then she burst out of the chair, almost knocking Elijah over and grabbing onto both of Anton's wrists, her face plaster white.

"OH MY GODS, SAMUEL!! We have to find Samuel!!"

An hour later, as Anton pulled the Audi out of MTF parking lot, he glanced over at her. "Are you hungry?"

"Starving," she admitted, nodding enthusiastically.

He smiled. "Good. Whatever you want, we'll pick it up on the way back to the apartment."

Mayla found her stomach tilt happily at the easy way he said we. Her mind went back to that kiss in the interrogation room. She'd known he was worried about her mind walking in the first place, but the depth of his concern still surprised her. A warmth spread through her at the memory of what it felt like to be sitting in his lap, wrapped in those arms. What had happened in that room certainly answered the question of whether or not he found her attractive.

She relaxed back into the leather seat, the low rumble of the car engine soothing in the quiet space. She closed her eyes and released a soft sigh. She sensed Anton glancing at her again, but this time she didn't react. He'd been doing that for the last hour, looking at her every so often as if to assure himself she was still okay.

Without opening her eyes, she spoke. "You can stop checking. I promise I am not bleeding from the ears, nor am I going to suddenly go crazy and try to jump out of the car or anything."

"Sorry, I just can't help it. You were so damn cold you were practically ice."

She heard him swallow hard. "It was disturbing. I just want to be sure that bastard didn't leave any of his darkness behind for you to have to deal with."

The concern in his voice had her opening her eyes, and she turned in her seat to look at him fully. His face was pale, his knuckles a tight white around the steering wheel. She reached over to place a hand over one of his and squeezed softly.

"Anton, I'm *okay*. Honestly, I feel amazing right now. For the first time that I can remember, my mind is totally clear. I wish I could explain it, but it's jut better. There's no darkness, no anxiety, just this amazing stillness that I don't think I've ever had before." She squeezed his fingers once more. "If that changes, even just a little bit, I swear I will let you know right away, okay?"

The tension in his body eased, and he let out a long breath. "Good. That's good. You do that."

Then his face lit up in a silly little smile that stole Mayla's breath. "Now, since I cannot read your mind, what do you want to eat?"

21

Mayla pushed back from the coffee table with a groan. "Ugh, I'm stuffed. If I eat another bite I think I'll explode."

She placed both hands over her stomach and sprawled back against the couch in dramatic fashion.

Anton chuckled and rose to his feet, gathering up the takeout containers.

"Anton, are you dating anyone?"

He lost his grip on one of the plastic bowls and it clattered back onto the coffee table. His ears reddened. How adorable, Mayla thought. But when he just stood there, blinking at her, she decided to soften her question a bit.

"I mean, it's none of my business, I was just curious. I didn't know if that's something Highbloods did, you know, the same way us boring Lowbloods do."

Anton looked at her a long moment before finally speaking. "I don't think you're boring at all. And no, I'm not dating anyone. You're right, with Highbloods it's just…different."

He lowered his eyes to his task before adding, "What about you? It's the empath thing, right? That's why you don't like dating?" He was purposefully avoiding her eyes, shuffling the stack of containers around in his hands.

She was strangely touched at his assumption that she didn't date because she didn't want to, not because every man she'd ever tried to start a relationship with had found her anxiety and intuition a complete turn off.

"Partly, yes. It's pretty hard to start dating someone when every thought they have makes you feel completely insecure," she admitted.

"I find that hard to believe."

"That I can be insecure? Oh I assure you, that happens pretty easily."

"But why? You're strong, you're resilient, you care for others more than yourself, and you're obviously gorgeous. What is there to be insecure about?"

When he finally raised those striking blue eyes to meet hers, Mayla's heart jumped in her chest. She felt her cheeks heat, but she didn't look away.

He thought she was gorgeous.

They stayed that way for a long moment, him on one side of the table, containers in hand, her on the other, their eyes locked on one another. Finally, he cleared his throat awkwardly and she dropped her eyes.

"Ahh, I think I'll just," he paused, shifting his weight, "go throw these away." He turned, and headed for the kitchen.

Mayla's mind was spinning. Had that been a clear invitation or was she imagining things? If it *was* an invitation did she have the nerve to take him up on it?

He was Highblood. She knew they had relationships, but it wasn't the same. They dated, got married and divorced just like everyone else, but it was a well-known fact that lust and mutual benefit ruled their relationships, not love. She rose to her feet and followed him.

As she entered the chrome and white kitchen, Mayla was intensely aware of his large body, so close in the confined space. She turned, leaning back against the counter, and watched him. She wasn't sure if it was the mind walking, the calm control she'd been feeling ever since, or the messages he'd been sending between the kiss in the interrogation room and the compliment just now. Whatever it was, Mayla decided she was done dancing around this.

She wanted him, and it was pretty damn obvious at this

point that he wanted her too.

"Would you like some juice?"

She shrugged, and he busied himself with grabbing a glass from the cabinet. He poured the juice and, unable to avoid looking at her any longer, his eyes met hers as he handed it over. Their fingers brushed as she took the glass, an electric tingle of awareness traveling up her arm. When she deliberately set the glass on the counter beside her and made no move to drink it, Anton settled against the opposite counter, crossing his arms in front of him.

"How are you feeling? Everything still okay?"

"I'm fine."

Those dangerous blue eyes dropped to her lips as she spoke.

"I feel more balanced than I ever have before. More in control. I really think using one of my magics without the other for a change was a relief to my system."

"Hmm, maybe." His eyes continued to fixate on her mouth, and when her tongue darted out to wet her suddenly dry lips, she watched his eyes briefly close and his chest rise on a deep inhale.

She had a clear effect on him, and his effect on her might be even stronger. She ached for him to kiss her again, to reach out with those amazing hands and pull her to him.

Her heart thundered into a gallop behind her ribs, so loud she could feel the vibration in her ears.

Anton sent a dark, hungry look down her body, and she felt a shiver dance along her spine. Immediately, he was beside her, his face concerned.

"Are you cold again?" he asked in a husky whisper.

She shook her head.

"No, I'm not cold," she rasped, giving him a long, almost pleading look, "I'm just...hungry."

The pulse in his neck jumped. "I can grab you something else from—," his large frame turned back towards the fridge, but her hand flew out lightning fast, catching his arm.

He turned back, his eyes searching hers. He felt it too, she knew he did, this intensity that was growing between them.

She wouldn't stay on this razor edge of need and want any longer.

"I'm not hungry for more food, Anton. I'm hungry for *you.*"

The flare of sudden heat in his eyes was scorching. He reached out a hand to capture her hip, pulling her hard and flush against him. The skin beneath her jeans tingled at just that simple touch. There was something about this man that lit her up from the inside out.

His voice was low and husky when he finally spoke.

"Are you sure this is what you want?" His lips pressed together for a moment, forming a hard white line. "You need to take a minute and really think about this."

His hand dropped from her hip and he took a slow step backward, the air between them cooling.

"I'm Highblood, Mayla. We aren't as human as you are, as much as I might wish it otherwise. I don't fall in love like you do. My relationships are built on respect, appreciation and," he slid his gaze up and down her body once more, "mutual gratification. So I need you to be very sure about this, because once I have you in my hands," his fists clenched at his sides and his jaw flexed.

"Once I have you in my hands," he repeated, "I don't think I'll be able to stop. I want you so damn much right now I don't trust myself. I might not be able to fall in love with you, but make no mistake, if you give yourself to me, you will be mine, utterly and completely. There will be no going back. No changing your mind."

Looking into his light blue eyes, raw, feral need stared back at her. Still, in that moment, she knew if she said it wasn't enough…he would walk away. He would continue to look for Willow, continue to anchor her when needed, but this intense attraction building between them? He'd shut it off like a faucet, and never speak of it again.

"Tell me right now, Mayla.

Are. You. Sure?"

It was a simple question, just three small words strung together. Three words that meant everything.

She wouldn't have his heart, but there was no rule that said she couldn't give him her own. She would have his body, his respect, and certainly his protection, he'd already demonstrated that. He would be possessive, demanding, probably even annoying at times. But she didn't care.

Not when, somewhere deep within her, she already knew this was right. If a Highblood relationship was all she could have of him, it would have to be enough.

She looked at him for another long moment, then nodded. "I'm sure."

Whatever the future held, she had to know him. All of him.

She watched him, leaned back against the opposite counter, strong arms crossed once more over that massive chest, neck tight as if he were holding himself back from everything he wanted in this universe.

With trembling hands, she reached for the bottom of her t-shirt, pulling it up over her head before tossing it onto the nearby counter. Her breasts strained against the pink lace of her bra, her nipples hardening instantly against the fabric. When she dropped her hands back to her sides, she was a jangle of nerves.

His shoulders clenched, his stomach quivering under his shirt as if a liquid shudder had gone all the way through him. His eyes drank her in, but he didn't move. Why was he was back to being so quiet and still? It was unnerving.

After what felt like an eternity, he reached down, yanking his own shirt over his head and tossing it aside. Her eyes reveled in the sight of him, that strong collarbone that had been tormenting her all day, the smooth plane of his chest and the hard, sculpted ridges of his stomach. When her eyes slid lower, to the band of his boxer briefs peeking out just above his jeans, and those sinful indents of muscle just inside of his hips that she'd known he'd have, she had to remind herself to breathe.

And when his desire hit her in a wave, sliding over her skin like velvet fire, she couldn't hold in her whimper of pure need.

The whimper was his undoing.

That single, soft sound set him loose like a lion after its prey.

In a flash he was across the kitchen and up against her, his mouth feasting on hers. His hands palmed her ass and lifted, her legs wrapping immediately around his lean waist. Another soft whimper left her lips as she felt the hard length of him brush against her sensitive core through their clothes.

She felt like fire and ice all at once, a delicious tingling heat beginning everywhere his skin touched hers. Her hands rose, one winding fiercely around his neck, the other tunneling into his hair to pull him closer, demanding and deepening their contact into one long, soul scorching kiss. She had the vague sensation of moving, but her mind was no longer focusing on the world around them.

All she knew was him. His name was a chant in her mind. *Anton. Anton. Anton.* Nothing else existed in this world, only the feel of his body against hers and the taste of his mouth on her tongue.

When he finally pulled back, she was breathless.

Their eyes locked as he walked her backwards, her back coming up against the cool marble wall of the hallway. He ground himself against her and she moaned, her head falling back so his mouth could trail a path of pure pleasure down her throat. He freed one hand from the curve of her ass long enough to yank her bra down under her breasts, releasing the creamy swells from their adorably pink confines. A ragged groan escaped him at the sight of those lush, rose-tinted nipples pushing upwards in invitation.

"Gods Mayla, you are…perfect." Lowering his gorgeous silver blonde head, he took one nipple into the warm heat of his mouth.

She felt heat pool at her core at his husky, half whispered words, but she shook her head."I'm not, I'm…"

The heat of his mouth disappeared and he lifted his head a fraction, looking at her sternly. His exhale brushed across her skin like cashmere.

"Do you want me to stop?"

His mouth was so tantalizing close, she could feel the heat of it tease against the rapidly cooling moisture he'd left behind on her pebbled nipple. Her words were jumbled, coming out in short gasps.

"No…I don't…I mean…don't stop…please."

"Then don't ever try to tell me you aren't perfect, Mayla." His tongue licked at her in one slow, languid graze, his eyes never leaving hers. "You are exquisite."

When he blew across her breast she could see his white cold breath, feel the frigid tickle against her heated skin. Her hips bucked.

He moved to the other breast.

"You are sensual."

Another slow, warm lick.

"And you are stunning."

More cold, crisp air.

Her head dropped back against the wall and her eyes closed, zings of sensation running directly from her breasts to the sudden slickness between her thighs. *Mother of gods*. His mouth would no sooner leave one breast that it would quickly capture the other.

"I cannot wait to be inside you," he growled, his head raising finally to her lips, his mouth taking full possession of hers. His kiss was hard, demanding, full of prolonged yearning and wicked promise.

This must be what it felt like to burn alive, she thought, it had to be. But gods, what a way to go.

When he lifted his mouth from hers and ground himself against her once more, she gasped.

"Anton. *Please*," she whispered.

Then his mouth was on hers again and all reasonable thought was gone. As he carried her down the hall and towards the bedroom, every step he took rubbed his hard length against her already weeping core through her jeans. Her hands flew over him, caressing every inch of flesh she could reach. They danced across his chest, then over his broad shoulders, kneading into his back before sliding up the back of his neck to dive into his hair.

She burned for him.

She'd had sex before, but it had never been anything like this. Each time it had happened it had been a quick, awkward fumbling - not this towering, blistering fire of sensation and unquenchable need.

And she wanted more. More skin, more heat, more everything.

Anton lowered her to the bed, kissing her thoroughly before pulling away to squat down and slide off her tennis shoes and socks. Mayla reached for the button on her jeans, anxious to remove those as well, but he reached up to put a broad hand over hers and shook his head.

He rose, leaning over to look her in the eyes. "You are a gift from the gods, Mayla. A gift to me."

Her heart swelled at his words, her eyes softening.

"Which means I will be the only one doing the unwrapping."

His words were delivered with a slow, sexy grin, his hands sliding under her back to unclasp her bra, her breasts springing free. He dropped a kiss to each before his hands made quick work of the button and zipper on her jeans. Sliding them entirely too slowly down her legs, he placed gentle, teasing kisses against her stomach, then traced the curve of her hip with his tongue.

She writhed. "Anton," she breathed, her eyes closing.

"Soon," he promised.

She heard the thump as he tossed her jeans to the floor, then wondered where his heat had gone as her flushed skin began to cool. She'd just opened her eyes when the heat of his mouth suddenly pressed against the soft cotton of her underwear, directly over her core. She arched off the bed, whimpering.

"First, I'm going to taste you right here."

He hooked a fingertip under each side of her underwear, tugging the scrap of material down her legs, as his eyes watched her. The heat in her core blossomed under his gaze, her hands clenching fistfuls of the sheets as she watched him in return.

He dropped to his knees.

Lowering his head, his lips brushed against the inside of one thigh and her body trembled.

Waiting. Expectant. Anticipating.

When that velvet tongue finally made a long, slow slide up her opening, her hips bucked involuntarily and her breath escaped her on a moan. Grabbing her behind the knees, Anton chuckled, tugging her closer to the edge of the bed before he dropped an arm across her hips, pinning her in place.

"You taste like peaches, Mayla. I love peaches. I could eat peaches…all…day…long."

Then he lowered his head back to the task at hand…and devoured her.

Mayla couldn't think. She couldn't even manage to open her eyes. All she could focus on was the way Anton's mouth was feasting on her, and the way her insides kept curling tighter, pushing her towards some unknown precipice.

She was flailing, her hands clenching and unclenching in the sheets, her head tossing from side to side. This feeling was exquisite, but it was too intense, and it just kept growing. It just kept building.

What was happening to her?

When Anton lifted his head, his words were gentle, soothing her frayed edges. "Don't fight it, Mayla, I've got you. Just relax. Don't try to control it, just let it carry you where you need to go."

She stopped thrashing, her body calming, settling into the sensations his mouth was creating. She trusted him, and whatever was happening, whatever *this* was, he would be there to catch her. The intensity within her began building once more, her core wrapping tighter and tighter.

Moments later, when that intensity finally exploded, she didn't fall...she flew.

22

Anton lay on his side next to her, his head propped on one elbow, his long fingers tracing lazy circles across the flat plane of her stomach as Mayla finally came back down to earth, her choppy breath slowly leveling.

"That was…just…wow."

A self-satisfied smile crossed his face, his fingers trailing slowly upward to tease tenderly across her breast.

"Thank you, I'll take that as a compliment. You've never had an orgasm with a lover before, have you, Mayla?"

She felt her cheeks heat. "No. I mean I've only had a couple anyway."

His fingers froze mid-caress, his shoulders tensing.

She hurried to explain. "Only two, they were both kind of quick and uncomfortable honestly."

His fingers started their slow tease once more, circling one nipple and then the other. It was such a small, simple touch, yet it felt so intimate, so powerful.

"Two lovers or two orgasms?"

Her cheeks were burning, and she turned her head away, suddenly shy. "Two different lovers, zero orgasms," she mumbled.

His fingers found her chin, bringing her face gently back to look at him. He pressed a slow, sweet kiss to her lips, then dropped another to her shoulder, his fingers sliding down to dance along her inner thigh.

"Never hide from me, Mayla. You have nothing to be embarrassed about. You can say anything to me, and it will never be repeated, I hope you know that. And again, there's nothing to be embarrassed about, I haven't had that many partners either. Certainly none as exquisite as you."

When his hand slipped upward and he slid lazy fingertip slowly along her opening, her stomach quivered, her eyes narrowing on him.

"I somehow find that hard to believe," she whispered.

He didn't respond, his finger continuing to tease and distract, his slow smile looking absolutely edible.

"How many partners have you had?" She pressed.

"Let's just leave it at…more than two." His finger deliberately pushed into her moist heat with excruciating slowness, pulling a soft groan from her lips. He was distracting her on purpose, but she couldn't bring herself to care. Her nerve endings sang, her skin heating. As his single finger slid in and out of her, his mouth captured her nipple, his tongue swirling around the tight bud in ever shrinking circles. She felt the tightening tension within her begin to build once more.

When he added a second finger she cried out in ecstasy, gripping his shoulder hard. She was flushed all over. Her blood felt like it was dancing in her veins, her body throbbing with need. When he curled his fingers just the slightest bit deep inside her, she cried out.

"Anton," his name was an invitation, both a plea and a demand as it dripped from her lips. "I need," she said breathlessly. She tossed her head back and forth, ebony hair spilling across the gray sheets. Her hands gripped at him, nails digging into his shoulders, insistant.

"I know exactly what you need, *milacek*," he promised, removing his hand to stand quickly and yank off his jeans and black boxer briefs. In just those few seconds she already missed the heat of him, needing the sensual brush of his skin against hers.

Then he was on top of her, every thought in her head disappearing as he settled between her thighs, the rounded head of him sliding sinfully against her folds. He worshipped her mouth with his own, his smooth, strong chest warm beneath her hands. When she slid her hands lower to tease across his abdomen he lifted his mouth from hers and groaned.

"I am going to spend entire days watching you come apart in my arms, Mayla. Days exploring your body and learning exactly what you like, but right now I can't wait any longer. I have to be inside you."

His eyes found hers in silent question and she nodded, tilting her hips up to meet him. He entered her slowly, splitting her slick, swollen folds, and they both moaned. He touched their foreheads together, ragged breaths twisting and weaving, but he didn't go any farther. His arms were braced on either side of her head, his eyes squeezed shut as if he were in pain.

She watched him for a short moment, suddenly unsure.

"Anton?"

"I don't want to hurt you," he ground out, teeth clenched, "I'm trying, very hard, to go slow with you, but fucking hell Mayla, you are so tight I might explode."

Hurt her? He wasn't going to hurt her. He was stretching her, yes, but it was the most delicious, most exquisite sensation she'd ever felt. But gods, wasn't it just like him to try to protect her, even in this? She slid her hands up to cradle the sides of his face. She opened the door in her mind halfway, picturing Anton standing just outside. Then she reached out, grasped his hand, and yanked him inside her courtyard with her.

His head shot up, eyes flaring wide before he looked down at her in awe.

"What did you just do?"

She pushed the blissful sensations his body was creating in hers towards him, wrapping him in the pleasure she was feeling, and watched his eyes widen even more.

"Mayla, I can - you're - I can feel you - in my head," he stumbled over his words, sucking in a gasp as she sent another wave of need over him.

"I can feel what you're feeling. I can—," his words cut off abruptly at the next wave, and his eyes closed in ecstasy, his breath shuddering out of him.

"Holy shit."

"You're in my mind now, Anton. So you'll know in an instant if you're hurting me." She clenched her inner walls around him and they both gasped. Her nails dug into his biceps and she raised her head to kiss his throat before whispering, "I want you to have my body and my mind. I want you to know all of me. To feel all of me." She rotated her hips, bringing her legs up to wrap around his waist, lines of raw need etched into her forehead. "Now for the sake of my sanity, Anton, please move before this aching tears me apart!"

Her words broke the tight grip he'd been keeping on his body, and his hips shot forward, seating him fully within her. He waited for a single heartbeat, then set a steady rhythm, pulling almost all the way out before slamming home again, their breathless moans mixing together with every hard thrust. Her hands pulled at him, her mouth trailing kisses across his chest, his shoulders, and his throat. When she wrapped her arms around him and scored her nails down his back he growled in delight.

He shifted them up on the bed, gripping the headboard with one hand and her hip with the other, the speed of his thrusts intensifying.

Mayla felt like she was burning alive. With every slide of his body sensations exploded within her mind. Her body coiled, the pressure building stronger this time, faster, fiercer. She pressed her mouth against his shoulder and whimpered in ecstasy.

"Not yet," he warned, feeling her tense, his chest glistening above her, "wait for me."

She leaned back, placing her palm against his heart, and watching him through hooded eyes. He was stunning, magnificent…

Hers.

The thought sent her skating along the edge of the abyss, pure pleasure reverberating over every inch of her skin. He was hers. She was his. Call it love, call it attraction, call it pure, stupid luck, she didn't care. They belonged together.

Somewhere, deep in the back of her mind, she felt a small, odd sensation. It felt like a key fitting into a lock, a sun-filled doorway opening wide.

Then Anton dropped his mouth to her shoulder and nipped before turning his mouth to hers, her thoughts refocusing in an instant. She tilted her hips upwards again, bringing him somehow even deeper, his groan raw in her ears.

"You are mine, Mayla. Forever and always."

The words sent her careening over the edge, and Anton followed after her on a roar.

Later that night, as the two of them lay sleeping, limbs tangled together on his massive bed, neither woke when a symbol appeared just above her heart, the soft blue light glowing in the dim room. Another, a perfect match to hers, appeared moments later on the left side of his chest. Both symbols flared, pulsing for a few heartbeats before fading, and then disappearing into the darkness.

23

The next morning, as Anton and Mayla drove through the outskirts of Miradea, he reached over and gave her thigh a little squeeze.

"You sure you're up for this? You could have stayed at the apartment to rest, I didn't let you get much sleep last night."

She leaned her head back against the leather headrest in the Audi and sent him a soft smile. "I'll sleep later. We need to find Samuel as soon as possible, there's no telling what that monster has already done to him."

Anton nodded.

After Mayla shared what she knew yesterday, and the details she was able to provide from Carl's memories, Asher had located a missing persons report for a six-year-old Samuel Whitaker. The child disappeared two nights ago from a friends birthday party at the most popular bowling alley in Miradea.

Using the details Mayla could recall from the images in Carl's mind, Callan had been able to narrow down the abandoned property to a list of ten strong possibilities. Asher was with the child's parents now, getting additional background, and would meet up with them when he was done to help with the search. Elijah had taken half of the list this morning, Anton and Mayla the other half.

"Alright, but why don't you try to rest for a bit, I promise I'll wake you if I see anything out of the ordinary. We've got at least a twenty minute drive to the next location."

She didn't answer, just lifted his hand to place a soft kiss against the back of it, then snuggled deeper into the seat and closed her eyes.

The touch of her lips to his skin sent a tingle of pleasure through his body, and he had to fight back the urge to sigh out loud. Gods but she was beautiful. If he'd thought having her in his bed last night would diminish his lust for her in any way, he'd been greatly mistaken. His skin heated as he remembered the night before. He'd taken her in the bedroom that first time, then again in his massive shower, her back sliding up and down against the warm, soapy marble. Sometime late into the night they'd both awakened, coming together with a sweet, slow tenderness that was even more powerful for all its gentleness.

He'd had his share of lovers, but Mayla was unlike any woman he'd ever known. Her body called to him, enticing his hands to reach out and touch, his lips to lean in and steal a kiss. It was silly, no doubt simply a side effect of being so intensely attracted to her, but he'd opened his eyes this morning feeling as if she'd somehow been made just for him, and he for her. From the moment he'd felt her snuggled against him, one graceful leg draped over his thigh, her hair mussed and completely adorable, he'd just felt…settled. Content.

He gave his head a quick little shake, focusing once more on the road ahead of him. He needed to turn off the bedroom part of his brain, and turn back on the detective part. Samuel Whitaker was out here somewhere, and they needed to find him as fast as possible.

Ten minutes later, as he glided the Audi around a corner onto a random, desolate stretch of road, Mayla sat straight up, wide-eyed and rigid.

"Anton, STOP!" She yelled.

He ground his foot into the brake, throwing a hand out to brace her and stopping the Audi on a lurch. "What is it? What's wrong?"

"I can feel someone! A child. They're nearby, they're very young, and they're very scared." She paused, her face going pale as she audibly swallowed down her bile.

"And Carl's face. I just saw Carl's face. It has to be

Samuel, right?" She looked down, her head tilting just a bit as she tried to focus inward. "I can feel his fear. I can feel that he's cold, but other than that it's just...darkness. What does that mean? Why can't I see anything else?"

She brought a hand up to cover her eyes, and wrapped her other arm around her stomach. "My head is spinning...I think I might be sick."

Anton threw the Audi in park, coming around to her door on a run, wrenching it open and helping her gently from her seat. Pulling her in tight against him, he rubbed her back in slow circles.

"Breathe, Mayla. Deep breaths in through your nose, then slowly out through your mouth."

Her knees wobbled and she squeezed her eyes shut. "Everything is spinning. You should move, I'm definitely going to be sick."

Bracing her with one arm, Anton leaned around her and into the car to pop open the glove box. A small box of prepackaged alcohol swabs sat inside and he snagged one, tearing it open with his teeth. Taking the little moist square between two fingers, he folded it in half and waved it under her nose.

Mayla's eyes immediately popped wide and she stopped weaving on her feet. She sent him a quizzical, *how-did-you look* and he shrugged.

"Trick of the trade. These little miracle workers keep me from throwing up at the worst scenes I investigate."

He felt her pull a deep, settling breath into her lungs, and he took a moment to look around them.

Three abandoned, dilapidated buildings lined the right side of the street, a run-down, fenced in junkyard on the left. A red, NO TRESPASSING sign dangled haphazardly from the junkyard's gate, and if the large padlock and heavy chain were any indication, the owner had clearly taken today off. The spaces between the three buildings were overrun with knee high weeds and littered with random trash. Prime real estate for enhancement deals and low end prostitution, and that was about it.

He felt Mayla tremble under his hands. Despite her earlier claims, he knew she was exhausted. They'd already hit three stops, and at each one she'd mentally reached out, fighting for any trace of information that might help them find Samuel. Her energy was fading fast. She looked at him.

"I think the dizziness might be Samuel. I think he might be hurt. Ugh!! I know I can feel him, why can't I just *see* where he is? I'm not good enough at this, I need to get better."

He shook his head. She was just as determined as any member of his team, just as invested in helping innocent people. His tenderhearted, stubborn, amazing Mayla. When she reached up and took the alcohol swab from his hand, he dropped a kiss to her forehead, happy to see she was still taking slow steady breaths.

"It's okay *milacek*, you're doing just fine. If he's here, we will find him."

She sent him a small smile. "You never told me what that means, '*milacek*'. You called me that a few times last night."

He chuckled, rubbing his hands up and down her arms to warm her chilled skin.

"Did I? I must have picked it up from Adriana, it's what she calls her husband whenever I'm over there for dinner. I'm pretty sure it means darling. When I was a kid it took me years to realize the man's name is actually Sven."

"I've never called anyone that before," he admitted.

Her smile grew.

"I like it," she admitted softly.

"I'm glad."

He lowered his lips to hers for a tender kiss, then straightened when she winced and grabbed the side of her head once more. He scanned the three properties quickly, deciding. They'd try the farthest building first. Maybe that's why she was seeing black, because it was just too far away. They'd go in together, he definitely didn't want Mayla on her own.

When she suddenly stumbled, weaving once more on her feet, Anton wrapped an arm around her waist.

Okay, new plan. They needed back up, and *fast*.

Mayla was done. If they did find the child somewhere close by - and please gods, he hoped they would - Mayla needed to go home and rest right after. And she'd need him to level out some of the exhaustion. He wouldn't be able to help them both.

"That's it. You need rest," he pulled his cell phone out of his pocket, tapping in a number before putting it up to his ear. "I'm calling in Asher. You are going to stay right here and relax before you pass out."

"But Anton I can—,"

Anton sent her a look, his brows furrowed, and she snapped her mouth shut. He was in full Chief mode, and she knew arguing wouldn't do her any good. After two rings, a low, familiar voice came over the line.

"I was already on my way. Where are you?"

"Southern edge of town, near the badlands. I dropped you a pin. Mayla thinks the kid is here somewhere, but I've got multiple potential properties and she's done. Bring a med kit just in case one," he eyeballed Mayla once more, "or both of them need it."

"Got it. I'm close by, be there in five."

After Anton hung up, he looked back at her. His expression softened, but not by much.

"We need to focus on Samuel right now. I can't do that properly if I'm worried about you at the same time. Asher will help me now, you've done enough."

His tone was firm and Mayla sighed, hating that he was right. This wasn't the time for her stubborn pride, Samuel was the only priority.

Besides, this tired was different from what she'd experienced before. It was bone deep, like she'd run a marathon and then tried to climb a mountain afterward. It wasn't pain filled or overwhelming like it had been in the past, it was just pure, utter exhaustion. She felt like a battery run down to it's last bit of charge. Just staying on her feet was a challenge.

Still, if she couldn't go looking for the child, maybe she could at least help him from here instead. She reached out again with her mind. It was him, it had to be. She found the terror and pain again, pushing as much warmth and safety as she could back. The tiniest light answered in her mind and she reached for it gently.

He was cold and so scared. What if the horrible fire man came back? He wanted to run away, but he was stuck. He wanted his Mommy and Daddy. He even wanted his little sister. She could have all his toys, she could break all his stuff. He didn't care anymore as long as it meant he got to leave this place.

Mayla sucked in a sharp gasp. Keeping her eyes closed to keep her connection to him as strong as possible, she reached out a hand.

"Anton, I think I've got him," she breathed. "I can hear what he's thinking."

"What, from here?" His larger hand grabbed hers, their

fingers intertwining, the shakiness she had been feeling leveled out. She could still hear Samuel, but she could feel Anton too. She felt stronger, more balanced.

"There's some kind of…metal pole? His wrists hurt."

Samuel's emotions were a blurry mix of reddish fear and muted gray exhaustion. A small sob escaped her at the brutality of it, but she pushed on. She would not let go of this child. There would be time to be upset about the situation later.

"The rope is too tight. His fingers are aching."

Vaguely, she registered the sound of Asher's old Chevy truck pulling up, the door opening on a whine, then shutting again with a bang.

Anton's hand squeezed hers, but he didn't say a word, not wanting to break her focus.

"His head aches, and there's sticky stuff in his hair from where the bad man hit him with the flashlight."

She felt Anton suck in a sharp, angry breath.

"His knee hurts and it feels sticky there too. He hit it when the cigarette man threw him down the stairs."

Asher's low growl rumbled beside her.

Down the stairs.

The scary man threw him down the stairs.

Mayla's eyes flew open and her nails dug into Anton's hand, her other hand clawing for Asher's arm before catching and gripping it tightly as well.

"Ouch." Asher clipped out, eyebrows raised.

"Stairs! Carl threw him down a set of stairs! It's cold and very dark, somewhere underground. The pole in the floor, it has to be a basement!"

Anton nodded, grabbing her in a quick hug and dropping a kiss to her lips.

"You did it Mayla. We've got it from here. We'll go find him."

Asher's reaction to their kiss was a simple crossing of his arms, a raised eyebrow and a slow smile.

Anton settled her gently back into the passenger seat of the Audi.

"We'll be right back. Stay here. Rest, relax, and don't

move. If you see anyone, you honk the horn," he ordered.

She nodded.

With the smooth efficiency of a team used to working together, Anton and Asher turned and took off at a dead run, Anton veering towards the house furthest down the street, Asher towards the one directly in front of them.

Without Anton's touch, fatigue crept back in, her exhausted trembling turning to actual shivers, but Mayla ignored it. She reached out to Samuel once more, sending him warmth, safety and as much comfort she could muster. He was dizzy, his head pounding, his hands aching, his knee hurting, and he was so very tired. His eyes were slowly drifting shut. He desperately wanted to sleep now. No! Without touching him, Mayla couldn't know if he was concussed, but her instincts were screaming at her that he shouldn't fall sleep.

Asher and Anton were each in one of the buildings now, she could hear them shouting Samuel's name from here, but Samuel wasn't registering that he heard anything.

There were no heavy footfalls above him, no one yelling his name. Mayla's eyes slid to the only other property, the building in the middle with a sign shaped like a pair of scissors.

He was there, he had to be.

She pushed herself up and out of the car, taking off in a stumbling run before she even knew her feet were moving. Moments later she was climbing the few stairs to front porch.

Sidestepping a rotted out hole, Mayla heaved a sigh of relief when she noticed the shabby front door had fallen off a good while ago and was now propped to one side. The faded lettering across it read *Shearly Amazing Salon*. Stepping inside, she saw two barber style chairs, the black leather of each torn and discolored with mold. Empty enhancement syringes littered the floor, along with leaves, twigs, and trash.

She ignored it all, stumbling down the hallway to wrench open doors one after another. Where was the basement? Her movements were becoming panicked and clumsy, her muscles so fatigued they fought her with every step. She found closet after closet, then two smaller rooms labeled Nails and Waxing. None led to the basement.

"Samuel!!" she yelled, praying he would hear her, hoping her voice would be enough to keep him awake. "Samuel, where are you?! Samuel!"

A wave of dizziness slammed into her, and she doubled over, bracing both hands on her knees, swallowing huge gulps of air to ride it out. She'd be no help whatsoever if she passed out on the damn floor.

When a small sound came from behind her, she turned, heading even deeper into the building. In the farthest back corner was another door, this one leading into a small kitchen.

Her eyes flew around the space. There!

A dull brown door covered in scuffs and scratches was hidden in the back corner of the room. She flung it open, banging it against the far wall and planting a palm in the middle when it threatened to bounce back at her.

Concrete stairs led down into pitch blackness.

She could feel Samuel's fear and his fatigue, but through it all, she felt his small, sparkling glimmer of hope.

"I'm here Samuel. I'm coming! Don't be scared, I'm here to help you!"

Stepping back from the doorway, she took a deep breath and screamed at the top of her lungs.

Anton exited the back door of the old mechanic shop, wiping his dusty hands on his jeans. Nothing to be found in there except garbage, rusted tools, and an old mattress with a handful of large brown stains caused by gods knew what. There were two recessed bays carved into the floor, no doubt once used to work on various cars, but no basement.

A fire blazed down his spine at the sound of Mayla's sudden scream, and he was running towards it in the same moment.

Asher appeared from the other direction, approaching at a loping run. Both of them ran, full speed, for the back door of the last remaining building. This last property had had a wooden privacy fence at some point, most of it now gone, with just a few stalwart boards still upright, trying valiantly to fight time and the elements. A shed sat in the back corner of the yard, partially hidden by the remaining fence.

As he passed both the fence and the shed, Anton's long strides stuttered to a horrified halt. Asher skidded to a stop in front of him and uttered only one word.

"Fuck."

A white paneled work van, an exact match to the one witnesses reported seeing at the baseball field, was tucked in neatly behind the shed.

Mayla's heart felt like it was going to pound straight out of her chest. Her fingernails split as she tore at the tight ropes securing Samuel's small hands behind him to the basement pole. The boy had been afraid when she first approached, then relieved, but in the last few moments he'd become almost listless, barely able to keep his eyes open. His head lolled to the side every so often, and he didn't respond when she called his name.

She had to get him out of here, and fast.

Finally, the ropes gave way in her hands and his small frame slumped forward. She caught him in her arms, scooping him up and carrying him as quickly as she dared up the stairs to the main floor.

She'd expected to feel all of his pain and fear as soon as she touched him, but instead she felt almost…nothing. His mind didn't seem to be processing what was going on around him anymore. This couldn't just be a concussion, and he hadn't simply passed out. She should still feel confusion, or a muted headache, something.

"Samuel, stay with me," she gave him a little shake, but got no response. "I promise I'm going to get you out of here. We're going to get you back to your mom and dad really soon. I need you to open your eyes for me."

When she laid him gently down on the floor, right in the middle of the main room, his head simply flopped to the side, his eyelids not even fluttering. His skin was an eerie shade of gray, his small hands loose and unmoving.

Shit. Shit. Shit! There was no time.

She didn't worry about creaking open the heavy door she'd created in her mind, had no time to worry about keeping anything separated.

Samuel was out of time.

She threw the door wide and got to work.

When Anton and Asher came barreling full speed through the back door of the salon a few minutes later, they found Samuel sitting up, wide-eyed and blinking at them. It wasn't until the child pointed to the far corner of the room that they turned around. And found Mayla, gray and lifeless on the floor.

24

Anton stood at the end of the hospital bed, staring down at his hands. They wouldn't stop trembling.

They'd stopped listening to him ever since he found Mayla on the floor of that filthy place, completely unresponsive. No matter how many times he told his hands to stop shaking, they simply ignored.

When he found her, she was still breathing, but no matter what he did, he couldn't wake her. He'd called Skyler immediately, carrying her out to the car and jumping behind the wheel.

Asher scooped Samuel up, wrapping him in a blanket and chattering away in a light, easy tone the entire time. The shifter swore he'd get the boy safely back to his parents, and check back in with Anton as soon as it was done.

On the way to the hospital Skyler had asked him a bunch of questions he didn't have the answers to, and promised he was already heading to meet them.

Miradea Health was the only hospital in the city, its primary role to handle life or death cases. With med units around every corner for quick fixes, and healers always on call for the right price, Miradea Health only took on cases needing extensive diagnostics or complicated surgery.

When Anton stormed through the front doors, Mayla limp and gray in his arms, the nurses had taken one look at his solid white irises, at the snow and ice trailing behind them in a dangerous swirl, and ushered them immediately into a room, paging the doctor on call.

Then they *all* started asking him questions.

He was sure they were expecting answers, but his mind didn't have the space for it. He couldn't turn his attention away from her long enough to focus. Couldn't stop watching the rise and fall of her chest under that stark white sheet and plain blue hospital gown.

It was all so surreal.

He felt like he was watching some terrifying, low-budget horror movie. Any minute now the credits would roll and this would all be over. Everything would go back to normal. Mayla would get up out of that huge bed and she would be fine.

He didn't know when Elijah showed up.

Suddenly he was just there, talking to the doctors. That was a good thing, because at least they stopped chattering away at him. Anton watched as they hooked Mayla up to machines, his eyes never leaving her as they scanned her head, lifted her eyelids to shine lights in her eyes, and took blood from her arm. Then they repeated the process. Over and over again. Every time a needle pierced that beautiful skin he wanted to choke the life out of someone.

But he didn't.

He stood.

And he watched.

And his damn hands kept shaking.

The rest of the team had arrived, and were now spread haphazardly throughout the room. Callan sat on the edge of a hard plastic chair, his hands clenched tightly together, his bright red jeans and sunshine face t-shirt glaringly out of place in the bleak atmosphere. Asher loomed darkly in the far corner, arms folded across his chest, one boot braced against the wall, everything about him utterly still.

When the last nurse finally left, assuring them the doctor would be in shortly, Elijah began pacing behind him.

Natalie flew through the door moments later, her eyes wild and her normally perfect hair in complete disarray. When she saw her sister, pale and unmoving in the huge bed, she stumbled, catching herself then standing in the middle of the room as if unsure of what to do. Her eyes scanned the room, then landed on Elijah. She made a beeline for him, wrapping her arms around his waist and burying her face in his chest to sob.

Elijah stood for a moment, startled, before bringing his arms up to pat her back awkwardly.

Anton looked at his trembling hands once more. Where the fuck was Skyler?

Skyler would fix all this. He would be able to reach her. He'd done it before, he could do it again. It would be easier this time, because she wouldn't be able to block him out. Skyler would reach her, he would find out what was really wrong, and then the healers or the doctors could get to work on fixing it.

As if his thoughts had managed to conjure the male into being, Skyler strode through the door, peeling off his gloves and immediately approaching the bed. He wasted no time putting his hands gently against the sides of Mayla's face and leaning in close.

Out of the corner of his eye, Anton saw Natalie stir as if she would to interrupt. Elijah shook his head, grasping her hand and whispering something in her ear. Surprisingly, the redhead settled, though her eyes continued to watched Skyler like a hawk.

The soldier leaned in close to Mayla, his eyes closed and his breathing slow and shallow.

Hope bloomed in Anton's chest. He had to be getting through. Skyler would fix this. Before they knew it, Mayla would be looking up at him again with those big, storm cloud eyes, smiling at him in that way that made him feel like he could take on the world.

She'd need to stay for a few more days of course, get some tests done just to be safe, but then he'd take her back to the apartment. They'd curl up together under a blanket on the couch and have the talk. The one that he'd been thinking about since this morning. The one about how he wanted to wake up next to her every morning. How he wanted to eat together and sleep together and live together every day. The one about how she drove him mad with lust even when she wasn't trying to. He'd crack a joke about even letting that damn cat of hers tag along if she'd just agree to move in. She would smile and laugh, and probably look away from him, the way she always did when she was feeling a little shy. But then he would kiss her, and she would kiss him back, and they would make love slowly, and sweetly, like they had last night.

Skyler opened his eyes, lowering his hands with a sigh and shaking his head. He looked across the bed at Anton, his dark brown eyes red-rimmed and raw with pain.

"I'm sorry Anton. I'm so sorry. I can't get through. There's just, there's nothing there."

A tall woman in blue surgical scrubs and neatly tied back blonde hair knocked on the open door and then entered, carrying a clipboard.

"Hello everyone, I'm Doctor McIntosh. I'm here to speak with the next of kin for," she perused the chart in her hands before looking back up, "Mayla Charles?"

Natalie stepped forward, her hand grasping Elijah's so hard her knuckles were white.

"That would be me. I'm her sister."

The woman's muted gray eyes glanced around the room, and then came back to rest on Natalie.

"Are we free to speak here, or would you like to go to a consultation room for more privacy?"

Natalie shook her head. "No, it's fine. You can speak here."

The doctor's eyes lingered on Asher, at his intense stare and menacing posture.

"Why don't we just go--"

Natalie's skin flushed red and her control snapped. "Spit it the fuck out, doc. That's my sister lying in that bed. I don't have the patience for your rules, regulations, or small talk right now!"

Elijah snatched his hand free of hers, waving it the air and blowing on it like he'd been burned.

Doctor McIntosh sighed, but took it in stride, glancing back down at her clipboard.

"I'm sorry to have to tell you this, especially in mixed company, but your sister has a considerable brain bleed."

Natalie's flush disappeared and her hand flew up to cover her mouth. Across the room, Anton's body jerked and he stumbled, catching himself on the corner of the bed.

"Unfortunately, the bleeding is so diffuse at this point, we are unable to pinpoint where it might have begun. This means we don't really have a viable surgical option. Our only remaining choice is to wait and see."

"Wait and see. You mean she could still heal on her own?" Natalie's voice came out on a squeak, high-pitched and hopeful.

The doctor pursed her thin lips together. Lowering the clipboard to her side, she gave Natalie an apologetic look.

"To be honest…a spontaneous resolution at this point is extremely unlikely. It's much more likely that the bleed will continue and your sister will pass on within a day or two. I suggest you make your peace with things and start saying your goodbyes." With that, the woman turned on her heel and left the room.

"What. An. Epic. Bitch," Callan muttered.

"It's not her fault. She's just doing her job," Asher reminded.

Natalie let out a ragged sob, and Elijah turned her back into him, holding her up when her legs buckled beneath her.

Asher shoved off the wall, beginning to pace in a long, angry lope. Callan stood and moved to look out the window, hand clasped behind his back.

"Its a long shot, but I could try to give her some of my blood. It's not something people really do anymore, but I don't know, maybe it could help with potential healing." Callan offered, not looking back at anyone.

"And what might that do? Risk her becoming some sort of vampire empath hybrid or something? Do we even know if that would actually help? What if her body rejects it and it just makes things worse?" Skyler asked from his position near the doorway.

Callan shrugged.

Anton stumbled around the end of the huge hospital bed, and took Mayla's hand in both of his own. His were still trembling, but he didn't even care.

He couldn't feel…anything…anymore.

It was as if his insides had simply been hollowed out, his heart and soul removed from his body and tossed away like garbage. He couldn't even feel his feet, though they were definitely still there when he glanced down. He barely registered when they lurched out from under him, only knew he landed in a chair that someone had shoved forward to catch his weight.

He felt like a sheet of glass that someone had hit with a sledgehammer. He was shattering.

Mayla couldn't die. She couldn't because he couldn't be here, on this earth without her. She couldn't die because if she did?

Then he was damn sure going to go with her.

"I love you, Mayla."

His voice came out on a croak, head dropping to rest on the small, cool hand he was clinging to like a lifeline.

All conversation in the room stopped, every gaze swinging to him.

"Wait, what?" Natalie whispered, pushing back from Elijah's arms, her face slack with shock. She turned an accusing eye to Elijah, poking him in the chest with a finger. "Highbloods don't do that. *YOU* told me that wasn't possible."

Elijah raised both hands in surrender and shrugged his shoulders at her glare, completely confused by his best friend's admission. He knew Anton was in full on lust for the girl, but love? How could he even know what that meant?

Skyler cleared his throat softly. "Anton, I'm truly sorry," his voice was low, comforting. "I know you're hurting right now. I know this is hard, but you're, I mean we are," he motioned to his own chest, and then around the room at the other males. His expression was pained.

"Highbloods don't really, we're not genetically able to—," he stopped talking.

His friend wasn't listening anyway.

Anton's huge shoulders trembled. "I love her. I treasure her more than my own life." His words were gravel and guts, the emotion behind them thick in his throat.

"SHE IS MINE. AND I AM HERS. ALWAYS."

Anton's head remained bowed, his forehead pressed against Mayla's hand. He didn't look up, didn't see the soft blue glow that lit up his left pectoral, the outline clearly visible through his shirt. He didn't see the blue continue to grow, didn't see it spread across his chest to travel down his arms in tiny rivers of light. Natalie gasped. Next to her Elijah stared, his mouth dropping open.

The symbol glowing on Anton's chest. The same one he'd seen all over his mother's research. The ancient symbol of eternal love. The Serch Bythol.

The symbol for fated mates.

"Sweet gods is that what I think it is?!" Callan asked, but Elijah waved a hand at him to shut it.

Asher slunk forward, wary but curious, his caramel eyes huge as he watched the scene unfolding at Mayla's bedside.

Anton spoke again, and a sudden, heavy power rolled through the room in waves.

"BY THE GODS OLD AND NEW, I CLAIM HER AS MY MATE. WHERE SHE GOES I SHALL GO. MY MAGIC IS HER MAGIC, MY HEART IS HER HEART. WHAT SHE NEEDS I SHALL ALWAYS PROVIDE. AND WHEN SHE MAY DIE…SO SHALL MY LIFE END."

The small blue rivers of light stopped flowing from Anton. They watched in stunned silence as the light moved up Mayla's chest, forming the same symbol right above her heart. The color pooled there for a moment before climbing the sides of her face to swirl in slow circles around her temples and forehead.

"WHAT IS HAPPENING TO HER?!" Natalie yelled, shaking off Elijah's arms and running to the other side of the bed.

Grabbing Mayla's free hand in hers, she brushed her sister's hair back from her forehead. She rubbed at the blue light there, but the light circling her sister's head never flickered. She hissed across the bed at Anton.

"What are you doing to her? Answer me!! I swear I will come across this bed and burn you to ash if you hurt her!!"

"Natalie. *Stop*. He's not hurting her, he's helping her." Elijah's voice was sharp and stern. He walked closer to the bed, his amber eyes locking with her hazel ones.

"Anton and Mayla are fated mates. They're fated, Natalie. See those marks?" He pointed first to Anton's chest, then to Mayla's.

"That's the mate mark. Their magics, their souls, even their lives, it's all one and the same now. Remember what I told you? About mates sharing their health if needed?"

Natalie stared at him, listening, her mouth quivering as she fought back tears. She gave him a tiny nod. His voice grew softer, gentling as he slowly removed both of her hands from her sister, holding them gently in his own.

"It means Anton is the only one with the slightest chance of helping her right now. He's acknowledged their mate bond. Maybe, hopefully, her magic will take what it needs from him and help her heal."

"But, Mayla's a Lowblood, how is something like this even possible?" Skyler sputtered, disbelieving.

"And she's not awake to acknowledge the bond," Callan let the thought drop, his voice dark and worried.

Elijah looked around to find everyone staring at him.

"I don't know," he shrugged, shaking his head. "The only thing I know for sure is that mark," he pointed to the pair of touching triskeles glowing above Mayla's heart, "is the fated mate mark. No one even remembers the last pair, it's been so long. So the only thing we know for sure, is that we don't know shit."

Asher prowled forward, his faded work boots silent on the linoleum. He placed a comforting hand on Anton's bowed shoulder, but the silver haired Highblood didn't flinch. Asher gave him a slight shake. No response.

"Anton." Nothing.

Asher's worried look bounced back to the others. "He's breathing, but I don't think he's asleep."

They all stayed silent a moment, watching the blue light swirling across Mayla's forehead. Both mate marks still pulsed like heartbeats.

Skyler spoke up from the doorway, his words soft and ominous.

"Well they're obviously connected now. Somehow the mate bond looks like it's been accepted. Which means either they'll both wake up eventually," he sent a long look to each of the others, "or...," he stopped talking, exchanging looks with the Highbloods in the room.

"Or what?!" Natalie demanded.

"Or we don't just lose her...*we lose them both.*"

25

The beeping of her alarm kept trying to pull her up out of sleep, but Mayla didn't want to wake up yet. She was in the middle of the most amazing dream.

She and Anton were spending the day in her sun filled courtyard, just the two of them. There were no interruptions, no phone calls, no stress, just the two of them and plenty of relaxation. They'd had a picnic, gone for a stroll, then dozed in the sunshine. She felt so warm and peaceful, resting her head on his chest, as they laughed together, sometimes stealing kisses just for fun. She felt so calm, so at ease. She wanted to stay here forever.

The steady, aggravating beeping continued, and she sighed, irritated. She really should get up and give Pan his breakfast. If she didn't he'd start mewling up and down the hallway in misery. Natalie would be furious if he woke her up again, and the relationship between those two was already tenuous at best.

She sighed. Fine.

She pressed a soft kiss against Anton's dream shoulder and opened her eyes.

The pain in her head registered instantly.

* * *

She slammed her eyes shut again, fighting the white hot lance of pain that shot across her forehead. What the hell happened last night? Gods her head was *pounding*. Was she hungover? She wasn't a big drinker, never had much of a tolerance for the stuff, but occasionally, when she, Natalie, and Willow got together…

Willow. Willow was missing. The Anord had taken her.

Anton and the task force were helping to look for her. They'd been at headquarters and then…Carl Richards. *Samuel*. The abandoned beauty shop. She'd carried Samuel up the stairs, but he'd been unresponsive. She had to help him, had to stabilize the boy but then…just like an old fashioned video at the end of its reel, everything went white after that.

What had happened?

When another stab of pain shot through her forehead, she sucked in a deep breath. The smell of crisp clove, winter and sandalwood wrapped around her like a hug. She'd recognize that scent anywhere.

Anton.

She cracked her eyes open once more, keeping them squinted against the blaring light. Wait, were they in the hospital? She didn't try to move, just looked slowly around, letting her eyes move while her mind took stock of any other aches and pains. Her head was the worst. Her body seemed okay, a little achy but no major injuries.

Her hands…

She looked down to find her fingers interlaced with Anton's and immediately the pain seemed to soften. He sat in a chair, his broad back curved over the side of the hospital bed, his head laying next to their joined hands. His face was turned in her direction, and his light blue eyes watched her silently. The love in his eyes was so strong she forgot about the pain in her head for a moment. She didn't move, a sense of warm contentment spreading over her like a warm blanket. All the words they would eventually say, all the knowledge of forever, hovered right there. Right where his icy blue wind and her dark blue ocean combined.

Hours later, as everyone sat around her bed in the cheap

plastic chairs Elijah had snagged from the cafeteria, Mayla couldn't stop the sudden swell of affection that flowed through her. They were all talking and laughing together, devouring burgers and fries like they hadn't had a real meal in forever.

Which, now that she thought about it, they probably hadn't.

With the exception of Skyler - who was still on active duty and had left to report back to base - the rest had only left this room long enough to grab coffee, visit the restroom, or pay way too much for crackers from the vending machine.

Anton had been out for two full days, and she'd woken up almost a full day later. After all the hugging and tears of relief, Callan had regaled her with how - shortly after the mate marks had appeared and Anton had become unresponsive - Asher had mobilized a protection team from headquarters to set up outside of Mayla's room. Even the doctor's hadn't been allowed in during those two days, no matter how much they pestered, threatened and cajoled.

Only after Anton had come to, was the hospital staff allowed back in to check them over. When a male nurse stuck a needle in Mayla's arm to draw blood however, it had taken Asher, Elijah, and Callan to keep a still groggy Anton from ripping the man apart with his bare hands.

His mate mark, as well as Mayla's, both flared bright blue during the scuffle, and the secret was officially out. Only after a solemn promise that no more needles would touch his mate, did Anton begrudgingly allow them to examine the now permanent markings. After the fifth doctor had been 'called in to confirm', Anton's eyes had turned white and Elijah had hurriedly ushered them all out of the room for their own safety.

Now, thanks to Callan and Asher running out to pick up burgers for everyone, they were all eating and smiling. They'd only have a few hours before the entire city found out about the newest pair of fated mates.

But they were all starving. So…food first…cultural phenomenon later.

Natalie was currently peppering Anton with questions.

"Right, but how did you know? How could you tell that you loved her? That she was your," she waved haphazardly at his chest and then her sister's, "whatever, your mate. Gosh, that is just so weird to say out loud."

Anton looked at her a moment, an indulgent smile on his face.

"I think it started when I first met her. I couldn't get her out of my mind, even for a moment. The more time we spent together, the more I started to pick up on what she was thinking. I could tell when she was nervous, happy, or even when she was tired. When Skyler told us how incredibly strong her empath magic is, I assumed it might be projecting things without her knowing it. But when she came to the apartment to be treated by Ariadne, something strange happened.

They were in the bedroom, I was in the kitchen. We weren't in the same room, but suddenly I knew exactly how she was laying across my bed. I could see the view out the windows the way she was seeing it. Then an image floated into my head. It was like a photograph, but of myself. That was my first sign that something else was going on."

Mayla swallowed a mouthful of soda and flushed red, trying to smother a giggle.

"I was thinking of you shirtless," she said on a half whisper. "That's why you dropped the mug, and why you couldn't look at me."

Anton grinned at her, his hand quickly catching hers, pulling it to his mouth to press a soft kiss against her knuckles.

"I knew she was in the other room, and that the image had come from her. When we met with Skyler," his eyes darted to a sudden tensing of Mayla's shoulders. She was worried he was going to talk about her panic attack. He gave her hand a small squeeze and sent her an ever so slight shake of his head.

"I knew when she needed a break, and when she was thirsty. When Skyler said I was her anchor, I decided maybe that was the reason for all of it, that anchor bond."

He didn't miss the easing of her shoulders, or the tiny, thankful smile on her face. "After we were," he cleared his throat, color flaring briefly in his own cheeks before he continued, "we were...together—"

"Oh my gods!! I knew it! You slept with him!" Natalie laughed, wiggling her eyebrows and gently swatting at her sister's shoulder.

Mayla dodged, grinning, and threw a French fry at her sister. "Don't be jealous."

Natalie snorted into her soda, her eyes sliding quickly over to Elijah, who was currently downing his third fully-loaded bacon cheeseburger, completely oblivious. Both women dissolved into gales of laughter as Asher and Callan exchanged tortured looks.

Elijah finally looked up from his burger. "What's so funny? Keep going, A, I want to hear the rest of the story."

Anton swallowed a grin but continued, "As soon as we were together, I just started to know what she needed all the time. I knew when she was awake or asleep, when she was angry or annoyed. I even knew when she was—," the color in his cheeks deepened, reaching his ears this time, but his eyes flared with heat, "when she wanted me."

Callan made a loud gagging noise and Mayla's eyes went huge before she lowered her gaze, pretending to be fascinated by the weave of the blanket over her legs.

The heat in Anton's eyes disappeared and the blue lightened dangerously. "But when we found her…at that salon…I tried. I tried to feel what she needed, what she was feeling, but I couldn't. And when the doctor said—" his voice caught, and he cleared his throat forcefully, taking a moment to swallow hard.

Mayla give his hand a tug. When he looked over at her, she mouthed, I'm okay and sent him a soft smile. He smiled back before continuing.

"When I thought I was going to lose her, the words were suddenly there, pounding in my head, demanding to be spoken. That's when I realized it wasn't her magic or the anchor bond. It was stronger than all of that. The idea of being here, or anywhere, without her was just, impossible. The words kept getting louder and louder in my head and finally I couldn't fight them. After I said them I have no memory of what happened.

The next thing I remember I was waking up, and it was back. I knew she was safe. My mind, my body, hell maybe it was even my soul, but everything in me said she was going to be okay."

He moved from his chair to sit next to Mayla on the bed, gathering her into his arms. She pressed her cheek to his chest and held on, hard. He lowered his chin to rest on the top of her head and loosed a long breath.

"Thank the fucking gods," he whispered.

Their mate marks gleamed.

Elijah rolled his eyes and let out a tortured groan. "You two are going to be all lovey-dovey disgusting and impossible to be around now, aren't you?"

Later that same afternoon, hours after Asher and Callan had been sent home with hugs from Mayla and strict instructions from Anton to take a day off and relax, Mayla found herself woken gently from her nap by a plump, gray-haired nurse.

"My dear, isn't it wonderful? Before they release you, the news station has come by, they're going to do an interview! The city wants to know all about how you saved that boy, and how you and that handsome fellow of yours are the first set of fated mates in centuries!" The woman rambled on happily, but Mayla felt her heartbeat quicken.

"An interview?" She rubbed the sleep from her eyes, sitting up in the bed. "I'm not sure I'm really ready for...," she trailed off as the door to her hospital room was propped open, a group of strangers filing in.

A well-dressed man with slicked back dark hair carried a microphone that looked way too big in his hand. A short balding man in an Atlanta Braves jersey followed close behind, a large video camera balanced precariously on one shoulder.

Natalie, sitting in a chair against the far wall and flipping quietly through a fashion magazine, rose to her feet.

"I don't think this is a good idea, she still needs rest," she began, taking a step towards the bed.

The cherub faced nurse waved her off. "Nonsense! The doctor said it would be just fine. She's stabilized and her test results are all clear, she'll even be released this evening to head home. Isn't this exciting? You're going to be famous! A mated pair hasn't been seen in my lifetime you know!" She patted Mayla's hand as she busied herself tucking the blankets around her legs, then fluffed the pillows behind her.

A severe looking brunette woman in a navy blue pants suit approached one side of the bed, waving a form at Mayla. "If you could just sign this release form my dear, it's just a formality. It allows us to air the interview not only tonight, but again at a later date if the network chooses to do so. Everyone is dying to see you and hear about how all this happened! Now, where is that mate of yours?"

Mayla's head started to throb. More people filed in, nurses, doctors, people in regular clothes that she'd never even seen before. They were all so excited and the sensation hammered at her. The room took on a pink glow and she felt a sweet syrupy tartness fill her mouth. That was new. She'd never been able to taste emotions before. She didn't have time to fully contemplate the new development, because her stomach somersaulted and she had to fight down a wave of bile.

Her eyes looked around desperately for her sister, but Natalie was blocked three or four people deep from the bed as more people continued to pour into the room. Even the janitor stood just inside the doorway. Mayla could sense her sister's frustration and the slow burn of her building anger. She caught a glimpse of long red hair as Natalie left the room in a huff, no doubt on her way to find an administrator and hopefully put an end to all this.

Mayla needed to close her eyes. She needed to go into her mind, make sure her door was shut tight. She wasn't using her magic, but her head still hurt so bad she couldn't afford to take any chances. Still, no matter how hard she focused, she couldn't find her courtyard. All she could sense was an orange throbbing heartbeat, and the rhythm perfectly matched the pounding in her head.

Her breath came quicker, her heartbeat jumping. The nurse patted the back of her hand, and the woman's excitement tingled up Mayla's arm. Suddenly she was trembling so badly her teeth were chattering.

Her skin began its telltale tingling, her palms going clammy. She could feel the emotions pouring into her. The fatigue from the reporter, well masked but still there. The greed from the suited woman still waving papers under her nose. The boredom rolling off the overweight cameraman. Her chest started to ache, her breaths scraping up her throat with every exhale. She needed to turn it off. To shut it down. She needed the opposite of all this chaos. She needed...

"An...An...Anton." It came out as a stuttering chatter, but the name was clear. When she got no response she tried again, louder this time, her panic gaining momentum.

"Anton?" she glanced around, desperate to find his face in the midst of this chaos, "Where's Anton?!"

"Anton? Oh yes dear, he's still here. He's out in the hall with the doctor I believe. He'll be back any minute, don't you worry. I'm sure the reporters have already sent someone to get him. They're going to want to talk to him too, you know."

The pudgy hand the nurse kept patting her with smelled like cheap, lavender lotion and the fake sincerity in her voice made Mayla's temples ache.

The dark haired reporter sat down on the right side of the bed, the blankets tightening across her thighs from the added weight. He smelled like cheap aftershave and stale coffee, and she could suddenly taste the dried-out sawdust of his desperation. Her stomach flipped and she tried not to gag. He motioned to the bored cameraman who took up a position over his shoulder. Her vision blurred and she blinked at the small red light focused on her.

"Now Mayla, is it okay to call you Mayla?" he began, sticking the huge microphone just under her nose. He continued without waiting for her to respond.

"Miradea is absolutely abuzz with the news that we have a brand new pair of fated mates! Would you mind showing us your mate mark? I know the entire city is just dying to see it!"

It was too much. Too much noise. Too many people. Too much, too much, too much.

Mayla felt it growing inside her chest until her ribs hurt, building until she could contain it no longer. It shot up her throat like a bullet and climbed out of her mouth on a scream.

"ANTONNN!!!!"

26

Anton stood in the hallway just around the corner from Mayla's hospital room, and thought seriously about digging his eyeballs out with a rusty spoon. It would be much less painful than trying to get actual information out of this doctor.

All he wanted to know was when Mayla would be released. He needed to get her home where she could get some real rest. They were all so exhausted and irritated from the constant in and out of the hospital staff today that even Elijah had gone in search of coffee.

The man didn't like coffee.

Mayla had finally dozed off, so while Natalie was keeping an eye on her he'd come looking for the doctor. He found her after about ten minutes of searching, but he still couldn't get a straight answer out of the woman to save his life.

"So far, the tests we've done do reveal some minor anemia and some definite adrenal fatigue, but her scans show she's made a complete recovery from the brain bleed. I have no idea how, but there's no trace of it anywhere. Her medicine regimen we've gone over already. When she heads home she'll need a strong multivitamin, and a healthy diet is an absolute must. I'd love to get some more blood though to run just a few more tests."

Anton's look had her backtracking in a hurry.

"That's not absolutely necessary at this point though, I'll admit. I will take a look at her records again when I get a chance and get back with you on when we can see about getting her discharged. I assure you there's nothing to worry about, once we've got everything ready on our end we'll let you know."

Anton seethed. Again, no actual answer. Just more hurry up and wait. So help him, if this doctor dared to pat his shoulder, he was going to send her surfing down the hallway on her ass, woman or no.

Realizing he was overreacting, he pulled in a deep breath, but it didn't help. He was on edge. His skin felt over sensitive, and his heart was thundering in this chest. Even his breathing had shortened into weird little gasps.

What was happening to him? Something was…strange. It felt like he were watching this happen to someone else. Which meant the feelings weren't his. The panic flaring inside his mind was coming from…

His mate.

He side stepped the doctor instantly, completely unconcerned as she sputtered after him.

"Sir? Sir. I'll need you to—"

Coming around the corner, he ran smack into Natalie, his hands shooting out to catch her by the shoulders when she bounced off his chest.

"Ooofff, gods you really are a solid hunk of man meat aren't you?" She rubbed at her forehead, her brows furrowed, looking slightly dazed.

"Hey, I need your help, the television station is here and they want an interview. I really think Mayla is still too exhausted to deal with something like this, but I can't find a single doctor or administrator willing to shut it down. Now they've let a bunch of people in the room and—"

"ANTONNN!!!"

When he heard his mate's scream Anton's entire body

jerked, his head immediately snapping towards the doorway to her room. He was around Natalie and through the door in the next second, his focus narrowing on one thing and one thing only.

Mayla.

He needed to get to her.

Right. Fucking. Now.

As he pushed through the throng of people gathered at the door, he had to fight to keep his magic leashed. His ice roared at him, itching to kill everyone standing in the way. Where had all these idiots come from? Anton barely registered a nurse in pink scrubs snapping photos with her cell phone before he snatched the device out of her hands and crushed it under his heel. When he was finally able to catch sight of Mayla over the heads of all the people gathered, his blood boiled.

She was terrified, propped up too straight on too many pillows, a panicked, nauseated look on her pale face. People crowded the bed, standing or sitting too close on all sides. A sleaze-bag reporter who reeked of drugstore aftershave was shoving a microphone of ridiculous proportions in her face, a smaller, rounder man pointing a video camera directly at her.

Elijah and Natalie entered the room just behind him, Elijah immediately dumping the two full coffees he carried into the trash, but Anton didn't have time to acknowledge them.

His only focus was Mayla. She needed him.

And all these people? They were standing between him and his mate. A very, very dangerous thing to do. He didn't look at their faces. They were no longer people, they were simply obstacles. He shoved, pulled, even picked up a few, tossing them unceremoniously behind him. The reporter was hauled off the bed by his collar and stumbled back, bumping into the cameraman who tried frantically to steady things with his one free hand. When the reporter protested, beginning to push forward again, Anton turned, arms folding across his massive chest. The smaller man opened his mouth, ready to argue, but Anton's ice white glare had him snapping it shut again and reconsidering his options.

Anton turned back to the bed. He could sense the fatigue and the headache battling within Mayla. Her eyes were squeezed shut and her breathing was jagged, coming in harsh gulps. She was too pale again, all the color she'd regained after eating earlier had disappeared. He could see she was trembling, her exhaustion riding her hard.

He should definitely kill the reporter, no question.

Anton took her hand gently, leaning over to touch his lips to her forehead. Gods but her hand was so cold.

"I'm here, milacek. I'm right here," he whispered against her skin.

Her eyes cracked open, and his heart ached at the immediate timid hope that sprouted there.

"Anton," his name was a whisper of relief on her lips, a prayer of salvation.

"What do you want me to do, Mayla? Whatever you need right this minute, just say it." He kept his voice low, his tone soothing.

"I need you to make it stop, Anton. Make the world stop. Please. Just, *get me out of here*," her eyes opened fully, and he saw tears of frustration gathering there.

"I'm too tired to find the barrier. I can feel all of it. All of *them*. It's too much, I just, I can't," she said, reaching for him.

In a flash he had her in his arms, the blanket tucked in tight around her, her head resting against his chest. Their mate marks flared as he turned away from the bed and the crowd let out a collective gasp. Camera's flashed and phones were lifted, the crowd pushing closer. He felt Mayla cringe.

"We need just a short video— "

"One more photo for the web page, it'll only take a second — "

"Gods, would you look at at that! The marks! I wonder what causes them to—"

Anton sent a quick, pointed look to Elijah, then threw back his shoulders, raised his chin high…

And unfurled his massive wings with a loud SNAP.

His left wing, by sheer coincidence of course, smacked the reporter in the head, knocking him onto the cold, vinyl floor. The right knocked a stack of papers out of the hands of a business woman with a tight bun.

And the room went deathly quiet.

His wings took up a lot of space, but their massive size wasn't what was terrifying everyone into silence. It was the dagger shaped icicles now edging every individual feather. Deep purple and interwoven with streaks of silver, the feathers looked both silky soft and razor sharp at the same time, their deadly intent crystal clear.

Anton looked slowly around, his glare a blatant warning. He unleashed a bit more magic and the temperature in the room plummeted, icy condensation spreading quickly across the windows, the pitcher of water on a nearby table freezing solid. Small white puffs of air escaped from the mouths of all the onlookers.

Mayla snuggled deeper into his neck, her breath coming in small, hiccuping gasps, and he couldn't resist lowering his forehead to hers for the briefest of moments. When he raised his eyes once more, his pupils had gone completely white.

"You will not get in my way, and you will not block my path. You will remain quiet and respectful or I will freeze every ounce of water in this room, including the water inside each of you."

The temperature in the room dropped another ten degrees, and the people quickly separated, clearing a path to the door.

As Anton rounded the end of the bed and quickly left the room, Elijah stepped right into the doorway behind him and unfurled his own wings, blocking the exit. The rich brown interwoven with gold shimmered in the overhead light. He clapped his hands together loudly before raising both well muscled arms above his head, revealing two black shoulder holsters lined with knives hanging out just under his jacket. His voice was loud, and obnoxiously cheerful.

"Good afternoon everyone! My name is Elijah and I am happy to announce that I will be your fuck-around-and-find out tour guide this evening! I strongly suggest you keep all arms and legs inside this room at all times until I give you permission to leave. Any arms, legs, or heads found outside this room," he looked pointedly at the reporter, who was trying to inch his way around them, "especially yours, Urban Aftershave Cowboy, will be immediately removed and happily returned to you at the end of the tour."

The reporter froze in his tracks, his eyes going wide. Natalie stood to his left with her arms crossed, her mouth grinning up at Elijah in devilish delight. He looked her up and down, loving the way a slight blush colored her cheeks at his attention, then gave her a slow wink before turning back to the people before him.

Lowering his arms, his hands unsheathed and palmed two knives so fast no one actually saw him move. He spun them in his palms and smiled wickedly.

"Now. Who's got questions?"

Out in the hallway, employees of the hospital gawked openly as Anton brushed past them without a glance, his stride quickly eating up the distance to the elevator. As they approached the doors, he pulled his wings down and around the two of them, shielding Mayla from prying eyes. The ice from earlier had disappeared, the feathers cocooning her in warm solitude.

When the elevator opened, the eyes of two masked nurses inside went saucer huge. They darted out of the way quickly at Anton's intense look, their heads lowered, and their eyes to the floor.

As he stepped into the elevator and turned, looking back down the hallway, Anton saw Elijah, gods bless the man, blocking the door to the hospital room with his own massive wings, trapping the chaos inside. He wasn't sure exactly what his friend was saying, but as the doors closed, the joyful peal of Natalie's laughter echoed clearly down the hall.

The next afternoon, Anton stood quietly at the doorway to his bedroom, watching his mate sleep.

His *mate*.

She looked so tiny, sound asleep in his king-size bed, gray sheets dark against the ivory white of her soft skin. She was such a deceptive package. Small, pale and soft spoken, and yet absolutely the strongest person he'd ever met. He didn't think anyone else could have survived an injury like that, mate bond or no. Yesterday, when they'd left the hospital after all the chaos, she'd fallen asleep in the car before they'd even left the parking lot, his right hand gripped tightly in her lap. When they finally arrived at home, she hadn't stirred as he carried her into the building, rode the elevator up to the apartment and tucked her into his bed. That had been almost eleven hours ago, and he prayed she slept for another eleven.

He needed her healed and healthy. Not for the case - screw the case and any other that might come along - he needed her healthy for his own peace of mind. He needed to see her laugh again, see a pink blush in her cheeks, see her happily living. It was the only way to yank his thoughts away from the dark horror that took hold whenever he recalled how close he had come to losing her.

He knew one thing for sure. Now that she was his mate, she would never be put at risk like that again. He should have stayed with her and let Asher handle the search. He knew better, but he'd been so worried about finding Samuel. Now of course, he realized it hadn't been just his own worry, but hers as well. Still, he'd learned his lesson.

From here on out he would protect her with his last breath if that's what it took. He was her anchor, her safe space, her buffer against the darkness of the world whenever she needed him. But she was also his moonlight, his beautiful ocean tide and his reason for existing in this world. He'd meant it when only days ago he'd stood in this apartment and told her he'd stop the world. Gods, if she decided she wanted him to stop this planet from turning on its axis he'd somehow make it happen.

She let out a soft sigh in her sleep and he smiled, stepping back into the hallway and quietly closing the door. He returned to the kitchen, files now cluttering the table. He'd slept next to Mayla for the first eight hours, her body tucked in close against his, and it had been the best sleep he'd had in days.

Once awake he decided to spend some of his down time going over everything they had on Carl Richards so far. He was searching for any clue regarding the old building Mayla had told them about, the one where Richards had been dropping off kids every so often. He still couldn't fathom what use the Anord might have for Lowblood children, much less why they'd need to be delivered on some kind of schedule. Since he'd completely stalled out on the why, he'd taken a step back to look at the big picture.

Tomorrow morning he'd put Callan on a deep dive for a thorough list of any larger buildings more than twenty years old still standing in the city. For today, absolutely everyone on his team was at home on mandatory time off. They'd stayed at the hospital watching over he and Mayla for days without batting an eye, without showering or eating or giving one second of thought to what they might need instead of what he and his mate needed. A swelling of pride filled his chest. They were damn good men, every single one of them.

And as for Natalie, well, she was starting to grow on him. It had taken him a while, but he'd finally realized the woman's fierceness only came from a place of intense love and protectiveness.

Something the two of them seemed to have in common lately.

There was a soft tapping at his front door.

Moving to the front hallway and pulling it open, Anton was startled when the woman he'd just been thinking about launched herself into his arms, squeezing him tight in a warm hug.

"It took me a while to admit it, even to myself, but without you, I would have lost my sister. Thank you, for saving her," Natalie whispered against his shoulder.

Anton relaxed, returning the hug. "You're welcome, but you don't need to thank me. She did much more of the work than I did. I'm pretty sure I was just a backup battery." He looked over her head to where Elijah stood in the hallway.

The man was carrying five - no six - bags, and he looked well past irritated. He shuffled past them into the apartment, unceremoniously dropping the bags to the floor. Natalie jumped back instantly, staring daggers at him.

"Be *careful* with those! There are breakable items in there!"

Elijah rolled his eyes, focusing instead on Anton.

"This pain in the ass packed half of her apartment to bring to her sister. Explain something to me. Why do women need three different kinds of shampoo? And what the hell is the difference between *lounge wear* and *pajamas*? It all looks the damn same to me! And, most importantly, why is frilly girl shit so heavy?"

Natalie's hands planted firmly on her hips. "Excuse me, Mr.-I-Have-Muscles-But-Apparently-They're-Just-For-Show. I didn't realize carrying bags filled with my poor, recovering sister's clothes would be so incredibly hard for you to manage."

Anton grinned, walking behind the two of them as they continued on into the apartment, bickering. He wondered absently if they would ever realize they were kind of made for each other. Then again, maybe the two of them being together really wasn't a good idea after all. Too many things might get destroyed. Lamps. Windows. Entire city blocks.

Mayla's sister and his second-in-command stayed just long enough for a cup of coffee for her and a soda for him. Natalie checked in once on her sleeping sister, then stocked his bathroom with all things female before leaving. She gave him explicit instructions on what to tell Mayla about the clothes she'd brought over - instructions he'd completely forgotten as soon as they were given - and then they left, Elijah agreeing to meet with him and the rest of the team the following morning at headquarters.

Some time later, Anton sat in front of his open laptop, scanning through a flash drive of photos that had been discovered during the search of Richards' studio apartment. There were 347 in all, most of them surveillance photos of children at various schools, parks and other locations. He'd already emailed to get a few officers working on digging out the timestamps for the photos and tracking down the kids as soon as possible. Unfortunately they had no other way of knowing if these were previous targets or potential ones.

When Mayla's soft hands slid over his shoulders from behind, he breathed her in, loving that wind and clean ocean scent. He'd known as soon as she woke, felt her small start of fear resolve quickly into peace and contentment once she'd recognized his bedroom. He loved that he could give her that.

Now she leaned warmly against his back, her arms draping over his shoulders and her chin resting gently on top of his head.

"Hi," she whispered.

He turned in his chair, pulling her around in front of him, wrapping his arms around her waist and pressing his head against her chest. He held her as tight as he dared, the only sound the soft rasp of their breathing. Her hands burrowed deep into his hair, her fingertips trailing softly through the thick strands. He thanked the gods that Mayla didn't try to pull away from him, that she was perfectly content to let him just hold her for as long as he needed. When he finally leaned his head back to look up at her, his arms still didn't loosen.

Their eyes met and she smiled down at him.

"I'm sorry if I scared you. After you and Asher left, I realized where Samuel was. My instincts told me he was hurt worse than we thought so I couldn't wait. Once I found him, when I touched him, I knew he was going to die if I didn't do something. I'm sorry."

Anton shook his head. "No. No more apologies. You don't ever have to apologize to me for helping someone, Mayla. That's part of who you are. Because of *you* Samuel is alive, safe and at home with his family right now. Because of *you* he will get the chance to grow up, maybe even have a family of his own someday."

"You sure you're not upset?" Her expression made her doubt clear.

"I'm not upset *with you*. I'm upset because I can't stop thinking of how close I came to losing you. I didn't realize until it was almost too late that you were my—"

"Your completely badass better half? Your reason for being? The calm and reasonable side of your crazy strong, overprotective attitude?" She paused a moment, the mischief in her eyes shifting to something deeper, warmer.

"Your fated mate?"

Anton stared at her a moment, then sighed. "I know you heard everyone talking about it at the hospital, but do you really know what that means, Mayla? For a Highblood I mean? I t means *I love you*. Now, forever, *always*. It means we can never be separated. It means there is you and *only you* for me. There's no one else, not ever. Are you ready for all that?"

Mayla ran her hands through his hair once more, a calming smile on her lips.

"Relax, Light Eyes. I know you Highbloods like your folklore, but lucky for you, even us Lowbloods are allowed to use the public library. I've read the histories. I'm sure there's plenty I don't know, and we'll have to figure some of it out as we go, but I know one thing for sure."

"And what is that?"

Her face went completely serious, all traces of teasing gone. "Anton, *I love you*. I was born to love you. I was meant to be your mate. I was put here on this earth to be with you, always." The mate marking above her heart glowed, emphasizing the truth in her words.

Suddenly he was out of the chair, she was in his arms, and they were moving quickly down the hall, back towards the bedroom.

She giggled. "Was it something I said?"

That small sound of happiness was heaven to his ears, easing some of his earlier terror. He looked at her, his gaze pure blazing heat, his eyes never leaving hers.

"The woman I love, my MATE, just told me she loves me for the first time. I think that calls for a little intimate celebration."

"Just a little?" She teased.

"Trust me, this celebration is growing bigger by the second."

Her laugh floated above their heads as he kicked the bedroom door closed behind them.

27

Anton and Mayla stood side-by-side in the kitchen, making sandwiches and cutting up fruit, both of them starving. Anton couldn't stop sneaking looks at her, loving the way his white MTF t-shirt hung to mid thigh on her and kept slipping down off one shoulder.

She was deliciously disheveled, long black hair loose around her shoulders, face pink with the flush of their repeated lovemaking. They'd planned to make lunch over an hour ago, but as soon as Anton had slipped on his gray lounging pants, not bothering with a shirt, his mate had gone absolutely feral on him. The raw lust in her eyes had him hardening again in an instant. Then she'd dropped to her knees before him, sliding those same lounging pants down before wrapping those amazing lips around him and pulling him fully into the heat of her mouth.

He'd almost exploded right then and there.

Her mouth was exquisite, all soft silk heat, and for a moment he'd forgotten his entire existence. His name, his sense of self, his whole world, there was nothing but the blissful torture she was inflicting on him with her hands and mouth. She'd drawn it out, pressing him back to lean against the wall, bringing him right to the edge before easing him away again, the wicked smile on her lips telling him she reveled in the complete and total power she was holding over him.

When she'd finally taken mercy on him, pushing him over that sensual edge to free-fall into ecstasy, his knees had buckled so hard he'd grabbed the closest piece of furniture to keep from falling on his face. When he accidentally snapped the corner of the dresser clean off, the two of them had fallen to the floor in a fit of laughter.

Now, back out in the kitchen, Mayla opened one of the cabinets, reaching up on tiptoe for a bag of chips, the edge of his t-shirt climbing just high enough that the globes of her ass barely peeked out beneath.

His breath punched out of his lungs. This woman was going to be the death of him and he was ready to die a happy man. He moved behind her, reaching over her head to retrieve the chips, the thin fabric of his lounging pants hiding absolutely none of his arousal as it pressed solidly against her backside.

She gasped, then giggled, peeking over her shoulder at him.

"As much as I love what you're thinking right now, we have to eat first, Anton."

He pressed a kiss to the side of her neck before he moved away, snatching the plate of fruit and carrying it over to the table.

"Eating is overrated," he groused, plopping into a chair and snatching a slice of apple with a petulant look.

Mayla grabbed the plate of sandwiches and the bag of chips, joining him at the table and laughing in earnest.

"You're actually pouting," she said, her expression delighted. "Do you know you're absolutely adorable when you pout?"

He cut his eyes at her but didn't respond, reaching instead for a sandwich and taking a huge bite. He groaned when the food hit his taste buds.

"Damn that is good."

Mayla nodded, raising her eyebrows at him across the table. "I told you. We need fuel before we get back to exploring any other mate bonding activities," she teased. Mayla reached for a sandwich herself, her arm bumping the side of Anton's laptop as she did so. A list of thumb-nailed images lit up the screen and she paused.

Anton moved to push the laptop aside, but Mayla placed a gentle hand on his arm.

"What are these? Are they...did you get these…from him? From Carl Richards?" Her voice was calm but oddly hollow, her eyes glazed.

"Shit, Mayla, you don't need to see any of this. I was just going over the contents of a flash drive that we found. I'm sorry, I didn't even think about you seeing these after everything you've been through. I'm an idiot. Let me just put it away."

He tried to close the laptop, but once more she stopped him. Her voice was suddenly eerily vacant, not like her at all.

"No need. I'm fine."

Her hand hovered over the keyboard, not typing, just barely touching. A few moments later she tilted her head, staring off into space.

"Photo 184."

"What?"

Her expression didn't change, but her tone grew more insistent. "*Photo 184.*"

Anton stared at her a long moment, then looked down at the laptop. Alternating between glancing at the screen and looking up at her, he scrolled until he found it. Photo 184 was a large brick building. An empty school perhaps?

"I found it, it's a picture of a building. Mayla…what is this? What does it mean?"

"Photo 184," she repeated, deadpan.

Her expression was so blank it was starting to terrify him. He reached over and grabbed her hand across the table, giving it a little shake.

"Mayla? Mayla look at me."

As soon as his hand made contact, her dark blue eyes cleared and she blinked. Her face was confused as she looked down at the sandwich on her plate, then back over to him. Sudden fear washed over her face.

"Anton?"

"Mayla," his response was slow and painfully gentle, as if he was talking to someone in shock at a crime scene. "Do you know what you just did?"

Her eyes were big, and worried. She shook her head.

"We were sitting down to eat when you saw these photos. After you touched the laptop you kept telling me 'Photo 184, Photo 184'. Repeatedly."

Mayla looked down at where their hands were clasped tightly together.

"I…I remember bumping the laptop. After that it felt like, like I was somehow back in Carl's mind. But that's not possible, right? There's no way that could be possible. They photos were spread out in front of me. They looked like a fan the way they were all laid out. That one jumped up and just hung in the air, right in front of me." Her voice trembled a little. "I don't even know how I knew the number."

Anton pulled her out of her chair and snuggled her into his lap, her worry starting to concern him. She was holding something back, he knew it. Something important.

He rubbed gentle circles against her spine, kissing her temple and then her cheek.

"What else? Talk to me, *milacek*. I'm right here and you are perfectly safe, I swear it. What else did you see?" he whispered.

"I can't say it. It doesn't make sense and it means I might actually be nuts," she whispered back.

"Well then, of course you have to tell me. I've made an entire career out of studying the stuff that doesn't make sense, remember? This is literally what I get paid to do."

A small smile curled her lips and she took a deep breath.

"Please Mayla. Just tell me."

"I think the place in the photo might be a psychiatric hospital. After I saw the photo and the number in my head, I kept seeing people in straitjackets. Some were strapped to strange machines and others were sitting in padded rooms. It was old, like a scary movie. I wanted it to stop, but I couldn't look away until you touched me."

She looked up at him, her eyes filling with worry.

"Do you think I might have damaged something? Up here?" She tapped the side of her head with one finger. "When I healed Samuel I mean?"

He pulled her against his chest, wrapping both arms tightly around her shoulders and pressing a kiss to the top of her head. After a long moment he stood up, setting her on her feet, then took her hand and led her back towards the bedroom.

"Anton, I'm sorry, but I really don't think I—," her tone was wistful and he knew exactly what she was mistakenly thinking.

"You and I are going to lay in bed and watch TV. I'm going to bring the food in too. We're going to put on some gods awful cheesy romcom while we eat, and then I'm going to hold you in my arms until you stop feeling scared and fall asleep."

He stopped, grabbing her other hand and turning her slowly to face him.

"It's too easy for you to think that you're somehow damaged or crazy, Mayla. *When* are you going to believe me when I tell you are amazingly, beautifully, phenomenally *perfect*?"

She looked at him, hopeful, but clearly doubtful.

"I am your mate, Mayla. That bond goes much deeper than husband and wife, or simple lovers. I know exactly what you're feeling, and right now your fear is stabbing me in the heart."

He pulled her in for a hug, his chin dropping, lips whispering against her hair.

"What you just saw would scare anyone, love, but it doesn't mean you're broken. It means your empath magic is strengthening. It's starting to branch out and try new things. Do you remember Skyler telling us about empaths in the past who could touch objects and get images from them?"

When she didn't respond, he gave her a tender, silly little shake.

She finally nodded against his chest. "I remember," she mumbled into his shoulder.

He smiled. "Now who's pouting? Tomorrow morning we'll have Adriana stop by just to look you over, but we BOTH already know you're perfectly fine. I'll call Skyler and get some afternoons set up where you can start practicing with all this and then it won't be quite so scary, okay? Then we'll go into headquarters, so Callan can find the location of that building. He'll prove to you that you're the most magical person I've ever been smart enough to fall in love with."

The next morning, Elijah clapped his hands together as he walked towards the white panel van taking up space in one of the numerous garage bays at MTF headquarters. It was too hot today for his usual bomber jacket, so his shoulder holsters were in clear view, stretched snugly over a skin tight black t-shirt that read I Like Knives and Maybe Three People.

A team of forensic techs were currently swarming the van like ants on a week-old donut dropped in the park. All of them wore standard, dark blue MTF shirts, some long sleeved, some short; And all wore standard issue blue latex gloves to avoid contaminating any evidence that might be found.

One of the ants approached him, her secret smile and slow up and down assessment of him oozing the confidence of someone who had already gone down that particular road. She stopped before him, closer than necessary, and tossed her black braids over one shoulder, clipboard in hand.

"Looking good this morning Elijah," she purred.

Elijah grinned back. "Francesca, *mi amor,* you look good enough to eat as always."

He caught her free hand, bringing it up so he could kiss her knuckles before nipping the skin just a bit with his teeth.

She gasped, snatching her hand back and looking around quickly as the toffee colored skin of her cheeks darkened. "You haven't called me lately, Elijah. A girl could start to feel a little neglected, you know.

Elijah let out a low chuckle, dropping her hand before rocking back on his heels, his face growing serious. "I am so very sorry gorgeous. I'm afraid I needed some recovery time after you ravaged me so thoroughly the last time we were together."

Francesca beamed. "Well as soon as you think you can handle another round you let me know, will you, handsome?"

"I absolutely will." Elijah looked pointedly over at the van and then down at the clipboard in her hands.

"Now my darling, what forensic goodies do you have for me today?"

28

"I don't know how you do it beautiful, but that magical mind of yours is heaven sent!" Callan gushed. "I was able to cross reference the schematics of all the brick buildings in the city that match - both in size and detail - to the building in that photo. Only one matched everything, the door placement, the overall building height, even the location of the few windows we could see."

Callan waggled his long, thin fingers towards a print out of the photo in question, propped up on his desk next to a half empty boba tea. Honey milk green tea with grape popping boba and chia seeds to be exact - he'd texted the pick up demand to Anton on their way into headquarters this morning. After tapping away at the keyboard for a few more moments, Callan leaned back, an older photo of the same building appearing on the large bank of screens above his desk.

"Ladies and gentlemen, boys and girls, I present to you… The Miradean Home for the Criminally Insane. It was built in 1932 by a ridiculously rich Highblood named Cedric Todesco. While the structure was being built, Cedric word vomited all over the news media about how he was 'just happy to be doing his part to make our city a safer place to live', and yada, yada.

Funny enough, Cedric failed to mention he was also getting a ridiculously large annual stipend from local government the entire time it was in operation. Lots of suspicious deaths, reports of torture, medical testing without authorization, you name it, this hellhole probably did it. I found a list of articles as long as my arm about families and residents voicing complaints, but the city government refused to do anything about it.

Finally, about thirty years after it opened, a patient came up missing who happened to be a distant cousin of a U.S. congressman. The congressman came to town dragging all sorts of bad press and national attention with him, so the city stepped in and shut the place down for good. Curious though, I couldn't find any information at all about Cedric after the closing. It's like he up and vanished or something? But the building, it still stands to this day." Callan looked over at Mayla and sent her a wink. "We probably wouldn't have even had it on our radar if it weren't for you."

Anton pulled a smiling Mayla in close and dropped a kiss to her lips.

"See? What did I tell you? Thanks to you and your amazing magic we've got our first solid lead on the Anord."

Asher leaned against the edge of Callan's desk, face upturned to the monitors.

"This *has* to be the hospital where Richards is dropping off kids, right?!"

Callan took a long, slow sip of his milk tea, nodded, and then grinned.

"I'd bet my entire collection of knock off Cartier cufflinks it is. It's so far out there the city has forgotten about it, and what better location for a bad guy hideout? Based on its distance from the city, our great grandparents clearly preferred their criminally insane out of sight and out of mind. Which is *exactly* where the Anord would want to be."

Elijah barreled through the door the next moment, waving a big manila envelope over his head. "Gather round people, we've got new info! Forensics just finished processing the van."

His voice went flat and completely sarcastic. "Total shocker, they found another black hoodie and red mask."

"It's at least confirmation the van was being used by the Anord like we thought,"Anton said, standing to his left, one arm draped casually over Mayla's shoulders. "What else did we get?"

"A cell phone. They found it stuck between the seat and the console. But it's beat all to hell, it would probably take some kind of amazing IT wizard to be able to salvage anything from it."

Callan appeared in a flash, snapped twice, and held out his palm.

Elijah grinned, digging into the envelope before pulling out a cell phone and slapping it into Callan's outstretched hand. The thing looked like it had been run over with a tank.

Callan tilted his nose in the air and studied it a moment, flipping it over once before rolling his eyes. "*Please*. This won't even be a real challenge," he complained, returning to his bank of computers and flopping back into his pastel pink chair.

"Mayla got us the location of a possible headquarters. I need about an hour to mobilize a full unit, but once they're ready we're headed out there to check it out," Anton said.

Elijah's smile widened until he was absolutely beaming.

"For real? Will I finally get to stab some bad guys? *PLEASE TELL ME I GET TO STAB SOME BAD GUYS*!!" His whine sent the entire room into gales of laughter.

Anton sighed in mock resignation, a big grin on his face.

"Yes Elijah, if there are bad guys you may stab all but one of them. I need at least one for questioning."

Elijah pumped his fist the air. "Hell yeah!! Oh, hey, almost forgot. There's one more thing they found in the van," he said, giving them all a gritted teeth grimace.

"What? What did they find?"

"Kobold venom. Lots of it. So much in fact, that Enwyn confirmed it had to have come from multiple beasts."

The Miradean Home for the Criminally Insane was a huge, three story brick monstrosity, it's twenty or so windows boarded shut, the sprawling concrete porch cracked and broken now in multiple places. The forest was doing its best to reclaim the area, climbing weeds scaling the building on all sides. Even the grass was knee high in every direction.

The two unmarked surveillance units Anton had sent over ahead of them reported another white panel van on location, identical to the one they'd found the day they rescued Samuel. No sign of people or additional vehicles moving in or out of the area so far.

Still, a flattened area of undergrowth and multiple tire tracks leading around the back of the building made it clear that someone, more likely a few someones, had been in and out of the location recently.

Pulling up in front of the old behemoth of a building, twenty MTF officers, led by Anton and Elijah, stepped out of four black trucks and looked around.

Everyone was in full tactical gear, and the tension was palpable.

For everyone *except* Elijah of course.

Elijah looked forward to dangerous situations the same way most people looked forward to an island vacation. He was practically giddy, bouncing from one foot to the other, huge grin on his face as he obsessively checked and rechecked his knives. After a moment he switched to carefully examining the Sig Sauer P365 now holstered at his hip. As he did so he chatted away to no one in particular, his five year old on Christmas morning attitude apparent.

"Dude! I have been waiting for this! I can't believe we're finally here! I bet we find some cool shit in there. I'd like a full roster list of Anord members myself, that would be prime. I could do a little door to door service if I had a list like that, you know?" He was completely unfazed by the fact that they had no idea what they could be walking into.

Anton however, had no such problem. He was already nervous about having Mayla anywhere near this scene, not knowing what to expect, but there had been absolutely no arguing with her. She'd flat out refused to stay behind, threatening to drive herself if she had to. They'd finally agreed that she she could come, but only if she waited in the truck with Asher back at the main road until he gave the all clear. Anton hated losing the shifter's phenomenal tracking ability and more than lethal fighting skills, but if there was any chance there may be Anord members still hanging around, he needed Mayla protected at all costs.

Asher had strict instructions to get the hell out of here if he heard anything go down on the walkie, and Anton knew from experience that the man would follow his directions no matter what.

As they split into five teams of four and approached the former hospital from all sides, Anton belatedly realized the panel van sitting off to the side had a flat tire. If the Anord had cleared out in a hurry - and he was starting to suspect they had since they'd met no resistance so far - repairing a flat wouldn't have fit easily into their timeline.

As they came up to the front door, weapons drawn, a loud thud sounded from within. He blew out a hard breath. So much for quick and empty then. Anton traded glances with Elijah and the other two men. He nodded once, setting into his haunches just in front of the door.

"Alright people, head on a swivel. No one dies today," he ordered, before stepping forward and kicking in the door with a loud crash.

Less than a mile away, sitting in Asher's truck on the side of the road with absolutely nothing to do, Mayla was fidgety. She was agitated at being made to wait 'somewhere safe'. What if he was attacked? What if something happened and she couldn't get to him to help heal him? He was her mate and she should be where he was, that's how it worked, right? Oh gods, what would she do if Anton was...killed? She couldn't stop the gasp that rose in her throat, and Asher's hand came to rest on top of her own, his long, lean fingers warm against her ice cold skin.

"Try not to worry too much. Anton is a pro, and he's had all sorts of training. He'll be just fine. He's done this sort of thing a million times."

Mayla nodded, sending him a weak, grateful smile, but she didn't respond.

"Besides, he's got Elijah and eighteen of our top guys watching his back." Asher paused for a moment, then grinned, considering. "We both know if anything heavy goes down Anton will have to get in line behind Elijah, that guy is just plain crazy."

Mayla released a small hysterical giggle, swallowing down her worry with visible effort. "From some of the stories Anton has told me, I think he really is. Does Elijah really enjoy hurting people that much? He seems like a good guy, and he's a lot of fun but sometimes his aggression scares me a little."

Asher sighed, stretching a lean arm across the back of the bench seat and thinking a moment before answering.

"No reason to be scared. Elijah is a decent guy, he just has a very strong sense of justice. I've never seen him hurt anyone who didn't deserve it. His motto is, if you've hurt an innocent, you deserve to be hurt worse in return. As much as he can be one sometimes, he really hates bullies."

Mayla nodded. "I guess that makes sense."

"He is definitely more bloodthirsty when it comes to the Anord though. You heard about what happened to his family?"

"I heard him say the Anord killed them when he was young. Is that true? Has the Anord really been around that long?"

Asher nodded solemnly. "Yep. Though no one knew who they were at the time. Elijah didn't even know for sure that they were responsible until he joined the force. The Anord ambushed his family on some backroad, way back when Elijah was just a kid. The case was flagged because it's one of the only times the Anord attacked Highbloods. Lowbloods are always their victims of choice so we assume it was a case of mistaken identity. But yeah, that's why he's always out for blood when it comes to these guys. I have to admit, if I lost my family that way? I'd be more than ready for a little payback myself. "

"Elijah also said you were adopted?"

Asher rolled down the driver side window, taking in a deep breath of clean, forest air. He stayed silent for a long moment.

"I'm sorry, I'm being nosy because I'm nervous, just tell me to shut up." She fidgeted in her seat, looking down at her hands.

"No, it's okay. I just...don't talk about it much. I am adopted. I never knew my bio folks. My adoptive parents found me wandering in Magnolia Park when I was only three."

He barked out a harsh laugh. "I had already learned to shift, so I was in my wolf form when they found me. I was literally the pup someone dumped on the side of the road." His tone was egg shell brittle, filled with pain and resignation.

Mayla inhaled, a sudden thought hitting her. "Magnolia Park, so the other day...the location just must have made everything that much worse for you."

Asher nodded, sending her a small appreciative smile.

"It certainly didn't help my frame of mind, no. Truthfully

though, my adoptive folks are the best. I couldn't ask for a better family. They couldn't have their own biological kids, so my mom likes to call me their 'miracle gift left by Fenrir'."

Mayla smiled. "The norse wolf?"

Asher nodded, his lips lifting into an affectionate smile.

"Mom's a big reader, loves all types of mythology and folklore. I never had the heart to remind her that Fenrir was more of a bad guy than a hero. She and my dad are Lowbloods. They have no magic, unless you count Dad's amazing talent for grilling steaks."

"I do count that as a certain kind of magic, actually. Let me guess, you like yours rare?"

Asher sent her an overtly wolfish grin. "You know it."

Laughing, they almost didn't hear the soft crackle of the walkie on the seat between them, two pained, whispered words escaping to rattle about in the confines of the truck.

"Officer down."

"Shit!!" The kobold sank a razor sharp fang into Anton's forearm, wrenching its head violently from side to side, and ripping a nice, deep tear down the muscle. The Anord left them a little welcome to the neighborhood present inside the hospital, and these bastards were brutal. Ignoring the searing pain as best he could, Anton kept his arms locked around the huge, slimy neck, focusing instead on pushing his ice magic deep into the beast's brain. Thankfully, this one smelled different the one in the park, and didn't appear to be able to secrete the sulfurous venom. Instead, it smelled more like rotten fish left out in the sun. Swallowing hard, Anton locked his wrist and cranked his grip down harder, his back slamming against the cement wall as the kobold flailed, fighting like hell to wrench him loose.

Not a chance, asshole.

Across the room, Elijah was engaged in hand to hand with another beast, this one a strange mud brown color with a slightly crooked spine. Falling back one moment, he leapt in close for a quick swipe with his knife before dancing away again. One dagger already protruded from the kobold's stomach, a trickle of green blood oozing down its body to dribble onto the floor. From the grunts, screams and cursing now coming across the walkie, the other teams were each facing a similar welcome.

As soon as they'd entered through the front door and seen the first beast, Elijah had emptied the Sig's full magazine into it, but the creature had simply blinked at him. A few small holes dribbling green ick were the only proof of his efforts. They'd been forced to give up on firearms and move quickly to hand-to-hand, or rather, hand to *claw*.

Refocusing on his own struggle, Anton closed his eyes, pulling even harder on his magic. The blood oozing down his arm solidified as the beast finally began slow, the reptilian skin under Anton's grip cooling quickly. Stumbling, the beast let out a strange hiss, breath exiting its mouth as ice crystals. The crystals dropped, shattering apart when they hit the hard, marble floor. One more stumble, and Anton felt the beasts' skin ice completely over, hardening beneath him. It took a final, lurching step, then the kobold spun, falling backward, with Anton's grip still firm around its neck.

He braced himself, understanding in a flash that he was going to be smashed between the marble floor and this massive hunk of reptilian ice. He sent up a quick prayer that he wasn't about to be popped like a grape, felt his head crack against the floor and an incredible pressure squeeze his chest…

And then his vision went dark.

Elijah spun, coming in close to cut a jagged tear at the kobold's armpit, praying he'd get lucky and hit something important. He'd fought a lot of men in his lifetime, battled a lot of different magics, but *this*? This was definitely a first. He had no idea what the internal anatomy of a kobold looked like, so he was stuck stabbing blind, hoping to get lucky and hit a major organ. Which was ridiculously frustrating. This was taking entirely too long and he was getting bored. When the creature's tail whipped out and grazed his shoulder, bony spikes slicing through shirt and skin, Elijah laughed with sudden joy.

"Okay you slimy fuck, you want to dance with me?

You're gonna regret it, but come on, *let's dance*."

Elijah palmed a second knife, spinning away from the creature to run across the room. The kobold hissed in frustration, its heavy legs ambling slowly after him. Out of the corner of his eye Elijah saw Anton and the second kobold fall to the floor.

Good, he hoped Anton turned that thing's mind into a sno cone.

He bounced from side to side, alive with expectation as the creature so dead set on killing him lumbered closer. Judging the distance for another moment, Elijah took off running towards the beast, the grin on his face growing. At five feet, he dropped to his knees, sliding easily through the green slime coating the floor, his wrists crossed in front of him, knives pointing straight out. When his knives sunk hilt deep into the slimy flesh of the creature's belly, he locked his arms and pushed the heavy beast upward, lifting it up off its back legs. In the next heartbeat, he yanked his knives apart, green blood showering down over his head, his knives eviscerating the kobold from gut to knees.

He flung the beast aside with a wet plop, and quickly stood, coming around to its head. It hissed at him, writhing on the floor but unable to regain its feet, insides spilling with a slow, wet thwack onto the floor. Elijah wiped his face on his sleeve, the tracks of green goo left behind looking like war paint. He leaned over the beast and sent it a cocky smile.

"Told you you didn't want to dance with me, asshole. I learned that move from Patrick Swayze." He straightened, waving one of his knives around like a professor giving a lecture to his classroom full of students.

"You know, come to think of, I really need to watch Dirty Dancing again. Epic fucking movie, truly. Taught me everything I know about women."

He paused a moment, contemplating. "Maybe I'll call Francesca and we can watch it at her place. Now *that* would be fun."

He tapped the bloodied tip of one knife to his chin twice before refocusing on the kobold. He narrowed his eyes as leaning closer, looking straight down into the creature's hissing face.

"Damn, aren't you dead yet?" He heaved a melodramatic sigh. "Here, let me help you out."

He placed both knives at the kobold's throat, gave the beast a slow and saucy wink, and ended it.

29

Asher shifted his ancient Ford pickup into park with a clunk and turned off the ignition, immediately reaching across Mayla to grab the door handle and trap her inside.

"We have to wait until we get the all clear. I shouldn't have even brought you over here, Anton is already going to kill me."

"Asher. My mate is in that building. He's hurt. I can't explain how I know, but *I know*. I am going in there. Now move your hand before you make me climb into your mind and convince you that you are not, in fact, a wolf, but some kind of brain dead tadpole instead, *BECAUSE SO HELP ME GOD IF YOU DON'T MOVE RIGHT NOW I WILL DO IT!!*"

Her stare was hard, fierce and full of promise. Her mate mark flared bright blue.

Shiiitttt.

Asher released the door handle, holding both hands up in surrender.

"Okay, I hear you. Let's just take a beat and think about this logically for a minute."

This mating bond stuff was intense, and the idea of being turned into a cold, slimy frog sent shivers of dread through him. He hated frogs.

He knew Mayla was upset, but he needed to figure out a way to stall for time until they could get an update over the walkie. In the space it took him to complete the thought, Mayla had the door open and was out of the truck, sprinting toward the building.

"Damnit!" Asher jumped out and took off after her at a dead run. She was already too close to the front door.

At that moment, Elijah and two other officers emerged, flushed and sweat-stained. Some type of disgusting green goo coated Elijah's hair and clothes. Asher watched as he caught Mayla by the shoulders, listening to her intently for a moment before nodding and letting her go, motioning her to continue inside.

He stumbled to a halt, releasing the breath he'd been holding on a whoosh, and . If Elijah let her in that easily, all threats had been dealt with and Anton was in one piece. Good news on both fronts.

He turned, heading back to shut the open doors of the truck. Something about this place was making his nerves twitch under his skin, the desire to shift into his wolf form almost overpowering. He'd noticed it as soon as they'd gotten within a few miles of this place, his skin itching the entire time he sat and chatted with Mayla. He wasn't sure why, but his instincts were screaming at him to have teeth and claws ready, just in case.

He pushed down the urge, reaching across the threadbare bench seat to grab his revolver and shoulder holster from the glove box. He avoided guns as a general rule, they were heavy and took entirely too much time to get the job done, but if his instincts were screaming and shifting wasn't an option, he was damn sure gonna have a back up plan.

He shut the truck doors with a creaking whine, heading towards the officers gathered at the front of the building. He'd get an update on what had gone down and then jump in and help with whatever clean up was needed.

He froze mid-step.

His head lifted and he sniffed at the air, glancing around. What was that scent? It smelled like…fresh water over smooth rocks in a stream, or the soft tang of new grass in the springtime. It smelled amazing and alluring, but at the same time, something about it was off. His wolf pushed him to the right, demanding he investigate. Asher might control his shift, but his wolf was the better tracker, and right now that particular scent had his wolf more agitated than it had ever been before.

Which meant it would drive him nuts until he found out where that scent was actually coming from. He turned to the right and followed his wolf,s lead.

The knee high grass was annoying, but it didn't slow him down. He hardly made a sound as he came around the back of the building, scanning the area with laser-like focus for a full minute. His eyes snagged on a small wooden shed tucked in just beyond the tree line. It was painted a dull, flat brown and splotched with green, as if someone had deliberately tried to make it blend in with the surrounding forest.

They'd done a good job, someone without his enhanced eyesight might easily have missed it altogether. He sniffed at the air. The scent seemed to be coming from that shed.

As he cautiously approached, the clean, beautiful smell grew stronger, but the hint of strange, salty bitterness increased as well.

It smelled like fear or desperation.

It smelled like...

Tears.

The door to the shed was surprisingly heavy duty, fully metal with a large, complicated push button lock. With just a glance, Asher knew he had no chance of getting that door open without major assistance from the tech squad or a righteous battering ram. In sharp contrast though, the rest of the wooden shed seemed old and not well maintained.

Taking a lap around the small building, he looked at every hinge and board, his eyes searching. Finally, on his second lap around, on the back side of the building and tucked under the shade of a huge oak tree, Asher found what he was looking for. Mold and mildew from the trapped dampness had saturated a number of the wooden planks there, and he pressed a hand against them firmly, smiling when they flexed beneath his hand.

He took a step back, let his wolf rise to the surface just a bit, and sent a fist straight through the boards. They gave way with a sickeningly wet crunch, chunks of the boards falling to the forest floor. The hole he'd created was only the size of a coconut, but the rotted wood around the hole hung limp, eager to give up its pitiful fight. A sudden noise from inside the shed had him spinning away and flattening against the building. He slid the revolver into his palm.

"This is Officer Ezhno with the Miradea Task Force. Identify yourself immediately," he called.

The wind rustled through the trees over his head, and an animal scampered somewhere deeper in the forest, but there was no additional sound from the shed. He thought about calling for back up, but he'd left his walkie in the truck, and from back here, no one in the main building would hear him yell. Plus, if he did get someone's attention and this turned out to be absolutely nothing?

A whimper reached his ears, and the scent of fresh tears filled his nose. His wolf howled inside his mind. He moved back to the hole he'd made, trying to peer inside.

It was dark within, only one small window high in the corner allowing in the tiniest amount of light. He could barely make out what looked like a cot, but when he saw something move on that cot, and distinctly heard a sob, his wolf stopped listening to caution, lunging for the surface. His nails lengthened, hooking into the wood as he grabbed handfuls of the boards, ripping them away and widening the hole as fast as he physically could.

He wasn't sure who, or what was inside, but whoever it was, they were upset, in pain, and his wolf was determined to protect them.

When the hole was finally big enough, he lowered his head and squeezed through it, grunting as the jagged wood tore at his white t-shirt and scraped at this broad shoulders. Pulling his legs in and getting his hiking boots back under him, Asher stood, thankful the roof was taller than expected so he didn't have to hunch. His fingernails retracted to their normal length. As his eyes adjusted to the dimness, he scanned the area, a few large boxes, a pile of dusty blankets…

And the brightest pair of utterly terrified green eyes he'd ever seen.

A slender woman was tied down to the threadbare military style cot, her jeans and t-shirt filthy, and her eyes sunken.

Asher immediately put both his hands up in a placating gesture.

"Hey, easy there, easy now. I'm not here to hurt you. I'm just here to help. I'm a police officer."

He could hear the breath sawing in and out of her nose and mouth, pushing through the dingy cloth that had been stuffed into her mouth and tied around the back of her head. When he took a step forward, she thrashed against her bonds, her movements weak but determined.

"No, no, hey listen. Shhhhh. I know you're scared," Asher tried to consciously soften his normal gravelly tone. "I'm not going to hurt you, I promise. I'm just going to reach over and take off that gag, okay?"

His hands stayed up in supplication. The woman was completely traumatized and there was no way he was going to make it any worse. They'd do this at her speed and no one else's. Those green eyes watched him intently, but when he didn't move, her struggling slowly eased.

"I'm with the Miradea Task Force. I promise I'm only here to help you."

He gave that a moment to sink in, and saw when the tiniest bit of hope flared in those eyes.

"I'm not going to hurt you, I swear it. I just want to take off the gag, okay?" He mimed untying something from behind his own head and removing it.

She watched him for another moment, then slowly nodded, still wary.

"Okay great." He moved closer to the cot slowly, hands still out in front where she could clearly see them.

She turned her head away to give him better access. When he touched the knot at the back of her head though, he saw her squeeze her eyes shut and watched her body tense.

When that amazing scent hit him again, he realized it was coming from her. She was what his wolf was so determined to protect. She wasn't a shifter, he'd have recognized that immediately. And while she didn't smell like she had any Highblood magic he was familiar with, she didn't smell like any Lowblood he'd ever been around either.

She smelled like the forest itself. Like nature and growth and rebirth. Like fresh air and everything that was good and clean in this world.

Yet someone had still done this her? His wolf prowled inside his mind, clearly agitated. Someone had abused her and traumatized her until the thought of another person getting close made her tremble in fear. Who had done such a thing?

He needed to know so he could find them and then kill them.

As slowly and as painfully as possible.

He swallowed down a growl that threatened to climb up his throat. He didn't need to scare her even more, and he was pretty sure growling wouldn't exactly give her the warm and fuzzies. He finally managed to untie the gag, pulling it gently from her mouth and flinging it into the farthest corner of the shed.

When she turned back towards him, those amazing eyes were filled with cautious gratitude. She tried to speak, but only managed a hoarse squeak.

He dropped to a knee beside the cot.

"It's okay. Take your time."

She swallowed painfully and tried again. When he finally heard her voice it was as cracked and broken as the chapped lips it escaped from.

"Wil…Wil…low. My name, it's Willow."

Mayla ran through the old hospital building, her eyes darting to scan the interior of every room she passed. The entire place was whitewashed, each room empty of people and unadorned. Inside were black metal bed frames, some with thin white mattresses, most without. All of them had a small, useless window high in the wall, barred and boarded up from the outside. As she approached the end of the hallway, a uniformed officer motioned to her, opening a door marked Procedure Room 7 and ushering her inside.

Entering, Mayla found Anton sitting on a metal exam table, his heavy tactical vest tossed aside. A female officer stood before him, wrapping gauze snugly around a large bloody gash on his forearm. She lurched to a stop, her eyes drinking him in from head to toe. His white hair was tousled, and there was a livid bruise coming up on his cheek, but he was in one piece. He was injured, clearly, but he was alive and not in any danger.

She took a slow, deep breath of relief, watching him. Then, almost without her intent, her focus narrowed to the female standing before him.

The one who was holding his injured arm in one hand and wrapping it with the other.

The woman who was tending to her mate. The woman who was touching her mate.

A blue flame of sheer rage flared so strongly through her gut, she made a tiny sound of surprise.

Anton looked up, his eyes immediately jumping from her, to the woman standing before him, then back again. He cleared his throat.

"Uh, that'll do, thank you Officer Marshall. I can take it from here."

The woman's eyes went wide as she turned, freezing for a moment before giving a quick nod, slipping past Mayla, and making a swift exit.

"Milacek, your eyes are glowing." Anton said in awe. He raised his hands from his lap slowly, opening his arms to her. "Please come here and stop terrifying my new recruits."

Mayla blinked, dispelling the glow, and sprinted across the room to throw herself into his arms.

Anton held her tight against him, his muscles tense, not from exertion, but from fear. *Her* fear, spilling into him through their bond. He cradled the back of her head against his chest and pressed kisses against her temple.

"It's alright. I'm fine, I promise. It's barely even a scratch. I'm sorry if I scared you," he whispered into her hair.

"I heard *officer down* and my heart stopped. My body reacted so strongly, I was terrified it was coming from you and that you might be—," Mayla broke off, sniffling against his black t-shirt and shaking her head in refusal. "I just had to find you. It was like I couldn't breathe until I saw you alive and in one piece."

She inhaled deeply, melting deeper into him.

He leaned back to look in her eyes, a soft smile on his face.

"I get it, I do. I felt the same way when you were in the

hospital. I guess this mate thing can be pretty intense. Try something for me, would you?"

She eyed him for a moment, but nodded.

"Close your eyes."

She complied.

"Inside your mind, try to focus here," his fingers tapped once, just above her heart.

"Do you feel anything new there? Something maybe more masculine than you're used to?"

When she didn't respond, he continued. "For me, it feels like I have a corner of my mind and my heart where you are. When I reach for you there, I can sense if you need me. I can sense if you're hurt. Did you feel something similar?"

Her lips creased into a slow smile and she nodded. "I think so. I can feel how tired you are, and that your arm is throbbing but you're trying to ignore it. I can also tell that you are absolutely dying to kiss me right now." She grinned at him and he couldn't help but grin back.

A moment later though, his grin disappeared, his expression darkening.

"Fredericks went down. He was rushed to the closest med unit. I haven't see him so I don't know how bad it is. We're still waiting for word."

Mayla squeezed his bicep. "I'm so sorry. If there's anything I can do?"

He shook his head. "No, he's my responsibility. Him and his new family. We'll stop by the med unit when we leave here and check on him."

Suddenly he straightened, pushing her back to arms length, his eyes narrowing.

"Wait, how are you already here? You aren't supposed to show up until we gave the all clear. You're supposed to be safely waiting with Asher."

She lifted one eyebrow at him, a sly smile escaping before she giggled.

"Don't be mad at Asher, it's not his fault. I didn't give him a choice. I threatened to scramble his brain until he thought he was a tadpole shifter."

Anton's eyes went huge. "Can you really do that?"

Mayla looked away, bashful. "No, but he didn't need to

know that."

Anton shook his head, his eyes bright with amusement. He slid a hand behind her neck and pulled her in, lowering his mouth to hers for a long, lingering kiss. His thumb rubbed slow circles against the side of her neck, her arms stealing under his to grip his shoulders and press closer. Minutes later, when they finally parted, he was still smiling.

"No one has ever threatened a wolf for me before. Look at me, falling in love with the sweetest, softest Lowblood lady - who just happens to be a total badass."

"Yeah well, this badass will do a lot more than just threaten the next time she finds Officer Marshall with her hands on you," Mayla grumbled.

Anton threw back his head and laughed.

30

Asher grinned.

Willow.

The Willow.

Though she obviously hadn't had an easy time of it, she was alive. Mayla was going to be absolutely over the moon. First things first however, he needed to get her out of this damn shit box and somewhere safe.

Working quickly to remove the restraints at her wrists and ankles, Asher bit back curses at the dark purple bruising he found there. He stayed on his knees so they were face to face, and he chatted aimlessly, hoping to help calm some of her terror.

"It's really nice to meet you Willow. I'm Asher. You know, my whole department has been searching for you. I've met your friend Mayla, she's been helping us look for you."

At the mention of Mayla's name, Willow's eyes went round and hopeful, a tremulous smile rising to her lips. Asher stood, trying the front door from the inside with no luck. Turning around, he eyeballed the jagged hole he'd made to gain entry.

"Cover your ears and close your eyes, I'm going to have to make that hole a little bigger so we can both get out of here."

She complied after a moment of consideration, and he pretended not to notice when she kept one eye slitted open. She had no reason yet to trust him, not after what she'd clearly been through, and he could understand her need to not be completely vulnerable.

Stepping forward, he sent a strong kick towards the top of the hole, the boards cracking and splintering outwards. He saw Willow flinch out of the corner of his eye, and wished that there were a way to do this without startling her more. Since there wasn't, he kicked again, then once more, until the boards finally gave way in an opening big enough for both of them to easily fit through.

When he returned to her side, quiet tears were pouring down her cheeks, her spring green eyes red-rimmed.

"I'm really sorry about that. Definitely not the chaos you needed after everything you've already been through, huh?"

She watched him, not speaking, but nodded. Gods, she reminded him of a frightened fox kit, cowering in its den.

"I'm going to pick you up now so we can get you outside, okay? From the looks of it you're badly dehydrated and I don't want you to fall. You've been through enough already."

He took one of her hands in his, feeling a small electric zing go through him at the contact. He smothered his reaction, instead looking at her quietly, and giving her time to adjust to the idea of his touch.

"If you can bring yourself to trust me, I promise you nothing else will hurt you. I swear it on my life."

She offered him a small, weak smile and nodded once. When he slid one muscled arm around her back and the other under her knees, she twined her arms around his neck. Pressed together like this, Asher could feel her heart thudding against his chest like a panicked, injured bird.

Once more, he swallowed down the burning desire to hunt down whoever had done this to her. He pushed away the thoughts of slowly dismembering the perpetrators and stored them for a later time. After a small jump out of the back of the dim shed, he carried her around the small building. Emerging from the tree line, the light from the gradually setting sun hit them both full force.

Willow blinked rapidly, her eyes immediately starting to water.

His heart twisted with the quick realization that she hadn't been exposed to direct sunlight in quite a while.

As they came around to the front of the building, a lone officer crossed towards one of the swat vehicles, and Asher lifted his chin, beckoning him over.

Willow turned her entire body into his, a tiny trembling beginning within her. His arms tightened and he lowered his face to hers. When he spoke, his voice was barely a whisper.

"NO ONE will hurt you, I give you my word. He's just a policeman, like me. He's going to help get us to a med unit so we can get you checked out."

The woman in his arms suddenly felt like she was made of concrete, her muscles instantly rock hard and tense.

"No. Please. I can't." The plea came out on a croak, and he felt as if jagged claws had ripped straight through his heart.

When she spoke again, it was in stops and starts, her voice shaky and terrified.

"I don't…want to go…to a med unit. There's…there's… too many people. Please I...I can't...I just," she stumbled over her words and her hands twisted handfuls of his shirt, her thoughts a traumatized jumble. She started to twist in his arms, seeking escape.

"Okay, okay," he whispered, tightening his grip so she didn't fall. "If you say no med unit, then we won't go to the med unit."

She stilled, listening.

"You promise?" She breathed.

"I swear it. What if I take you somewhere safe that's very quiet? Somewhere where there aren't any other people. Would that be okay?"

She watched him suspiciously, but nodded. Asher began walking towards the truck, calling out instructions to the officer as they passed.

"Run in and update the chief. Let him know I've located a missing person. Tell him it's Willow, he'll know who you mean. Tell him he and his mate can find us at my place, but they are to bring no one else. No one else, is that clear?"

The officer nodded, surprised, but turned around immediately, taking off back towards the building at a run.

When they reached his truck, Asher managed to get the drivers door open with one hand, lifting Willow gently into the seat. He climbed in quickly beside her, as the death grip she kept around his neck didn't appear to be easing anytime soon.

Snatching his flannel jacket from behind the bench seat he

wrapped it around her, leaving her tucked up against his side as he started the truck and drove away.

When Asher opened the front door of his cabin a few hours later, the blur that shoved past him looked vaguely like Mayla. He caught the light blue of the sweatshirt she'd been wearing earlier, and a wave of black hair before she was down the hallway and out of sight.

"Second bedroom on the right, next to the bathroom - be gentle please!" he called after her, knowing the woman would likely tear his house apart looking for her friend.

Anton stepped inside and Asher shut the door quietly behind him. The two men headed into the kitchen, Asher grabbing two bottles of beer out of the ancient fridge and popping the caps off before passing one over. His white haired friend held it, but didn't bring it to his lips, staring at the bottle a moment before he looked over, his expression somber.

"How is she?"

That was the best thing about Anton. He didn't bother screwing around with small talk.

Ever since the two of them had met three years ago, they'd just sort of clicked. They were on the same page about so many things, and neither of them bothered with unnecessary small talk, mutual understanding coming easy to them both.

But how was *anyone* supposed to understand something like this? What kind of sense could you make of the world when an innocent woman was taken, held against her will and brutalized?

Asher ran a hand through his jet black hair. "Honestly? Not good. She's completely traumatized. She looks to be in one piece, but I think she's still in shock. She barely talks, and refuses to let me or anyone else check her over for injuries. I offered to bring in a female healer, but she's adamant she doesn't want to see any other people.

From what I did see, she's been restrained for a long time. She hasn't said as much, but I'm willing to bet they kept her in that shed since she was first taken. She's underweight and weak and sensitive to light. Her arms are riddled with bruises and track marks from needles, but she doesn't seem to be on anything or detoxing, so I don't think they drugged her. Maybe they were taking her blood or running other tests on her for some reason?"

Anton closed his eyes as if the thought put him in physical pain.

"The forensics team is doing a full sweep of the building now. Before we left they found evidence of all sorts of genetic testing. We think the hospital is where they were creating, or at least modifying the kobolds. It's likely they were experimenting on her for some reason as well," Anton admitted.

Asher stared at him, the blood in his veins going ice cold. He'd suspected, but hearing it confirmed first hand? That cut.

Setting his beer down on the countertop, he took two long strides and sent a fist into the wall of the log cabin. His knuckles split on impact, but the wall looked none the worse for wear.

"Gods damn it! Anton, when we find these mother fuckers I swear...," He let his words hang in the air, sucking in deep breaths and grappling with his self control.

Anton nodded. After a few minutes of stony silence, Asher spoke up again.

"I tried taking her some food but she only stared at it. I told her she was more than welcome to take a shower, but as soon as the words were out of my mouth, she ran to the opposite side of the room trembling like she was waiting for me to attack her."

He blew out a frustrated breath and his voice dropped an octave, the horror in his own voice raw and raspy. "Whatever experimenting they did to her in that shed? It was bad Anton. It was very, very bad."

31

Mayla knocked softly on the door to the bedroom. Her nerves were jittery with anticipation. Asher's stunning log cabin home had taken her by surprise. She'd somehow imagined him living in a studio apartment or a simple bachelor pad, not this rustically beautiful, well-crafted home settled back in the woods like some kind of fairytale.

Her eyes traced the scene of a wolf sitting under a full moon that had been so delicately carved into the wooden door. She wondered idly where he'd found a craftsman with such incredible talent.

She blinked, listening, but there was no response from inside. Her thoughts were spiraling. She wanted to see for herself that Willow was okay, but she was terrified to shove open this door and possibly scare her friend even more after all she'd been through.

When the officer had approached them back at the hospital to tell them Willow had been found, Mayla had been over the moon with excitement. She'd needed to get to her friend and hug her immediately.

But shortly after that, Asher had called. When Anton hung up, he'd pulled over, turning in his seat to face her.

His eyes were serious and slightly sympathetic when he looked at her. "It sounds like Willow has been through quite a lot. Asher says she's badly traumatized."

Mayla's skin tightened and she raised her chin, her eyes filling with tears.

"They *hurt* her?"

Anton swallowed, reaching a hand out to wipe at her tears. He nodded. "He said that physically she is a little weak, but she doesn't seem to have any other injuries that he can see. She won't let us take her to the hospital, so it will be up to you to see if you can make sure of that, okay?"

Mayla nodded, her tears spilling over at the thought of anyone hurting her friend.

Anton cupped her cheek. "*Milacek,* please don't cry. Whatever they did to her we will all help her get through it. We just have to be patient and let her share everything with us in her own time, okay?"

When her tears splashed against his wrist he stopped talking, unclipping his seatbelt, then hers so he could pull her against his chest into a hug.

"I'm sure just seeing you will help her more than you know."

Mayla leaned back, swiping forcefully at her cheeks to wipe away the remaining tears, sudden determination in her eyes.

"Willow will get better," she proclaimed. "I know she will. I know it because she's special, she's one of a kind. And she'll have all of us to help her."

Anton nodded his agreement, then froze when Mayla's eyes narrowed, their ocean depths swirling into a raging tempest.

"But I'm telling you right now. When we finally find the people responsible for all this?

I'm going to climb into their minds and drown them SLOWLY with their own most terrifying fears."

Now, half an hour later, standing in front of this beautiful door and going over that conversation in her head, Mayla was even more determined to help Anton hunt down the Anord and put an end to this chaos once and for all. Gone was the fragile, anxious part of her that constantly second guessed every decision. The Anord had not only attacked her mate twice, they'd kidnapped and traumatized her best friend.

These monsters stole children, blew up buildings, and were responsible for countless deaths here in the city. She knew Anton might try to prevent it, but she was done being a bystander in all this. If she really was the most powerful empath in Miradea, it's was past time she started acting like it. She would climb into whatever mind she needed to, chase whatever clues she could, and help stop the Anord for good.

She pulled in a breath and focused on pushing her angry thoughts aside. The time for vengeance was coming, but right now Willow needed her calm support, not her blazing and bloodthirsty anger.

She knocked again. Still no response.

Mayla turned the knob and opened the door slowly, hoping against hope that her best friend was resting.

She wasn't.

Instead, Willow sat on a king sized, wooden framed bed, wrapped up in a white down comforter so large she seemed to be disappearing into it. She sat tucked against the far wall, as far away from the door as possible. Just from her face Mayla could tell she'd lost weight, her cheeks were pale and hollow, and her normally shining green eyes shadowed by dark circles.

Mayla's heart shattered like a glass dropped onto concrete. What had they done to her? Had they even bothered to feed her? Willow didn't turn to look at her, and Mayla could see the comforter trembling from across the room. She slowly approached the bed, careful to be as quiet but as deliberate as possible. When she spoke, it was barely a whisper, just enough for the two of them to hear.

"It's me, Willow, it's Mayla."

The woman on the bed leaned forward, the comforter slowly slipping from her shoulders, hope sprouting in her eyes. Her voice was hoarse, raspy, and the most beautiful sound Mayla had ever heard.

"May? Is that really you?" When Willow dissolved into tears, Mayla threw herself onto the bed. She wrapped her friend in her arms and rocked her slowly back and forth, whispering over and over.

"It's okay. You're safe. I've got you now. You're safe."

The huge, tormented sobs that tore out of Willow shattered her heart. She kept rocking and kept whispering, her arms tight around her best friend.

She would never let go again.

Deep inside Mayla's mind, the enraged part of her grew, pulsing with the promise of retribution. Every single person who'd had a hand in making Willow feel this way was going to pay. And pay dearly.

When Willow's loud, heartrending sobs reached the ears of the two men in the kitchen, Asher dropped his beer once more, his caramel eyes raw with pain, his face going dark with fury. His hands clenched, and Anton watched his nails elongate into his palms, blood drops forming as they punctured the skin. The man's lip curled and his canines protruded before he rushed out the back door, throwing himself down two short steps into the yard.

Coming to stand at the door, Anton watched him complete the shift, marveling when a massive ebony wolf with honey colored eyes stood staring back at him. The beast sent a pleading look over his shoulder and Anton nodded, understanding the request without words. He would stay and look over Willow until Asher returned. At his nod, the wolf took off at a run, making it two full strides before he disappeared into the dense forest.

Anton had never seen his friend unable to control his shift before. Shifter magic was its own special kind of burden, but he'd always heard control of the shift was up to the person, never the magic.

He made a mental note to sit down with Asher in the next few days and check in, something was clearly off. When his phone rang a moment later, he was still standing by the back door, still staring out at the forest lost in his thoughts. He pulled the device out of his pocket and accepted the call.

"Yeah."

"Hey Chief. I was able to get into the cell phone, but it didn't give us much. I got a few addresses, some completely rando photos, and a chat history that looks to be encrypted. A few more hours and I should have that cracked as well. You want me to send over copies of everything or just leave it here at headquarters for later?"

Callan's voice was quiet and all business, with none of his usual sass. As much as he liked to pretend otherwise, the vampire worried when the team went out in the field, especially when there was any kind of physical risk involved.

Anton paused. Asher shifting, Callan's demeanor, even Elijah had been quieter than usual after this morning's events. It had been a rough few days, that was true, but was that all that was was going on?

"Chief? You still there?"

Anton nodded, though no one was around to see it. "Yeah, I'm here. Send me everything. And I want more techs sent out to the mental hospital. I want them going over that whole place with a fine toothed comb. No trace is too small. Bag it, tag it, and test it. If they don't find any additional evidence the first run through, have them do it again."

Another racking sob echoed from the back hallway and he stiffened, his eyes burning a hole into the forest where Asher had disappeared. The Anord were directly affecting his team now. His Lowblood mate, and her friends and family were at risk.

He was done playing cat and mouse games.

"One more thing. Send out a notice to the entire department. From here on out, I'm approving the use of deadly force on all cases regarding the Anord."

"You want me to clear that with the city government?"

"No. I'll handle that part myself."

"Sure thing."

"Callan, remember that file that only you and I know about?"

Callan was silent a moment before responding.

"The one with all your father's business records and contacts?"

"That's the one. I need you to get it out and start doing some digging."

"Are you sure about that, Chief?"

Anton took a long slow pull of his beer and then stared at the forest once more. He let out a sigh of resignation.

"Yeah, I'm sure."

Willow finally drifted off about two hours later, settling into the deep, heavy sleep of utter exhaustion. When Mayla tucked the comforter gently around her friend and left the room, slipping silently out the door, she was bone tired. She'd spent those two hours sending Willow soft memories of happier times, covering her with gentle feelings of safety and security, and talking softly about nothing in particular. Willow hadn't responded much, so it would remain to be seen if what she'd done had been any real help.

When she entered the living room, Mayla wasn't sure what had happened between Anton and Asher, but she couldn't miss her mate's repeated intense looks in Asher's direction, or the wolf shifter's concerted attempts to avoid them.

"She's finally sleeping. I don't think she'll wake up again tonight, she's exhausted."

Anton crossed the room and lifted her chin gently in one hand, forcing her to meet his eyes.

"She's not the only one from the looks of it."

Mayla nodded. "I did my best to try and help. It was the least I could do for her."

She leaned into Anton's embrace, pressing her face against his broad chest, but turning her face to look at Asher.

"Thank you. I don't know how you knew where she was, but I'll always be grateful to you. Always."

Asher nodded. "My wolf found her. I'm not sure how he knew, but he took me straight to her."

"Speaking of," Anton said, looking at him over Mayla's head, "I need to take Mayla home. She's still recovering and needs to rest. Can we trust your wolf to behave or do I need to make arrangements to have Willow moved?"

Asher's eyes blazed at the question, his caramel irises taking on a softly translucent glow. When he spoke, the pitch of his voice was low and rumbling, his and strangely not his at the same time.

"She will stay here. Where she will always be safe. Both with me and my wolf."

Whatever Anton's hesitation had been, Asher's declaration seemed to appease him. As they said their goodbyes and headed for the door, Mayla wondered what all that had been about. She knew that Willow was right where she needed to be.

She couldn't explain *how* she knew, but she'd never been more certain of anything in her life. The safest place for Willow right now was with Asher.

Later that same night, Mayla trailed a slender finger across Anton's bare, chiseled chest. She sat next to him as he relaxed on the pile of blankets and pillows they'd tossed onto the living room floor. They'd stopped to eat after leaving Asher's place, but barely made it through the appetizer before asking for the rest to go and heading home. Making small talk over that table, they'd both felt the exact same thing. The desperate need to lose themselves in something other than the growing darkness that seemed to be spreading in their lives.

A need to lose themselves in each other.

In the elevator, the doors had barely closed before they'd been locked together, kissing, touching and fumbling until they reached their floor and fumbled to unlock the apartment door. They'd made love fast and fierce right there in the hallway, eventually ending up on the couch and then the living room floor.

Now, as moonlight shone through the giant windows and danced across their bare skin, Mayla marveled at the mate mark on Anton's chest, and at the soft, translucent glow coming from it. She glanced down to see her own mark doing the same.

"We're glowing," she whispered, as if afraid speaking too loud might break the blissful cocoon they'd managed to create. Anton smiled at the awe in her voice, his fingertips playing with the tips of her inky black hair, loose and shimmering in the moonlight.

"It happens sometimes when mates are intimate with each other."

She tilted her head at him, curious, her fingers continuing

their feather soft strokes across his chest.

"Really? Does it happen every time?" She asked, watching her own hand as it trailed up over his shoulder, then back down his chest to slide across his abdomen. The ridges of muscle quivered at her soft touch.

"I'm not actually sure," he admitted, sitting up, his hand sliding into her hair to pull her close for another kiss.

"But I am *absolutely* on board with finding out."

When their lips finally parted, Anton leaned his forehead against hers for a moment, breathing her in before laying back against the pillows once more.

Mayla's mouth curved into a smile and he found himself transfixed by the way her eyes twinkled as she watched him. She went back to slowly tracing every line of his body, taking her time. He wanted to grab her, wrap her in his arms, flip them both over and bury himself deep within her, joining them in both body and soul. But he held back, letting her draw out her delicious torture instead.

She was happy.

There was a new boldness growing within her, he could feel it, a steely determination that was just starting to show itself. Right now, as her fingers explored his skin and made his heart jump in his chest, his mate was content.

Let him burn if it made her this happy, let him burn for days. He'd still die with a smile on his face.

One of her hands slid up his neck, her palm softly caressing his cheek, and he lost his breath at the tenderness of it. He'd never know this feeling before her. This feeling of being treasured, of being desired above all others, of being utterly and entirely complete. He leaned his face against her hand and briefly closed his eyes, losing himself in the feel of her fingers.

His mate.

His love.

His *Mayla*.

Her eyes softened as if she were once again reading his mind.

"We are the beginning of something important, Anton. I don't know how to explain it, but I know you and I were destined. Highblood, Lowblood, none of that matters. You are *mine* and I am *yours*. We were born to find each other."

He drank her in, her open, loving expression, those

serious dark blue eyes and the midnight hair falling over the soft cream of her bare shoulders. Her expression lifted, chin tilting farther to the side and eyebrows raising as if she would ask him a question, but she didn't speak.

"What is it, milacek?" He tucked a strand of dark hair her behind her ear and waited. Whatever she wanted, he would find a way to get it. The rarest tea in China? Fruit from a solitary island in the South Pacific? A three-legged Arctic nymph? He wasn't sure there was such a creature, but if there was he'd damn sure find one for her.

A slow, seductive smile crossed her face. "Do you think you could you do one thing for me?" When her voice dropped an octave and her tongue slid out to moisten her lips, the need blazing through him went up another twenty degrees. He suddenly knew, in his chest and in his heart, exactly where her mind was headed.

He leaned in, his lips against her ear.

"And what might that one thing be, my love?"

She shivered, letting out a small sigh, then pulled back a bit so those dark blue eyes could blaze at him.

She reached between them, wrapping her soft hand around that most sensitive part of him and his hips bucked upwards, a groan escaping into the night.

"Show me again how much you love me."

He wrapped his arms around her, flipping them both before settling himself snuggly between her eagerly parted thighs and sliding home.

"Always," he whispered, lowering his head to kiss the column of her throat.

"And forever," she whispered back.

32

Two days later, Anton stood inside the wood paneled office they'd discovered in the farthest recesses of the Miradea Home for the Criminally Insane, and felt his gut twist. If it hadn't been for a fresh faced recruit desperate to find a bathroom after his first kobold cleanup job, they may never have found the secret door hidden inside one of the supply closets. And they certainly wouldn't have found this massive office, which had clearly been the center of Anord operations out of this location.

Anton stood with his legs braced apart and his hands clasped tightly together behind his back. It was the only way he could manage to keep from putting his fist through the wall.

This was…it was just…well, there weren't bad enough words for what this was. A clusterfuck of epic proportions came close, but it still didn't fully cover it. He'd been debating telling everyone, struggling for a few hours over whether it was worth it to keep them safe through the simple lie of omission. But that's not how his team worked. They didn't hide from anything, they faced it all together head on, as a unit.

In the end he'd called everyone and asked them to drive back out here. They deserved to know, and they were absolutely going to have to see it to believe it anyway. His eyes scanned the massive oak desk he stood in front of, then lifted to the massive wall to wall bookcase behind it. He blew out a hard breath. This was going to leave a very big, very nasty mark.

Mayla and Callan entered the room chatting away, iced lattes in hand. The vampire had picked up his mate first thing this morning with exactly zero advanced notice. He had simply announced that the two of them were going shopping, and that Anton was expressly not invited.

With plenty of work to do here, he hadn't put up much of a fight. He knew his mate could do with a normal, low-key day, one with no criminals or mythical beasts to deal with. Plus, there was absolutely no chance she'd be in any danger from the Anord while with the vampire. Though he tended to avoid physical altercations like the plague, Callan's senses were actually so much better than everyone else's they were borderline annoying.

Natalie had driven over to spend time with Willow, the latter still steadfastly refusing to have anything to do with the outside world, preferring instead to stay holed up in Asher's cabin.

When the shifter entered the room with Elijah a few minutes later, Anton suspected that Natalie's presence at his home was the only reason Asher had felt comfortable leaving in the first place. Currently, Elijah was regaling the man with the details of his kobold kill.

"They're slow as shit man. They just lumber around on those stubby reptile legs and wait for you to get close enough. I did end up with twenty or so stitches in my shoulder thanks to that bony ass tail the thing had though. It took me longer than I expected, but when I finally decided how I wanted to take it out? When I say it was done with utter finesse man, I mean I wish I'd recorded it just so I could show everyone at the Christmas party this year. Anton just went brute frosty, as always. I've really got to get him into the gym more so I can show him some other techniques."

"Quiet, Elijah."

Mayla sent a concerned look to her mate, the hard edge in his voice raising immediate flags. When she opened her mind, red anger was rolling off him in waves, and there was an underlying thread of…was that sorrow? She moved quickly to him, sliding an arm around his waist before glancing up at him quizzically. His tightly clasped hands immediately released, one well-muscled arm coming around her, pulling her snugly into his side. She sent comfort and calm back to him, hoping to lighten the load he was clearly shouldering.

Elijah immediately stopped talking, his eyes watching Anton intently. When he remained patiently quiet, Mayla knew Anton's second-in-command had decided something was off, just as she had. Quiet was not in Elijah's normal repertoire. Asher moved to one side, a strange tension seeming to hover around him. Probably still a little overwhelmed with having a woman he didn't really know living in his house. She glanced over at Callan, relieved when he sent her his signature saucy wink, but her attention snapped back when Anton took a big step away from her, turning to address the group.

"Now that everyone is here, there's something you all need to see." He paused a moment, looking at each of them in turn, his eyes lingering longer on Elijah. "And I have to ask you to brace yourselves, because it's bad, guys. *It's very bad.*"

As each of them nodded, he stepped behind the desk. Reaching up, he pushed the wall to wall bookshelves apart. They split in the middle and slid away smoothly, mounted on some type of rolling track.

Behind them was a huge wall covered in maps, photos and diagrams. Most of the maps looked to be parts of Miradea, nothing too surprising there. But the photos, those were...disturbing. Many looked like photos of ancient fae creatures that Mayla had seen in books. There were a few pictures of kobolds, still more of what she had always pictured Sluaghs would look like, with their leathery wings and emaciated bodies. Others were of creatures that simply defied explanation. A few were...headless, but still somehow standing?

The medical diagrams were even worse. Mayla covered her mouth with one hand, her breakfast threatening to make a reappearance. Hand drawn images of modified prosthetic parts, attaching to bones and muscles were everywhere. They almost looked like parts of some kind of robot, if that robot happened to be the main character in a horror movie. Muscles and tendons on a mechanical jaw, a metal spine connecting to rib bones, a skull that looked that it had been cut clean in half and then welded back together. All with disturbingly precise and detailed notes written next to them. Mayla turned her eyes away.

"Anton what in the *hell* are we looking at?" Callan asked,

his face pale. "This looks like the planning board for a horror movie."

But Anton didn't answer.

Instead he watched Elijah, concern etched deep into his features.

When Elijah stepped forward for a better look, the ground shifted beneath him, and his vision blurred.

This wasn't possible. It just...*wasn't.*

Why couldn't he couldn't feel his legs? He lurched awkwardly, Asher darting forward to catch his elbow and steady him. Without acknowledging the assist, Elijah snatched his arm away, his nostrils flaring and his eyes going saucer wide as he continued to stare at the board.

There was no way he was seeing what he thought he was seeing. Those meticulous, drawn to scale diagrams, the clear bold strokes in that awful black pen. Each titled with a specimen and version number. Specimen Four, Version Sixteen. Specimen Twelve, Version Twenty Seven.

The handwriting.

The labeling technique.

That fucking black pen.

It was exactly the same. He'd seen the exact same things in his father's office as a boy. The detail, the nuance, even that mother fucking signature in the top right corner.

A. Barrett.

Atius Barrett.

Father of Elijah and Isabelle Barrett, husband to Melinda Barrett, and one of the most celebrated molecular biologists of his time. Or at least he had been before he'd been *fucking KILLED* along with his wife and child along a dark, abandoned road nineteen years ago.

Anton's voice broke the heavy silence. "Elijah, I'm sorry. It could be a copycat, someone just trying to make us think it's him."

He raised a shaky palm in Anton's direction, and silence

once more filled the room. He continued to scan the diagrams lining the wall, stopping to read a page of notes written in that eerily familiar hand. His father was dead, he had been for years. Not only that, there was no way, even if his father was alive, that the man would be working alongside the same people who killed his wife and child. It just wasn't possible.

But it *was* possible, and somewhere, deep in his gut, Elijah *knew*. A bone burning sense of rage was building inside him, traveling through his body and hollowing him out completely. His mind flashed back to that night so many years ago. The night when he'd been terrified, sitting there on the side of the road. He'd been so focused on his own fear, he'd never stopped to think about the way his normally timid mother had slapped his father. About the way she'd been so visibly angry at him. As if it had all somehow been *his fault*. As if the whole thing had been planned, but something had gone wrong. His blood turned to ice in his veins.

Asher's voice was gruff when he spoke up, his watchful gaze never leaving Elijah. "This is what they were doing out here? Working on creating more of these genetically engineered creatures? Why? What's the end game?"

"It looks like the Anord didn't have time to pack up everything in their haste to leave this place. From the few files we've gone through already, they are attempting to recreate and modify lethal fae creatures from ancient times. Most of what you see here are early stage trial runs. We don't know exactly how far they've gotten," Anton answered.

"But we do know about the slimy shit that attacked those kids in the park, and the ones waiting here to ambush you all a few days ago," Callan pointed out, his brows furrowed in anger.

Anton nodded. "We've compared the beast at headquarters to the ones we fought here. The one released at the park was the most advanced by far. None of the creatures we encountered here could excrete the neurotoxin, and only a few had functional modifications. Which does nothing to explain all the extra neurotoxin that was found in the van.

We have to assume there are more out there somewhere. Likely quite a few more."

"*Son of a bitch,*" Asher grumbled under his breath.

Anton acknowledged the comment but continued, waving a hand back towards the board.

"The one thing we found consistent in all the notes," he shot a quick look at Elijah, "that this person left behind, is that there is only one main objective. Every creature is engineered to target, and then eliminate, Lowbloods."

Elijah's sudden dark chuckle echoed in the deathly quiet room. Anton opened his mouth to speak, but it Elijah beat him to it.

"My *father* is using his skills to try and kill every Lowblood in Miradea." His voice was flat and cold, his features chiseled in stone.

Mayla made a small noise of distress and Callan was next to her in an instant, their hands clasping quickly together.

Anton watched her a moment, assuring himself she was okay, then returned his gaze to Elijah. His best friend since childhood was still staring at the drawings and diagrams.

"I always knew the guy was a top tier asshole, I guess I just never really understood how far up that ladder he'd managed to climb," he admitted.

"We'll stop him," Anton assured everyone, "we'll figure out a way to put an end to all of this."

"*WE* don't have to figure out anything," Elijah said calmly. When he turned to face the rest of them, his eyes sparked with rage, but his face was eerily calm.

"My father will never get the chance to kill every Lowblood in Miradea."

Asher nodded. "You're damn right. We'll stop him, and we'll shut down the rest of these Anord assholes for good."

"You guys focus on the rest of the Anord. We're finally making progress, we can't afford to take our foot off the gas now," Elijah said, planting both fists on the desk before him, and leaning his weight on his knuckles. His amber eyes were lethal, determined.

"You leave my father to *me*. He killed my mother, my baby sister, and he *clearly* thought he'd killed me. Now he thinks he's going to get away with killing people I have sworn to protect."

He let out a low, ominous chuckle, his normally easygoing expression twisting into a frightening sneer. "So you guys really don't have to worry about this. I can promise you, my father won't be creating any more creatures. He won't be putting the city at any more risk. I'll be killing him *very, very slowly* before he gets that chance."

www.ingramcontent.com/pod-product-compliance
Lightning Source LLC
La Vergne TN
LVHW090559110826
845146LV00001B/195